ALSO BY IAN MOORE

Death and Croissants
Death and Fromage
Death and Papa Noël

A FOLLET VALLEY MYSTERY

IAN MOORE

First published in 2023 by Farrago.

This paperback edition published in 2024 by Farrago,
an imprint of Duckworth Books Ltd
1 Golden Court, Richmond, TW9 1EU, United Kingdom

www.farragobooks.com

Paperback ISBN: 978-1-78842-497-4
eBook ISBN: 978-1-78842-406-6

Cover design and illustration by Patrick Knowles

For Niv, my all-time inspiration.

Chapter One

The sun was a quarter way over the horizon, its weak, early morning beams just beginning to flood the distant Follet Valley like a transfusion of blood, giving the place life. It was mid-September and for Richard Ainsworth, the best time of the year for this usually quiet corner of the wider Loire Valley. The mist that clung like cobwebs to the trees and the fattening vines would be burnt off by late morning, and the day would be as warm and languorous as at the height of summer, only without the tourist crowds – allowing the locals to reclaim their quiet land.

But that would be late morning, still half the day away. Richard had no trouble with early mornings: as the owner of a high-end *chambre d'hôte*, or 'posh B&B' as one of his recent guests had called it, causing a small part of him to die inside, an ability to get up early was the most basic of qualifications. What was unusual about today though was the enthusiasm with which he had bounced out of bed, almost causing him to rick his neck in the process. Today was the first day on a new job and while enthusiasm to Richard was a deceitful, potentially dangerous state of being, for once he couldn't suppress it. He hadn't been able to shake the wide grin he'd had since getting up, and though it used muscles that normally lay dormant, it was simply beyond his control. For once in his life he was going to let himself enjoy the moment and if jaw ache, cracked cheekbones, or a potential change of wind direction led to permanent grinning-idiot status, then bring it on.

Something crackled behind him, footsteps on the gravel perhaps and there was a muffled voice giving someone a dressing-down. Pretending he hadn't heard it, he bent to move the large metallic flight case at his feet, the dozens of red FRAGILE stickers on it making him think twice about touching the thing at all. There was another crackle and more muffled exhortations, and this time he stood, rubbing his neck, leaving the fragile coffin-sized strongbox glowing in the rising sun as though it were possessed. He turned around but saw nothing as the dawn sun reflected off one of the dozens of windows opposite him. Then the crackle came again, still from behind him though, and he realised it was the walkie-talkie in his back pocket, and the impatient, hectoring voice was that of his friend of uncertain status, secret object of desire and highly demanding, Valérie d'Orçay. Glamorous and exotic, she blinded Richard like the sun on the windows. She was also his new business partner, though in truth the word 'partner' was doing an awful lot of heavy lifting in that description. By trade, Valérie was a professional bounty hunter and possible assassin of international repute, while Richard was a maker of tourist breakfasts and a former film historian. He was also of international repute; he had a doctorate to prove it, though it was of little use in their new business of Private Investigators and Personal Security. It had been her idea and he had, naturally, gone along with it.

He plucked the walkie-talkie from his back pocket and replied to the snappy crackles. 'Yes, Richard here. Over.'

'Over what?' was the testy reply.

'No. Over. You say over when you're… over.'

There was a pause and he suspected a deep breath had got lost somewhere in the ether. 'I did not know you had used a talkie-walkie before.' She was trying to sound patient while at the same time letting him know who was really in charge. Also she'd used the word 'talkie-walkie' which was French for walkie-talkie, one of those peculiarities of the French language where they had taken an internationally recognised word yet still tried to retain control over it. Either way, talkie-walkie was a very pleasing twist.

'We'll be over in twenty minutes,' she said seriously.

'No, you put the over at the end,' he joked, immediately regretting it. In the past few months they had spent a lot of time together and still Richard hadn't been able to eradicate flippancy or sarcasm from his conversation – two things that usually flew straight over Valérie's head, like a perfectly executed tennis lob.

'Richard?' she crackled again, the crackle not all atmospheric. 'We shall be with you in twenty minutes.'

'I'll be here,' he replied seriously and he heard the radio go dead.

He sat down on the big flight case wondering what to do in the next twenty minutes that would indicate to the imminent Valérie that he'd done anything at all. It wasn't actually his responsibility to be moving the flight case, he just felt like he should do something. It was dawn, there were very few other people about, but he really should make an effort. After reappraising the size of the case,

3

however, and the fact that its four wheels meant nothing on the gravel beneath them, he decided to sit and rest instead for the next eighteen minutes at least. Keep an eye on things. As nominal Head of Security, it was the least he could do.

Sitting on the case he turned again to the sight of the slowly rising sun reflected in the windows and the ornamental pond that stood between him and the west wing of the magnificent Chateau de Valençay. From where he sat, he could see the three main stages of its construction: the Gallo-Roman, the Renaissance and the Enlightenment; the two great domes on its west wing loomed large in the dawn light. The chateau smacked of wealth and power, of opulence and riches, of political intrigue and history-defining moments stretching back nearly a thousand years. He liked that; he wasn't one for the supernatural but to him it gave off an energy. What was it Orson Welles said about the Borgias in *The Third Man*? For thirty years they had warfare, terror and bloodshed and produced the Renaissance, while in Switzerland they had five hundred years of brotherly love and produced the cuckoo clock. Richard sighed. He felt a bit under pressure knowing that the Chateau de Valençay, itself the result of warfare, terror and bloodshed was, for the next twenty minutes or so, solely his responsibility. He'd have preferred to guard a cuckoo clock.

He gulped nervously just as a peacock somewhere in the manicured gardens woke and began its morning squawk. It sounded mocking to Richard, another sign of the other-worldly luxury of the place, and he missed his calmer, less brash hens. What right had he to be Head of

Security for the Chateau de Valençay anyway? This really hadn't been his idea at all when Valérie had first mooted the idea of a detective agency. They had had two prior adventures, cases, investigations – he wasn't sure what to call them – but he had been very much dragged along in Valérie's tempest of a wake, for the most part happy to hang on to her impeccable coat-tails and just, really, to be with the woman who was as intoxicating, mysterious and enchanting as the waking chateau he was guarding.

They had had a few enquiries for business initially, but they were all to do with marital infidelity which, while it got their business off to a flying start financially, was also beginning to lose Richard drinking partners in the local bar and gain him stony looks in the market. They had swiftly rebranded to say that they didn't do 'marital' work and the Follet Valley, worried about the fallout, had breathed a collective sigh of relief. Business had been quiet since then until this job came in, and though not strictly within the boundary of the Follet Valley itself, Valençay was close enough to be local. This job now had Richard guarding a thousand years of French and European history, and a few hundred thousand euros of film equipment ready for the production of *The Master Servant*, a new Hollywood blockbuster. At the same time Valérie was personal security and bodyguard to one of its main stars, the fragile, beautiful Lionel Margaux who was playing Napoleon's second wife, Marie-Louise of Austria.

It had been at Lionel Margaux's request that Valérie, and nominally Richard, become her personal bodyguards and on-set security. Her mother and Valérie were friends, and when the young Lionel Margaux had become the victim of a stalker while filming in Paris, it was decided that the production would move to Valençay, at great expense too, though with a smaller crew. This film was a Franco-American production, the actress representing the best of the Franco part, so money was no object. Besides, the publicity department had said, what could be better than filming the interior scenes where they had historically taken place?

Richard looked at his watch and wondered if he should just take a look around the courtyard and the entrance bridge that came over the long-dried moat, check for snipers or something. Do stalkers use snipers? Do snipers use stalkers even? He had no idea but he should take a quick look anyway and tip-toed, for no good reason, through the central welcoming arch under the keep. It was all eerily quiet, even the gargoyles seemed half asleep, and he turned and went back the other way where he'd come from, past the pond in the Cour d'Honneur and out towards the Jardin de la Duchesse which had, in the daytime anyway, a magnificent view over this side of the valley.

He descended the stone steps into the garden and for the first time felt tense. The two statues in each of the symmetrical flower beds were half-lit by the morning sun and it made them look threatening. Richard tightened the grip on his heavy torch, trying not to focus on the fact that if a couple of statues were giving him the shivers, a potentially murderous stalker was probably not his department at all, and maybe in future he should offer to stick to the admin side of the business.

'You there!' The voice was deep and immediately authoritative, stopping Richard in his tracks. The clipped English tones were slightly softened with a continental edge, but that didn't detract from the voice, and presumably the person behind it, being very used to power and to wielding it. 'What do you think you're doing, prowling around my gardens at this time of day, eh? I should have you thrashed!'

Richard turned slowly as a man emerged from the shadows behind the stone steps, a pronounced limp making his movements look laboured.

'Well? Explain yourself, monsieur!'

The aristocratic bearing and even the language were early nineteenth century, the powdered wig the same; but the low-slung jogging bottoms and trainers were definitely not period, and for a moment Richard thought he'd chanced on the stalker. A nutcase with an Enlightenment fetish and a leisurewear addiction.

'The emperor arrives today, man. I won't have strangers cluttering up my gardens!'

The man kept coming at his slow, debilitated pace. Of medium to small height, the wig high on his forehead, his skin was pale and though smaller than Richard, his air of authority made it feel like he was taller. Then Richard almost dropped his torch. This wasn't a stalker at all, this was Dominic Burdett, Hollywood star since he was eight years old and one of the great movie actors of his generation. His commitment to his roles bordered famously on dangerous obsession as his method acting had at times brought him close to breakdown with drastic changes in weight and punishing, sometimes dangerous research, all in the name of his art. So while this wasn't a stalker, in an odd way it wasn't Dominic Burdett either. This was, to all intents and purposes, His Serene Highness Prince Charles-Maurice de

Talleyrand-Périgord, owner of the Chateau de Valençay and the subject of the film itself. Burdett was in character, leisurewear notwithstanding.

Back up the steps Richard heard a motorbike come loudly through the keep arch and skid to a halt in the gravel. *Dammit*, he thought, *that's where I should be!* And he ran halfway up the steps before stopping and turning back to the figure below. 'Er,' he said, 'excuse me, Your Grace.' And continued with haste to the courtyard.

A motorbike with two riders had stopped right in front of the set entrance, and Richard's heart beat faster. Both riders wore heavy biker leathers and still had their helmets on, classic modern assassin get-up he decided, basing his conclusion on nothing more than something he'd read somewhere. Should he approach them? I mean, it was his job after all. But if his instincts were right, his job didn't, as far as he was aware, entail martyrdom.

'Erm, excuse me, but you can't bring that bike in here.' As a confrontational opening gambit towards two potentially desperate killers, it left something to be desired, and he regretted his actions as the lead rider slowly started to remove their helmet.

'Ooh, you're scary! Change of plan, didn't madame tell you?' The redoubtable Madame Tablier, his long-time cleaning woman, scourge of germs and social niceties, looked around her. 'I wouldn't want to have to clean all those windows,' she said as Richard let out a sigh of relief. Then the pillion passenger shakily removed their helmet too and shook her long blonde hair. Lionel Margaux, the hottest name in French cinema, though with a haunted, delicate fear about her. A fragility that was almost transparent.

She looked at Richard, terror in her eyes. 'I never want to go on a motorcycle ever again!' she said, on the verge of tears. 'I think I'd rather live with a stalker.'

'Well!' Madame Tablier huffed. 'That's gratitude for you!'

Chapter Two

Richard took Lionel Margaux's helmet as she stepped off Madame Tablier's motorbike. If the idea had been for her to arrive without causing attention, then her figure-hugging bike leathers and her long blonde hair billowing from under her helmet would have undoubtedly had the opposite effect. Richard wouldn't be surprised if she'd left a trail of motor incidents from rubbernecking farmworkers and early morning *vignerons*. The contrast with Madame Tablier's Johnny Hallyday-painted, sleeve-tasselled leather bike jacket was marked. As was the fact that Madame Tablier was still wearing her apron underneath, ready as always for any cleaning action that might be had.

His radio sparked into life again. 'Has Lionel Margaux arrived yet?' Valérie's tone was serious, and she spoke slowly making sure there would be no misunderstanding.

'Yes.' Richard replied equally clearly. 'Lionel Margaux has arrived safely. Over.' He enunciated every word, giving each one a crisp 1950s BBC announcer's flourish.

'Why are you talking like that, Richard?' A few seconds later Valérie was standing in the doorway of the chateau right behind him, a perplexed, slightly fractious look on her face, which had a golden glow thanks to the rising sun.

'I… er…' he gulped, tearing his eyes away from her with difficulty. 'How did you get here?' he asked, pulling himself together as best he could, an attempt at control lost entirely as he was continuing to speak into the walkie-talkie.

Valérie didn't offer an explanation; instead she shrugged the most Gallic of shrugs as if the question was irrelevant. She lowered the inevitable sunglasses into place, and raised her profile slightly to catch the sun. She was wearing a beige two-piece tweed trouser suit, the trousers baggy, the one button on the jacket buttoned up, and her black roll-neck matched her black beret, completing the look perfectly. Richard had no idea if what he was now calling 'Resistance Chic' was a practical ensemble for film set security – neither were his areas of expertise in truth – but as a Marlene Dietrich-style wow 'bloody hell' entrance, he doubted it could be bettered.

'My dear aunt,' Lionel said, unzipping her jacket and addressing Valérie, 'you realise I could have you banned from the set looking like that? You are upstaging the beautiful, glamorous star!' Her humour was warm and genuine, and a long way from the media reputation of the actress as being cold and unapproachable.

'Oh, you know, these are just working clothes,' Valérie replied, her false modesty hanging in the air like the mist on the vines.

'Mine too,' cracked Madame Tablier. 'Now, if you don't mind me, and you usually don't, I'll get back and clean up.'

'Could you feed Passepartout, please?' Valérie asked urgently. 'I let him sleep in this morning.'

'I suppose so; what does he eat these days, filet mignon?'

Valérie either ignored the older woman, or thought the answer was an obvious yes. 'And take him out for a little walk too, if you could. Thank you, madame.'

Of all the sights and images rattling around Richard's head that morning, the one with Madame Tablier in Johnny Hallyday leathers, a biker's helmet and a pampered Chihuahua on the end of a bejewelled lead was possibly the most arresting, but he wasn't allowed to dwell on it for long.

'Now, Richard,' Valérie said, 'I will take Lionel into make-up, and I want you to keep an eye on the set.'

'Yes, sir!' Again it was lost on Valérie, though he caught the brief smile on Lionel's lips. 'What am I keeping an eye on exactly?'

'On the people; particularly look out for strangers.' She turned and led Lionel through the door.

'But they're all strangers to me! What am I supposed to do? Just wander on set and introduce myself?' He was saying this to the backs of the two women moving away from him and down the corridor.

'Brilliant, Richard!' Valérie said, without turning round. 'Let everyone know that you are in control.'

From anyone else it might have sounded flippant, but Valérie d'Orçay didn't do flippant. He followed them through the main door, but whereas they turned left towards make-up and wardrobe, Richard turned right through a small vestibule and into the main dining room of the chateau, the setting for the scene being filmed today. He entered cautiously; the quiet work of professionals setting up the room was like drone bees – a hum of satisfaction, everyone knowing their role and getting on

12

with it. But the visual scene itself, what stood before him, was so familiar, so comforting to him because it was the scene he'd had in his head since he was a boy.

Richard wasn't given to wild fluctuations of emotion, he was steady as she goes. A sort of grumbling contentment was his default setting, but if there was one thing guaranteed to make him smile, to bring the child in him to the surface, it was the tableau before him now. The room's windows were blacked out, making it feel like evening. What illumination there was came from an enormous film light, a key light he knew it was called. Occasionally someone would walk in front of the light and be silhouetted by its glare – and that was the image for him and briefly it took his breath away. It was an image Richard had always loved in the books about 1930s Hollywood that he'd collected as a boy. It promised so much, contained so much romance and intrigue and glamour, and he saw it just as it appeared in those old books, he saw it in black and white. He sat down carefully on a nearby director's chair, unable to take his eyes off the wonder of it all; it felt like he had been waiting for this all his life and he was utterly lost in it, a boy again.

'Ooh, get you sitting down already; some of us have work to do.'

Strong as the vision in front of him was, it was never going to withstand an icy blast from Madame Tablier.

'I thought you'd gone back,' he whispered, not looking at her.

'Don't worry, I'm on my way. I forgot to give you this; you left it on the table when you should have been clearing up.' She thrust a piece of paper at him, placing it in his eye-line to get his proper attention.

It was a list of cast and crew he'd put together the night before, using some newly bought reference books, some of his own knowledge and very studiously, some might say stubbornly, avoiding his online nemesis and film-historian-job destroyer, the Internet Movie Database.com. 'Ah yes, thanks,' he said, taking the paper without looking up, still the look of wonderment and childish innocence on his face.

'Have you got wind?' Madame Tablier asked, a note of genuine concern hidden somewhere beneath the hard crust of her personality. Richard's attention was elsewhere, however, so she tutted and turned to go. As she did so she walked straight into an enormous man, almost bouncing off his rock-hard body. She steadied herself by putting a hand on Richard's shoulder, removing it quickly but finally tearing him away from his set watching.

He looked up to see the giant towering above Madame Tablier. He was well over six feet tall, built like a small mountain range and wearing shorts, industrial work boots, a tight T-shirt and a loosely hung tool belt around his paunch. What was even more noticeable about him though was the mass of hair on his head. Long grey hair, combed back upwards which at some point, around the arms of his glasses Richard guessed, met his equally enormous beard. He looked like an ageing lion. Richard glanced at his list: Alain Petit, chief gaffer and grip, the film set's handyman and nicknamed, ironically considering his mane, 'Le Loup', the wolf.

'Wire cutters,' he growled down at Madame Tablier.

'What about 'em?' she growled back up at him, which caught him a little off guard.

'Where are they?' He decided to fight fire with fire.

'How the hell do I know?'

Richard knew there was only one winner here.

'Well,' Petit was hesitating fatally, 'you put something down around here and it just disappears!'

She looked him up and down, which could easily have led to the kind of neck pain Richard was suffering from. Then, having apparently made up her mind, she said, 'I've got some spare in my tool box. Follow me.'

Alain 'Le Loup' Petit, the self-proclaimed hard man of film, who'd once knocked out Burt Reynolds because the star had disrespected one of his technicians, somewhat meekly did as he was told.

Richard turned back to the film set in front of him. It was the image of old Hollywood in this quiet corner of rural France, so his two worlds had collided. The shadows danced as the skeleton crew quietly, professionally continued with their specific tasks. He shook his head, trying to concentrate his mind, and decided this was a good opportunity to put some names to faces. He opened up his list of cast and crew. Some were immediately obvious; the cinematographer was Brian Grace, a slight man, about sixty with bouffant white hair. He was dressed all in denim but with a flamboyant silk scarf tied loosely around his neck, making him look French, though Richard knew he was actually Australian and a triple Academy Award winner. He stood behind the large camera, occasionally leaning into it and talking to a tall woman standing next to him. She was wearing headphones around her neck, her long, dark hair hanging loosely over her shoulders and onto a gilet with dozens of pockets on it, all laden with tools and tape. This was Stella Gonzales, sound recordist,

Spanish and also a multi Oscar winner. There must be quite a budget on the film to afford talent like that, Richard thought, yet he knew they had all moved down from Paris with just a skeleton crew for these location scenes.

In the corner stood a harassed-looking man of about sixty whose shiny, tailored suit seemed out of keeping with the setting. He was wiping sweat off his forehead, his swept-back receding hair greying at the roots as the obvious black dye grew out. He stopped wiping his forehead and used the same cloth to clean his thick-rimmed glasses. He was also chomping on a large unlit cigar. If you had to describe the stereotype of a jumpy, ulcer-suffering Hollywood producer then Ben-Hur Friedman was it. Named after the classic film, he was Hollywood royalty, the grandson of legendary producer Isaac Friedman, one of the founding fathers of the golden age of cinema. Next to Friedman, and looking equally harassed, was a smartly dressed woman rubbing her hands anxiously and clearly trying to explain something to Friedman that he didn't want to hear. Richard wasn't sure, but he suspected she was Dr Amorette Arthur, former TV historian, now located permanently in Valençay and advisor on the production; she clearly wasn't happy about something.

Sitting on a director's chair behind these two was a serious-looking woman in a baseball cap, also wearing glasses and holding what Richard assumed was the script in one hand and a pencil in the other. He knew this was Sacha Vizard-Guy, one of the great new breed of European film directors, long feted by Hollywood but who had held out, stubbornly sticking to small budget arthouse productions. She was unsmiling and in total contrast to the young man standing next to her, also pointing at the script. He looked almost as excited as Richard was to be on set, a bundle of energy. He must be the assistant director, Richard concluded, and looked at his list of names: Samuel Friedman, so presumably related to the producer. Occasionally they would both look up and point at the grand dining table in the middle of the room, and the subject of the next scene.

The calm of the set was broken by Napoleon himself, who could be heard shouting in the corridor as he approached, swearing at minions in a very un-Napoleon type American accent. Reed Turnbull's name had once meant automatic box office gold; an action hero, a romantic hero, a sex symbol and a man's man, he was still a big star, a world star and it was obvious he liked to let people know that too. He was also what they called 'difficult', and he seemed determined to live up to his reputation.

'If he was so goddamn powerful, why did the guy dress like a lady? These things aren't pants, they're nylons!' Something smashed on the floor, but nobody seemed to notice, and just let it go. 'I'm sitting down in this scene for Chrissakes; do I have to wear this stuff? You – yeah, you – go ask the lady director if I have to wear this stuff.'

The only person paying any attention to this was Dominic Burdett who had wandered in from the gardens and now sat at the dining table, a look of paternal embarrassment on his face. It was a look, Richard knew, that his character Talleyrand would wear if Napoleon himself was throwing a tantrum. Standing over Burdett was the French actor, Gilbertine, young and good-looking but not in a fine-boned way, a chunky way, and therefore perfectly cast as the famous chef Marie-Antonin Carême, inventor of profiteroles if Richard had his facts right, and Talleyrand's personal chef at the Chateau de Valençay.

There was just one person left and she arrived hurriedly, sitting opposite Burdett and holding a pair of glasses like they were a magnifying glass, studying the script. She looked nervous, more nervous than you would expect someone of her experience and talent to be, but then Jennifer Davies was making a comeback. A well-publicised breakdown and divorce, drying-out clinics and her career-hindering interviews about the cruel treatment of actresses 'of a certain age', had damaged a once stellar career. She was playing Laetizia Bonaparte, Napoleon's mother, even though Jennifer Davies and Reed Turnbull were the same age and had made their names as romantic teenagers in a hit film of the 1980s.

'Hello, mother!' Reed Turnbull smiled cruelly as he appeared on the set. It was almost a snarl and Richard expected the poor woman to crumble, as she seemed panicky enough as it was.

She looked up, making a play of looking through her glasses at Turnbull. 'Oh Reed, I still think you look the wrong size to be playing the great emperor!' Turnbull puffed his chest out. 'Napoleon was so much taller.'

Turnbull's face went puce and he stalked off. 'Where's my chair?' he shouted. 'Where's my goddamn chair?'

Richard looked around him trying to see in advance who was going to cop the next outburst from the star. Then, with a deepening sense of embarrassment and impending doom, he realised it was him. He was sitting in Reed Turnbull's chair.

'What the hell do you think you're doing in my goddamn chair?' he screamed. 'Just because you French are paying for some of this picture, you think you can do what ya like, don't ya?' It seemed an odd thing for Napoleon to say in Richard's opinion, but Turnbull wasn't finished and he now knew that everyone on set was giving them their full attention. 'I am so sick of the lack of respect I'm getting on this movie! Friedman!' He shouted without looking over his shoulder. 'Friedman, I want this guy thrown out, and I don't give a damn if he's the goddamn president, ya hear?'

Silence came over the set, the tension unbearable, just then Richard's walkie-talkie crackled back into life: 'Richard,' Valérie's voice was inadvertently broadcast to the room, 'try to be discreet around the actors, please, they are quite temperamental I think. Can you do that?'

Chapter Three

'Mr Ainsworth, is it?' It was the producer Ben-Hur Friedman, who took Richard gently by the elbow and steered him away from the lava flow of Reed Turnbull's anger. 'Security, right? I have a job for you.' Richard allowed himself to be led away, trying to look as unconcerned as someone in security might look if confronted by a small man with a Napoleon complex dressed as Napoleon. He was also trying to hide his cringing embarrassment at upsetting the world-famous Reed Turnbull.

'My name's Ben, I'm the producer.' Richard liked the way he pronounced the word as *prodooser*, and that the man also looked harassed, which he could strongly identify with and which put him at ease immediately. 'Don't worry about Reed,' Friedman said, forcing a laugh and pushing his heavy-framed glasses back into place. 'You're not part of the film family until Reed Turnbull has balled you out. Come with me, I'd like you to meet someone.'

He led Richard to the other side of the set, well away from the still venting film star, but their path was blocked by the petite, studious figure of historian Amorette Arthur. She removed her glasses to signal her frustration.

'Monsieur Friedman, I really must…'

'Yes, in a second, Amorette, maybe a minute.' He brushed past her, still guiding Richard by the elbow. 'That lady won't leave me alone, er…' He stopped and looked at Richard.

'Richard Ainsworth. Security.' He repeated his job title almost as a question, gently letting go of any delusions of authority.

'Richard. Right. Security. Right.' They moved off again. 'Know anything about the movies, Richard?' He didn't wait for a reply. 'That lady is historical advisor; hysterical would be more on point. Don't get me wrong, she's a brilliant historian so I'm told, passionate about her subject. But!' He stopped again. 'She knows nothing about the movies,' he was almost pleading. 'Just 'cos a movie is set in the past doesn't mean it needs facts, right?'

Richard was caught, as usual, on the fence, but sensed that Mr Friedman wanted backing up a little. 'Not necessarily, no,' he said, making sure Madame Arthur was out of earshot. 'I can think of many that were a bit loose on fact: *Anne of a Thousand Days*, Von Sternberg's *The Scarlett Empress* – both good films though.'

'You see!' Friedman beamed through his unlit cigar, and held his arms out wide.

'Of course, there's always John Wayne playing Genghis Khan, ha!' Richard continued, laughing before trying one of his John Wayne impressions, 'For good or ill, she is my destiny!' he quoted, then laughed some more before noticing that Ben-Hur Friedman wasn't joining in.

'My grandaddy was on that picture,' he said, sounding wounded.

'Great film!' Richard replied quickly.

There was an awkward moment while Friedman weighed Richard up, then he beamed once more. 'Hey though, it's great to have a real film fan in the family!' He led him away again, past the actors at the table who were either concentrating on their lines or being fussed over by Samuel Friedman. Brian Grace and Stella Gonzales were still in deep conversation about lighting and sound, while Sacha, the director, seemed to make a point of not acknowledging anyone.

'Sam, you got a minute, maybe two?' Friedman called Samuel over.

'Hey, Unc!'

'This is Richard, he's Security.' Richard felt that his title was becoming more ridiculous by the minute. 'Richard, this is Sam, he's the AD – assistant director, but I guess you knew that. He runs the show, anything you need, Sam's your go-to guy. Now, Sam, where's the old man?' Samuel beamed a broad smile at Richard and pointed to the corner where a tiny old man sat, incongruously dressed as Napoleon as well but also wearing a battered old black beret.

'You speak French, Richard? 'Course you do. The old guy there, erm…'

'Corbeau,' Samuel said, looking at his notes, 'Régis Corbeau.'

'That's right, Corbeau. He's gonna sit in for Reed in this first set-up. He's the oldest man in Valençay, he's…'

'One hundred and two.'

'One hundred and two, that's right. One hundred and two years old, isn't that something?' Richard looked at the old man. It certainly was something; he actually looked older. 'We did this thing with the local guys here,' Friedman continued, 'because we came from Paris at the last minute; we didn't want to upset folks so we said "can we get some of you in the picture?" And this guy, er…'

'Corbeau, Régis Corbeau.' Samuel helped him out again.

'Yeah, Corbeau, well, it's good publicity. A war hero and all.' He looked at Richard conspiratorially and continued in a whisper, 'He's about the same height as Reed too.'

'Not far off the same age either,' Samuel added, also in a whisper. 'I'll take you to meet him, he's a little scared I think, maybe you can put him at ease.'

'Ben!' It was Sacha Vizard-Guy, the director, who was now holding her copy of the script as if about to swat a fly. 'We need to start clearing the set please.' Her deep voice and heavy French accent gave her speech an extra authority.

'Yes, Sacha.' Friedman went into harassed mode again. 'That's the problem with a skeleton crew, Richard, I get to pitch in and do the menial tasks. Sacha, this is Richard, Security.'

She gave Richard an uncomfortable, very penetrating stare to the extent that he felt like he was being X-rayed. 'Security,' she said slowly. 'You're a little late.' She didn't take her cold eyes off him, leaving Richard feeling very guilty about something, though what that something was, he hadn't the faintest idea.

'Come with me, Richard, let's go meet Monsieur Corbeau.' Richard felt grateful to Samuel for the intervention and also that Monsieur Corbeau might potentially be an ally in this highly fraught situation. A local, as was Richard, sort of.

'Monsieur Corbeau?' The old man was sitting on an antique-looking chair in the corner of the room when Samuel approached him. He was looking through a gap in the blacked-out windows, a look of longing on his face. A longing to be anywhere but here. He looked up at Samuel and a nervous smile broke out on his face. 'Monsieur Corbeau?' Samuel repeated. 'Richard Ainsworth.' Then he rushed off, hearing his name called from across the set. The old man stood up quickly, despite his age and offered his hand to Richard. A spritely smile opened up his previously worried face and his eyes watered in friendly warmth.

'Monsieur Ainsworth,' he said. 'This is a great honour.' Richard smiled back and shook his hand.

'It's OK, Monsieur Corbeau, I'm not famous. I live in Saint-Sauver.' Richard spoke French, putting the old man at ease, who then giggled, his eyes watering even more.

'That's a relief.' He patted Richard's chest. 'I've been introduced to a lot of people today, and they all seem to think I should know who they are.' He sat back down and shook his head. 'I should be at home; I have things to do in the garden.'

Richard found a chair and sat next to him. 'It wasn't your choice to be here then?'

'Oh no! This isn't me at all!' He indicated his Napoleonic tunic. 'I'm a hundred and two years old, I've fought uniforms all my life,' he grinned again, 'and now, now they finally get me in one!' He shook his head, smiling as he did so. 'Monsieur Ainsworth? Never get old. And if you get old, don't be the oldest! Round here they use you like a trophy, dusting you off for ceremonies!' He giggled again. Richard liked him enormously. A man caught up in a situation he had no control over and battling it quietly in his own shoulder-shrugging 'what can you do?' way. Richard knew a kindred spirit when he found one.

'Hopefully they won't take too long,' he said, noting already that Reed Turnbull's temper meant people liked to move quickly.

'I hope not,' said the old man seriously. 'I have a doctor's appointment at eleven. He held up his left hand showing a filthy bandage. 'I have to get this re-dressed. I cut my finger helping old Marchant with his vines last week. It keeps leaking.' He looked suitably embarrassed.

'Well at least you're playing Napoleon,' Richard joked, 'you can hide your hand in your tunic!'

They both laughed, the old man wiping his eyes as he did so.

'Monsieur Corbeau?' They both looked up to see Ben-Hur standing above them, the usual worried look on his face. Richard stood up, assuming that's what 'Security' would do in this situation and the old man followed suit. 'Monsieur Corbeau, I have the honour of introducing you to one of our stars, Mr Reed Turnbull.' He stepped aside as Richard translated, and revealed the scowling, diminutive Turnbull wearing the same tunic as old man Corbeau, with more authority it had to be said, though that didn't seem to bother Corbeau at all, who looked him in the eye and smiled. 'It's an honour, monsieur,' he held out his hand which the actor either didn't see or just ignored, concentrating instead on trying to stand taller than his 'double'. It didn't work and Corbeau giggled and sat down.

'Monsieur Corbeau,' Samuel approached the group, 'we're ready for you now.' Corbeau stood up again and removed his beret, placing it neatly on his chair. He smiled a watery-eyed smile at Richard and was led away.

'Ah the magic of the movies,' Friedman senior said, himself smiling. 'The camera will be behind the old man concentrating on the others, you'd never know it wasn't Reed in the shot.' He leant in closer to Richard. 'Except it will probably go more smoothly.'

Samuel sat the old man down, and Brian Grace and Stella Gonzales stood behind him, camera and sound at the ready. Valérie came into the room with the stunning, but very pale, Lionel who sat opposite Corbeau and in-between Napoleon's mother, Jennifer Davies, and Prince Talleyrand himself or, at least, Dominic Burdett, which is as close as it could come. Sacha Vizard-Guy directed things quietly from the side, frowning in concentration. Samuel made some last-minute adjustments to the table arrange-ments on Amorette Arthur's fussy involvement, moving a decanter of wine slightly to the right, wiping a glass and positioning finger bowls to the side of the decorative dessert, which Richard knew was a *croquembouche*, a pyramid of profiteroles. Sacha ordered Samuel to put everything back as it had been, a matter of centimetres, and the historian flushed with anger. Despite the minor disagreement, the attention to detail was very impressive, and Richard felt like holding his breath.

'I hope that's not real wine in that bottle,' Turnbull quipped from the shadows. 'We don't want *my mother* sauced before the end of the scene.'

'Are you still here, Reed?' Jennifer Davies replied calmly. 'Shouldn't you be putting your heels on?'

'Quiet on set!' Sacha barked. 'And action!'

26

It was all over in a few minutes, a couple of takes just for publicity Richard guessed, and he could see that Corbeau was relieved it was over. Valérie appeared immediately at Lionel's shoulder and nodded seriously at Richard. A job well done, she seemed to be saying, which made him feel like he'd just averted a major incident.

'OK, Monsieur Corbeau.' It was Samuel, quickly at the old man's shoulder. 'That's a wrap for you!' Corbeau didn't understand, but he guessed it was done and he stood, still smiling. He turned to move away but the ornate lace table cloth had become attached to a button on his tunic and he began to pull the bottles and glasses with him as he moved. Noticing the problem, he turned smartly to stop any spillage, whipping his bandaged hand out of his tunic as he did so. He was just too late though as the decanter fell into a glass and the bowls, spilling the wine. He looked mortified, and tried to mop up any damage, apologising profusely as he did so.

Samuel kindly put his arm around his shoulder and gently led him away towards Richard, who saw that his eyes were still watery, but in impish mock embarrassment. Monsieur Corbeau caught Richard's eye and, without being seen by the others, rolled his eyes and gave him a pixyish smile. He hadn't wanted to come in the first place and now this, he was saying. But also, that it wasn't the end of the world. Richard put his hand on the old man's shoulder as he silently put his beret back on. Corbeau looked once more at the set and everybody stared back, embarrassed for him. Stepping forward Richard saw that Corbeau was about to say something, probably along the lines of 'don't take yourselves too seriously,' but instead his face became tortured as he opened his mouth, his eyes widening in horror. He stumbled slightly and grabbed his chest as he did so. Richard noticed the pulsating veins in his neck and leapt forward, managing to catch the old man just before he hit the ground. He was still too late. Monsieur Corbeau was dead.

Chapter Four

Richard helped close the door to the back of the red medical-response vehicle and it shut with a heavy thud. He leant forward and rested his forehead on the closed door, gently banging it. The young uniformed *pompier* tried to offer him a sympathetic smile whilst making sure she kept a safe distance as her training demanded when confronted with a grieving angry relative.

'These things happen, monsieur,' she said softly. 'Heart attacks are very common and he was a very old man.'

'He was a hundred and two,' his needless confirmation was muffled into the vehicle's paintwork.

She shrugged her shoulders in a 'well there you go then' way and breaking the rules, placed a gentle hand on his shoulder. 'Did you know him well?'

'No.' She removed her hand immediately while Richard, for his part, tried to shake his head, but merely succeeded in wiping his forehead on the paintwork instead. 'I just met him.'

She looked at him askance, unsure in that case of why he seemed to be taking the whole thing quite so badly. The truth was that Richard knew *exactly* why he was taking it so badly. Yes, of course, old Monsieur Corbeau was a hundred and two and maybe the excitement or the stress had played a bigger role than his demeanour had let on. But it was the rank injustice of the whole thing too, that's what was annoying Richard. The old man had been under his 'security' for just less than five minutes, and bang, he'd dropped dead. And while he felt sorry for the man, and no doubt a thousand relatives, it was bloody unfair of Corbeau to go like that on his watch. I mean, couldn't he have waited? It was Richard's first day as personal security, bodyguard, call it what you will, and so far he had a one hundred per cent record of failure. He banged his head on the door again. Bafflement, annoyance and the feeling that he was some kind of jinx led Richard to his favourite place. He could get through this if he imagined that the old man was actually John Mills in the 1978 remake of *The 39 Steps*; that he'd been assassinated by foreign agents just before imparting crucial, secret information to our hero, Richard Hannay.

Richard Ainsworth sighed like a punctured air-bed; he didn't feel like a hero, he felt like a berk.

'Tch!' he said, suddenly standing up straight. 'Bloody typical!'

'I have a couple of things to do.' The *pompier* obviously thought he was something of a lunatic but was being very gentle with him, especially as he now had vehicle grime on his brow. 'Go and see my driver and he'll have a number for counselling. You know, if you need it.' It was clear she thought that he did. 'And here…' She handed him a tissue and pointed at his head.

Oh God, he thought, *she thinks I'm going to cry*. 'Right,' he said definitely, aware that he was in danger of causing a bit of a scene, especially as Sacha had removed her director's cap and was watching him intently. 'Things to do.' He decided to do as he was told and moved off to see the driver, still in something of a haze and not really paying attention.

'Bad luck, old man.' Martin Thompson leant out of the driver's window, an artificial look of condolence on his face. 'Still, he had a good innings by all accounts.'

'What are you doing here?' Richard sighed, unable to hide his irritation. Martin looked hurt, but after a brief pause decided to put it down to stress.

Richard's eyes narrowed in suspicion, not necessarily at Martin Thompson himself, but at his surreal appearance at the Chateau de Valençay. He hoped that it was all a dream, that his first ever charge as a security 'expert' wasn't actually dead, that in a minute he, Richard, would wake up, make breakfasts for his B&B guests and spend the rest of the day hiding from life, just the way he liked it. He looked around for Gennie, Martin's wife, knowing they always came as a pair. He knew them both well, too well in his view, and had done since he and his now estranged wife, Clare, had moved to France a few years earlier. On the one hand, Richard wanted absolutely nothing to do with them. On the other, where Martin and Gennie Thompson were concerned, forewarned was forearmed. Keep your friends close, and your enemies closer and all that. Not that they were enemies at all, or even unlikeable; although Martin's constant search for an inappropriate double entendre could grate, they just operated in a different world to Richard and one that he was wary of. They also owned a *chambre d'hôte*, and while others may have thought that Richard's antipathy towards them was based solely on business rivalry, it wasn't. Martin and Gennie's establishment was 'specialist', catering for holidaying couples 'with a sense of adventure' as Gennie had put it. 'Swingers' Martin had confirmed bluntly. And, astonishingly to Richard's admittedly more staid outlook, business was absolutely booming.

He continued looking about him. 'Looking for the wife?' Martin beamed. 'She's not here. I'll say you were curious though.' He winked and Richard felt nauseous.

'What are you doing here?' he asked again, almost a touch of desperation in his voice.

'Ah!' Martin looked very pleased with himself. 'Well, you know, volunteering for the community, and so on and so forth…' He tailed off, and ran a finger under his recently grown military-style moustache. He reminded Richard of Leslie Phillips in his 'Hello, ding dong' pomp, though without the comic charm or veneer of innocence.

'It's the uniform, isn't it?' Richard asked, a sense of ennui seeping through the question like a disappointed headmaster cutting through a lie.

'It is!' Martin beamed. 'The old girl loves a uniform. She always said she could see you in a uniform, old man.' An image flashed through Richard's mind of Gennie and him for some reason dressed as amorous traffic wardens. Martin suddenly adopted a more serious tone. 'I mean obviously, it's not just the polished buttons, it's nice to give something back, etc.'

'But it's mainly the uniform?' Richard no longer bothered to hide his contempt with Martin, who was utterly shameless anyway so never saw it.

'Well. About ninety per cent, I'd say.'

The young medic hopped into the passenger seat alongside Martin, signalling it was time to take the body away.

'Did you give monsieur the number for counselling?' she said, concerned.

'I'll be fine,' Richard interrupted, 'thanks anyway.' Though the truth was, he always felt the need for advice and counselling after even the shortest of conversations with Martin – advice, counselling and a shower.

'Richard...' Valérie appeared at his side.

'Hullo, Val!' Martin grinned.

As with Richard, she looked momentarily confused by his appearance. 'Martin,' she said coolly, 'you look very smart.'

Richard's heart sank as Martin winked at him again. 'You see?' He smiled. 'The uniform!'

The vehicle pulled away slowly through the stone arch entrance, leaving them standing, watching as it left. 'What does he mean, "the uniform"?' Valérie scoffed. 'Silly little man.'

The Thompsons had helped them out on their 'cases' with the occasional use of some inappropriate handcuffs and their handy S&M dungeon as a temporary prison, and though she had a soft spot for Gennie, Valérie remained less impressed with Martin. In truth, she had still not got over Martin greeting her naked in his garden for cocktails. Gennie had been naked too, but had been less offensive on the eye in Valérie's opinion.

'He likes uniforms,' Richard said enigmatically.

'Well at least he is dressed!' she snorted. Then she turned to face Richard. 'Richard,' she said quietly, 'we need to talk.'

He'd been expecting this obviously. When you go into partnership in a personal security business, one of the early pitfalls to avoid is a death within the first few minutes of your shift. A shudder ran down his spine, not just at old man Corbeau's death, but at the very real, distinct possibility that he might just be about to get the sack from his own business.

'I know,' he sighed. 'Still, look on the bright side, when I left the film set there were, I think, still some people alive.'

For her part over the past few months, Valérie had been trying to come to terms with Richard's gallows humour. It was a fatalistic response to a world which constantly challenged him, she'd concluded. She had even tried to match him, and she thought she would try now.

'Yes, there were. Not all though.' It had to be said, the early results of her rare forays into satire and acerbity were patchy at best and Richard looked briefly crushed by her comment. She produced a tissue, leant forward and wiped his forehead clean. It was a gesture that, if he wasn't still reeling from his sense of rank injustice, would have sent him reeling further. She smiled at him, put her arm through his and guided him gently into the gardens, away from the chateau and the film set.

Chapter Five

Richard and Valérie stood together at the furthest wall of the garden where he'd first met Dominic Burdett as Talleyrand just a few hours earlier, though it felt much longer. Beyond the wall, the valley fell dramatically some one hundred feet into a narrow lane below where a few houses were scattered. In the distance, directly opposite the chateau, stood a grand domed hunting lodge, originally part of the chateau grounds, but now divided from them by the less regal D956 road to the town of Châteauroux.

The hunting lodge had been used to luxuriously imprison members of Spanish royalty who were, in theory at least, the main thrust of the film, their release forming part of the Treaty of Valençay in 1813 and bringing an end to the Peninsula War. Though, in fact, Richard hadn't seen any actors for the Spanish roles, this Hollywood interpretation of history concentrating more on a hypothetical ménage a trois between Talleyrand, Napoleon and Marie-Louise of Austria. It was a somewhat old-fashioned style of Hollywood history-telling, two older leading men vying for a younger leading actress, and went against the new way of thinking since the 'Me Too' movement. Even to

Richard, a mostly staunch supporter of old Hollywood, it jarred somewhat.

That's what he had felt when he'd glanced at the script the night before anyway, but that wasn't on his mind right now. 'How are you feeling?' Valérie asked gently. They stood less than a metre apart; she had her back to the hunting lodge and was leaning elegantly against the wall. Richard looked in the opposite direction, directly forward, also leaning but heavily, his head bowed and his hands on the wall. He looked like he was contemplating leaping over it.

'How am I feeling?' he repeated, a little petulantly; then he hung his head down and sighed. 'I'm feeling...' He paused. 'I'm feeling incompetent.'

Valérie span round immediately. 'Oh no, Richard!' She seemed genuinely confused. 'What you did this morning was brilliant!'

Richard looked at her out of the corner of his eye. He was aware that recently she had been trying to accommodate him, if that was the right expression, but he was also aware that she was incapable of hiding her real feelings. Though if she were doing so now, she was making a damn good fist of it. Lionel must have been giving her acting lessons.

'Brilliant?' he puffed, like a customer tired of a salesman's dubious flimflam. It wouldn't do in his eyes, he could take his medicine and when a fellow cocks up, you should tell the fellow he cocked up.

'Yes, brilliant.' He went to interrupt, but she rode over his objections. 'Our main job here is to protect Lionel Margaux; well that is my role. Your role, this morning, was to protect the others on the set.' She looked at him as if that were explanation enough.

'You mean, because none of the actual film company expired, my morning's work was a triumph? That's a bit of a stretch, don't you think?'

'Richard, I know about security.' She was very serious. 'We put a ring around the people we protect. You protected our employers from a… I don't know, what would you call it, a trauma?'

He thought about this, and at the same time looked for signs that Valérie hadn't been taking an evening course in mendacity and was just trying to make him feel better about himself. She was, of course and as always, deadly serious. It was also true that while the cast and skeleton crew had made all the right noises and so on – except the the toxic Reed Turnbull who'd complained about having to wait around when they could be getting on with things and Sacha who had at least made it outside – they were were mostly too obsessed with themselves to feel that the old man's death was actually anything to do with them. Maybe that was why Richard felt partly responsible; it was also Valérie's reasoning behind his so-called 'brilliant' work.

'It's true,' he mused, 'no one seemed all that bothered. Sad really.'

She stayed silent for a moment. 'There was nothing anyone could do, I suppose.'

'No.'

'He was an old man.'

'A hundred and two.'

'The stress of the film set, and then being caught up in the table cloth and upsetting the glasses. It must have been too much for him. He must have been very upset.'

Richard thought about this. It was the same conclusion that the young medic had come to, and it basically boiled down to 'he was a hundred and two and distressed; what do you expect?' He shook his head.

'No,' he said, quietly.

'No? No what?'

'He wasn't stressed or anxious or troubled. I spoke to him beforehand and he thought it was all a bit of a nonsense, people taking themselves so seriously, dressing up.'

'But that was before he upset the dining table, yes?' Valérie wasn't convinced.

'And after.' Richard continued, remembering the scene in more detail. 'After he'd been disentangled from the tablecloth, he walked towards me and he smiled…'

'A nervous smile probably. Embarrassment.'

'No. No it wasn't that, it was almost mischievous…'

'I don't understand, Richard.'

He turned and looked seriously into her eyes, unsure whether he was trying to convince her or himself. 'It was all a bit of silliness to him, I think.'

'He spilled the table deliberately?' Valérie felt this had gone far enough.

'I'm not saying that. Only that it really didn't matter to him. Don't cry over spilt milk and all that. Or in this case, fake wine, some plastic profiteroles and a couple of finger bowls. He even winked at me! I don't think he was at all stressed.'

Valérie thought about this for a moment, then took his wrists in each hand and held them as though he needed to be protected from self-harming. 'Richard.' Her tone was motherly. 'This sounds like one of your wild goose chases.'

There are times in life, no matter how gregarious a person you are, or how confident in yourself you may be, or, like Richard neither of those things, when something hits you like a tsunami of affront. A great wet haddock of injustice slapped to the forehead, knocking your axis bandy and rendering you utterly, utterly speechless. He could say nothing, he almost gasped for air at the accusation. In the end, he sort of just whimpered like a small dog mistakenly blamed for the misbehaviour of another dog. *His wild goose chases? The bloody cheek!*

'Now,' Valérie ignored, or didn't see, the effect her words had had on him, 'are you sure that nobody else was interested in the tragedy?'

They began to walk up the steps and towards the catering van which was setting up in the courtyard. Richard, a few paces behind, was determined to remain injured and sullen but something in Valérie's question also sounded like a test of his observational skills, and he thought back through the events of the morning again. Everybody, literally, had a role. Turnbull the bully; Burdett lost in his character; Sacha the moody arthouse director; Brian Grace and Stella Gonzales concentrating on camera, lights and sound; Jennifer Davies coolly defending herself; the preening French actor Gilbertine, fussing in his role as Carême; and Amorette the historian, flouncing off set. They were all like bubbles, disconnected but occasionally bouncing off each other and Friedman and Samuel were trying to make sure that none of them hit each other hard enough to burst.

'They're such an odd bunch,' he said, playing for time. 'And I think all of them are just too self-obsessed to be affected by an old stranger's death, no matter how close it was too them.'

'All of them?' Valérie replied enigmatically.

'Well, I…' He put his hand to his forehead in classic slapstick fashion. 'Of course! Lionel!' Valérie nodded slowly. 'I noticed when you brought her on set that she looked very pale. I put it down to make-up and, I don't know, the nature of her role.'

'And?'

He paused before continuing very slowly, 'And it wasn't the make-up or the nature of her role?'

'That's right, Richard.' She stopped walking and grabbed his arm. She had that wild-eyed excitement in her eyes that he already knew heralded the start, in her head at least, of a problem, a case, an adventure. She positively thrived on it even if it was someone she regarded as family who might be in danger.

'What happened?' He was trying to sound calm, assuming his regular role in their relationship as a sponge mopping up her excessive enthusiasm.

'Someone left a message for Lionel in her dressing room!' He thought her eyes might pop out of her head, and he knew that meant her excitement levels were being ramped up.

'I'm assuming it wasn't fan mail then?'

'No!' She carried on looking at him, deep into his eyes, as if this was all the information he needed to join her in her ecstasy.

'Well, what was it?' he asked eventually.

'A threat!' she shrieked.

'Madame d'Orçay!' He wasn't always this demonstrative and Valérie suddenly calmed down at the full use of her name, like a child who hears a parent add their middle name to a command. 'Now calm down, and tell me what's happened, please?'

She smiled at him warmly. No, he hadn't used her name like that since they had first met, but she knew that Richard adding the ineffably polite 'please' to the sentence meant that he thought he had gone too far.

She took a deep breath. 'There was a message, left in lipstick on her make-up mirror,' she whispered as they neared the catering van, her calmness restored. 'It said *CACHE-CACHE.*'

'Cache-cache? Hide-and-seek?' He frowned.

'You know what this means?' Valérie was deadly serious now.

Again Richard sighed heavily, and his shoulders slumped. 'It means that whoever was stalking Lionel in Paris has followed her here.'

'Yes. Precisely, Richard.'

They both became aware of a third party lingering close by. It was Jennifer Davies, still in costume and make-up, holding a Styrofoam cup of pale greenish liquid, steaming and with a fennel teabag label sticking limply to the side.

'I just wanted you to know, Monsieur Ainsworth...' She paused, obviously waiting for Richard to say something, which it took him a moment to work out.

'Oh, ah, call me Richard, please.' He nodded, almost bowing in deference to the costume; he was speaking to Napoleon's mother after all. He missed Valérie's slight smile at his formality.

'Oh, Richard, and call me Jennifer. I wanted you to know that I have spoken to Monsieur Corbeau and...'

'You have spoken to Monsieur Corbeau?' Valérie couldn't help herself.

The look on the face of Jennifer Davies was as if she hadn't known that Valérie was even there. It's a brutal world, Richard thought, not for the first time.

'Not directly, madame,' the actress said coldly. 'His body is dead. I spoke with his spirit.' She broke off and stared into the distance. 'His spirit wishes us to carry on with the production; he is our Guardian Angel now.' She turned her eyes back onto Richard and Valérie who stood rigidly still, somewhat stunned.

'Oh. Right-o,' Richard said eventually, forcing a smile.

'I just thought you should know.' Jennifer turned flamboyantly away and walked back towards the chateau.

Richard and Valérie both breathed out deeply as they turned to the counter on the catering van. Richard was shaking his head and Valérie was, rarely for her he noticed, speechless.

'*Bonjour*, Richard,' came the deep voice of the caterer. 'I hear you killed Napoleon this morning!'

Richard recognised the voice immediately and looked up to see René DuPont leering down at him. René, owner of the Café des Tasses Cassées in Saint-Sauveur, was a good friend to have. Former feared scourge of bad debtors right across the Paris region, he had settled comfortably into the catering trade, but still carried with him the weight of menace. As such, no one really had the heart to tell him he was totally unsuited to his new calling. The coffee was awful and both Richard and, to a lesser extent, Valérie tried to hide the fact.

'What are you doing here, René?' Richard asked, getting off the subject of his supposed assassination of the emperor.

'I'm the caterer for this nonsense.' He swept his Popeye-like forearms wide as if unveiling his kingdom. It was indeed eye-catching: a converted old Citroën van with the side opened up to reveal a serving hatch. 'I won her in a game of cards,' he said proudly. 'Well, I say "won".' Richard was impressed but couldn't help feeling that if this production was jinxed already, then having René DuPont as the provider of meals and drinks was surely the indigestible proof in the pudding.

'He's also an experienced extra pair of eyes and ears for us, Richard,' Valérie said decisively. 'Very useful. And, you're going to keep watch tonight, René, aren't you?'

'No.' René would have some pretty dark stories to tell about his former life of crime, but Richard saw him move towards the back of his van and away from Valérie's gaze at his change of plan. 'I can't. I'm double-booked.' He wiped some surfaces clean.

'But this could be a matter of life and death!' she hissed dramatically.

'I know, mine!' He tried to laugh it off. 'I'm sorry, madame, but I promised to cater for the *guinguette* this evening. There's not many of the old folk still dancing now, I don't want to let them down.'

Richard saw the man's dilemma. The *guinguette* is a tradition in France, usually an open-air dance floor, next to a river where old couples danced to the old accordion-backed French café songs of Piaf, Trenet, and so on. The numbers had dwindled in recent years, and now it was mainly old women dancing with other old women, the weaker men having expired. Richard knew that it wasn't that René didn't want to let them down necessarily, it was that they were, even to René, a formidable and terrifying group.

'Right.' Valérie was making quick calculations and Richard knew, even from limited experience that he was about to cop it. 'Richard, you go back home and get some rest. I think you should do night duty tonight.'

'But I have to do breakfasts in the morning!' He decided token resistance was the least he could do.

'Oh we can sort that out.' And with that she marched off back to work, as both Richard and René, an unlikely pairing, watched her go.

'She is some woman,' René said eventually, and not entirely in admiration. 'Another coffee?'

Richard thought about it. It had been a tiring, harrowing, put-upon day. Yet another in his estimation, but it still hadn't hit the depths so badly that he needed another of René's coffees.

Chapter Six

In the moonlit gardens of the chateau, Richard crouched awkwardly and thought of his treasured hens as he did so, in particular his late, beloved Ava Gardner. Outwardly life was normal, or as normal as life in Valérie's circle would allow, but the truth was that he still harboured a fair amount of indignation over the mafia assassination of Ava, even if the 'adventure', as Valérie now referred to it, had brought the pair together. Obviously, he knew that in the grand scheme of things it was unlikely he would, or could, take on the entire Cosa Nostra over the murder of what was at best an infrequent layer, but it still irked him. Valérie had bought him a replacement hen which he'd named Olivia de Havilland, and in doing so Valérie had dropped the bombshell that the real Olivia de Havilland, who was the last living link to the golden age of Hollywood, and therefore to Richard a goddess, was in fact a neighbour of Valérie's in Paris and that they occasionally shared an afternoon patisserie. Olivia de Havilland, the actress, had died aged 103 not that long ago, but Olivia de Havilland the hen, was settling in nicely with the others, Lana Turner and the feisty Joan Crawford. It was a comfortable arrangement. They relied on Richard, and Richard relied on them. They were his comfort, his go-to 'space', outside of a late-night black-and-white film classic obviously, and he doted on them. It was odd then, how one creature from ostensibly the same species, if not genus, could be completely different to another under the same zoological umbrella.

Take peacocks for example. They were, to Richard's currently jaundiced eye, vicious bullies. Hens and peacocks are both fowl, though this one was definitely more so. This peacock, whose name he'd been told was Clovis, roamed freely around Valençay's large grounds and didn't, on the face of it, like his territory threatened. Richard had been left with pretty vague instructions about keeping an eye out for somebody wandering around, presumably with lipstick and thus revealing themselves as the person who'd left the rather haunting message on Lionel's dressing-room mirror, but Clovis currently had him cornered, and had a look in his eye that suggested mercy wasn't in his nature.

'Nice peacock,' he said cautiously and for about the tenth time. 'Nice peacock.' His attempts at fraternal bonding with the creature were proving pathetically inadequate and it also struck him that this potentially murderous, or worse, amorous bird was making a far better fist of night-time chateau security than he was and, more than likely, on higher wages. Why would anyone even need security with a ferocious beast like this wandering in the gothic shadows?

The bird shook its feathers in what Richard knew was a show of grace, courage and beauty designed to render any passing peahen weak at the knees. That he also now felt weak at the knees was not due to falling under some romantic spell, however, but the hideous vision of him still being penned in a corner like this at dawn when the cast and crew would reconvene, and that wouldn't do. That wouldn't do at all. Richard decided to change tack and cautiously laid his torch down at his feet, making sure the beam was on him, then he spread his arms wide and shook himself in what he hoped was an imitation of peacock courtship that was so bad the bird would feel neither threatened nor amorous and go back to strutting in the darkness. His nemesis looked at Richard, his head tilted to one side, confused by Richard's awkward, flailing-arm-belly-dance routine. He then squawked harshly, in what sounded like a stream of foul, or fowl, mouthed invective, shook his feathers again, scraped at the ground and turned his back on Richard, before strutting away, the victor.

Richard waited for a second, then quietly whispered to himself, 'Oh no, it wasn't the airplanes. It was beauty killed the beast.' He suspected Clovis would lap up the *King Kong* reference.

He picked up his torch, pleased with himself, then immediately dropped it again when he heard his name called. He stood stock still, trying to dismiss the idea that the peacock was in fact one of Valérie's operatives in heavy disguise and that this had been a test of courage and ability under fire.

'Richard?' The voice came again. It was an American accent and he realised he could also smell cigar smoke. 'Has that goddamn bird gone?' Ben-Hur Friedman emerged from the shadows, the lighted end of his cigar looking like a warning beacon in the night. 'Why are those things always so angry? Jeez.'

Richard had no idea how much Friedman had seen of the last few minutes but decided he could probably get away with it. 'Yes, well you just have to know how to deal with them, that's all.' He dusted himself down and picked up his torch again. 'I didn't know you were still here, Mr Friedman.'

'Call me Ben.' He drew on his cigar and the orange glow became more intense. 'You know what they say about the captain of a ship, Richard? That he must go down with his crew.'

His words were slightly slurred, and he sounded morose. 'Is the ship going down, er, Ben?'

The producer sighed heavily. 'I don't know for sure. But we've been chased out of Paris, that old guy died today… the guys with the money back home are getting nervous. You know what one of them said to me this afternoon?'

'No, what?'

'*Waterworld*, Richard. He said, *Waterworld*. Jesus Christ. That set Costner back twenty years.'

Richard didn't know much about the film; it was, as he liked to say, 'after his time'. But he knew what Friedman was getting at. If a film production starts to get a whiff of difficulty it would become easy prey for the vultures, and unlikely to recover from that. The film would be the story.

'Is it as bad as that?' he asked gently.

'They seem to think so.' Friedman produced a hip flask from his inside pocket, and offered it to Richard. 'Here, even though you're on duty.'

Richard took the flask, his nerves still somewhat shredded by the peacock incident. He was expecting a rough bourbon taste, but instead it was a warming cognac of very high quality. Friedman followed Richard's sip with a mighty gulp before refastening the lid.

'I need this picture, Richard. I need it. It's my last chance. I don't have Costner's stamina. If this doesn't get finished, or it's a turkey… I'm finished.' He drew on his cigar once more. 'I always wanted to make a costume movie. A real, old-school Hollywood movie like my grandaddy and my old man. No CGI, just great stars and great writing.' He breathed smoke out, filling the air. 'Instead,' he said slowly, 'I'm in charge of a crazy house and I'm trying to keep my actors from tearing each other apart.'

'Can't the director help you there?'

'Sacha? You'd think, huh?' He opened the flask and took another swig before handing it to Richard. 'You notice how she doesn't talk to the cameraman, or rather he rarely talks to her?' Richard hadn't noticed.

'Brian Grace?'

'Yep. A genius, no doubt. No one frames a shot like Brian, no one. That's why he's won the awards.' He paused. 'I gave him his first job as a director too. You ever see the movie *The Sidewalk Romantics*?' He chuckled. 'Of course you didn't. Nobody did. That film is buried somewhere underground with nuclear waste. The man is an artist, but not a director.'

'He wanted to direct this film?'

'Yep. And he got real sore when he didn't get it. But Sacha wrote the script. It was her project when she came looking for the money, and she insisted that she was part of the deal.'

'That seems only fair.' Richard was hoping that he would remember all this in the morning.

'Fair? Maybe. But she's one of these arty directors, a real European, know what I mean? No offence. In real life these characters, Napoleon, Talleyrand, Marie, there was a tension, a jealousy, a lack of trust, right?'

'Probably, yes.'

'Well she wants the actors to feel that for real.'

'Is it working though? Is it good?'

'It's good only if it gets finished, Richard, and I'm the sap who has to hold it all together.' He emptied the flask. 'Let's go get another.' He walked carefully across the gravel, perhaps to hide his inebriation, his shadow looking enormous in the chateau courtyard lights. Richard wasn't sure if his job as nightwatchman was supposed to entail getting drunk with the producer, but as – in name at least – he was a co-owner of the as-yet-untitled detective agency he and Valérie had set up, it was definitely in his remit to collect the gossip. He followed Friedman down the garden steps to the back of the chateau, where the French doors were open on a room at the bottom of the building and where a pale light flooded into the grounds.

'I didn't know anyone was staying in the chateau itself,' Richard said, keeping it light and trying not to provoke Friedman's gloom. The producer stumbled in through the open doors, pausing slightly to regain his balance. He re-emerged quickly with an ornate bottle of cognac, holding it by the neck. Richard could just make out the name in the light, a Frapin Millésime cognac and about two hundred euros a bottle. He gulped, savouring the aftertaste that had lingered from earlier.

'Officially I'm not staying here, I'm in one of the trailers like everyone else, but I negotiated it with Amorette,' he said. 'This was the private apartment of Dorothea von Biron, Princess of Courland. And Talleyrand's mistress.'

'You know your history,' Richard said, encouragingly.

'She was a kept woman, a courtesan. Not only with Talleyrand, but with other powerful, rich figures.' He sighed heavily. 'I know exactly how she felt. Damn, I forgot the glasses.' For a brief moment Richard thought he was going to neck the cognac straight from the bottle. 'Here hold this,' he said and disappeared back indoors.

'You didn't want to stay with the rest of the cast and crew in the grounds then?' Richard asked when Friedman came back into the garden.

The producer sat down heavily on a low brick wall and puffed on his cigar again. 'No. I'm their sheepdog during the day, and if I'm really needed I can sort things out. But I need my time too. Even the captain has to lock himself in his cabin sometimes.'

Richard got the distinct impression that Friedman was a depressive drunk, railing against the world when the world wasn't watching him. He had a lot of sympathy with that. He sat down next to him and Friedman poured out about fifty euros worth of top-notch cognac.

'Look on the bright side,' Richard began. 'Tyrone Power died three-quarters into the filming of *Solomon and Sheba*, and that still made money!'

Friedman turned towards him, studying his features carefully. 'You really know your stuff,' he said, impressed.

'Well, I'm a film historian,' Richard replied, 'a doctor of film actually.' It was something he usually hid but the cognac had excessive mouth-loosening properties.

'Is that a fact?' Friedman mulled this information over. 'You speak French?'

'*Oui.*'

Friedman scraped his light stubble, and put his hand on Richard's shoulder. 'Richard,' he said. 'I'm promoting you.' Alarm bells immediately started ringing in Richard's head. Now what had he done? 'Can you deal with the press tomorrow? The boys back home will be impressed with a real doctor handling the press for them this end. Real impressed.'

Richard didn't know what to say. Well, he did know what to say and what he wanted to say was 'no bloody way, thank you very much'. On the other hand though, it was either deal with journalists or spend his nights in a duel with a rapacious peacock.

'Well...' he said, still hedging his bets.

'Come on, Rich, this calls for a celebration! Remember what W. C. Fields said: "I drink therefore I am!"' And he quoted the old comedian with a tone-perfect impersonation. Richard smiled his assent. 'Good!' Friedman beamed at him. And with that he disappeared back inside presumably looking for more alcohol.

Fifteen minutes later Richard was still sitting there, drifting off himself. He stood unsteadily and went to the French doors. On the sofa Ben-Hur Friedman was lying face down, his glasses hanging in his hand. Richard's first thought was 'oh no, not again!' Then he heard the American snore loudly and he decided to leave him to it.

Chapter Seven

It was not the best of Richard that made his way back to Les Vignes *chambre d'hôte* just before dawn. It wasn't just the realisation that at his time of life a good night's sleep was as essential as his reading glasses, but that at the bare minimum he should have less to do with either drunken Hollywood producers or sociopathic wildfowl. The latter of these had attacked him again near the maze, cutting his hand in the process and this was, for Richard, pretty much the straw that broke the camel's back. 'Enough's enough,' he'd said to the angry creature, threw a stick as a distraction – which hadn't worked – and resigned his post as nightwatchman forthwith.

He was even, rarely for him, looking forward to serving breakfast, and then of course hiding behind his breakfast bar and spending some quality time with his hens. It was not to be though. Valérie had commandeered the place and breakfast had begun without him. It was true that all the guests were working on the production anyway, not that he had as many guests as usual since Valérie and Passepartout had moved permanently into one of his three rooms. One of the others was taken by the increasingly pale Lionel Margaux and the other by Alain 'Le Loup'

Petit. The enormous, wild-looking Petit was presumably there as extra security but Richard couldn't help feeling that, though this was probably a good insurance policy, the amount of hair left behind when he eventually checked out would be hell to clear up. What was more remarkable, however, was that breakfast was being served, not by Valérie, but by Madame Tablier. Usually, on the rare occasions that Madame Tablier was asked to fill in on serving duties, she did so in a way that would make a stroppy teenager look enthusiastic, being to customer service what Dr Crippen had been to the bedside manner, yet here she was pouring coffee and offering croissants. Was she wearing her hair slightly differently too?

Richard wasn't keen on change and sloped into the salon with an air of suspicion before slumping into a chair in the corner. Everybody stared at him and he suddenly became aware of just how dreadful he must look. A middle-aged man who's gone a night without sleep gives off a stench of defeat at the best of times, but one who has also over indulged in cognac, albeit high-quality, after being bullied into the bushes by a violent peacock and who is bleeding from a cut hand thanks to said angry bird is, under any normal circumstances, to be pitied. These were not normal circumstances.

'Could I have some of that coffee please, Madame Tablier?' He tried to affect an air of pre-guillotine dignity.

'Broken your legs have you?' was the unforgiving response.

He sighed and nodded to himself.

'I'll get it for you, Richard.' It was Lionel Margaux who made the offer and again, under normal circumstances,

Richard would have been absolutely delighted and awkwardly honoured that a beautiful, major international film star was acting as his Samaritan. But he had very little left in him for such emotion.

'Thank you,' he said weakly. 'It's been a long night.' He was aware, though trying not to show it, that Valérie and Passepartout were both staring at him, and that they had exactly the same look on their faces. There was an element of concern he guessed, but it was definitely in the minority, overwhelmed as it was by a total lack of comprehension.

'Have you been fighting, Richard?' Finally Valérie spoke and he thought he detected a slight hint of guilt in the question. She obviously hadn't banked on him being the victim of a night-time assault.

'You could say that, yes,' he replied somewhat tartly, wrapping a paper napkin around his bleeding hand for added effect.

Lionel poured his coffee. 'I am so sorry,' she said. 'This is all my fault. I have brought whatever it is, whoever it is, with me here.'

'It's all in a day's work,' he said, heroically.

'How many of them were there?' Alain Petit clearly had experience of these things.

'Who was it, Richard?' Valérie sat next to him and was now showing genuine concern.

'I didn't catch his name.' He felt this had gone on long enough but couldn't think of a dignified way to get out of it.

'You are very brave. Thank you.' Lionel put her hand on his shoulder and went back to her table.

Valérie held Passepartout closer. 'Did you get a good look at him, Richard? Would you recognise them again?'

Richard let out a deep breath, stirred some sugar into his coffee and said quietly. 'It was Clovis.' Everyone turned to each other in confusion. 'Clovis, the peacock.'

There was a stunned silence in the room.

'But you…' Valérie began.

'It was the peacock OK? It was the bloody peacock! Vicious bugger too.'

The silence remained for a split second and then Alain erupted in a huge auditorium-filling guffaw. Even Madame Tablier laughed, and she hadn't been on record as even cracking a smile since the turn of the century. Lionel was trying hard not to laugh, Passepartout quite clearly would have laughed if he could and Valérie didn't know what to believe, whether Richard was indeed being stoic about his heroism or that he had actually had a fight with a bird. Alain stood up and made his way over to Richard.

'I salute you, monsieur,' he said, wiping the tears from his eyes. 'I'd rather fight ten men than fend off a peacock on heat!' He made for the stairs to get ready, still chuckling. 'Madame,' he said to Lionel as he passed, 'I can take you this morning if you like, and if it's agreed by the security?' He glanced briefly at Richard who flushed. Valérie, the boss, nodded her consent.

Twenty minutes later Lionel and Alain had left, leaving Richard, Valérie and Madame Tablier awkwardly sitting in silence. Richard and Valérie didn't know what to say to break it and Madame Tablier was enjoying the strained atmosphere. It was none of them that broke the mood in the end as Commissaire Henri LaPierre came through the door and before even saying '*Bonjour*' poured himself a coffee. He then leant on the breakfast bar, Richard's breakfast bar, and surveyed the room. He looked at each one of them in turn before finishing with his eyes on Valérie.

'Natural causes,' he said, without preamble. 'Now, Madame d'Orçay,' – his formality, as one of Valérie's innumerable ex-husbands, was not lost on the room – 'I do not know why you ask me to waste my time in this way. I say to myself, "Well, she has a nose for these things, so maybe…" Your nose has lost its way, madame.' He shot a quick glance at Richard, leaving no one under any illusions as to the cause of Valérie's current lack of nasal direction.

'It is best to be certain, Henri, don't you think?' Her own lack of formality was designed to puncture the policeman's pomposity, but Richard guessed it would take more than the use of his Christian name to achieve that task.

'What was natural causes?' Madame Tablier asked gruffly, resorting to her default mode now that 'Le Loup' had left.

'The death of Monsieur Corbeau, madame,' was the stiff reply. 'It was natural causes.'

'Well he was getting on!'

'He was a hundred and two,' Richard confirmed automatically. He was secretly quite chuffed that Valérie had taken his vague suspicions and had the authorities investigate to be sure.

'Well, Henri, thank you for confirming that for us.'

'I now owe a few favours,' the Commissaire wasn't letting this go. 'And I am not entirely sure why you wanted a post-mortem. It was really very obvious that the old man had a heart attack. The medics said as much at the scene, you said that yourself.'

Richard went to share his doubts with Lapierre but Valérie got there first. 'It is our first major assignment Henri…'

'Ah yes, the *security* business!' He scoffed, emphasising the word security and giving Richard a haughty look.

'The Les Vignes Agency, Commissaire, will thrive. It will reduce your workload, most probably, allowing you more time for fishing, which was always only your ever real passion.' Lapierre blushed. 'And, we take our duty of care very seriously indeed. Do we not, Richard?'

'Absolutely!' Richard gushed, though this was the first he'd heard of the agency name and might have known Valérie would keep her name off the title.

'I see.' The Commissaire grumbled, knowing from experience that arguing with Valérie was futile. 'And I wish you luck.' He looked pointedly at Richard. 'For my part I still do not see why you had any doubts over Monsieur Corbeau's death. He was very old…'

'A hundred and two,' Richard interrupted, aware that he was repeating himself incessantly with the man's age.

'Yes, a hundred and two. And he had apparently upset the table; it was inevitable that he would suffer from the stress!' He slammed his hand down on the breakfast bar, almost repeating Monsieur Corbeau's spillages.

'Pah!' It was Madame Tablier who was having none of it. 'Old Antoine Corbeau stressed? Absolute rubbish.' Everybody looked at her. 'Everybody knows that Antoine Corbeau did not get stressed about anything. He was ice cold.'

'What do you know of this, madame?' The policeman's interest was reluctantly piqued.

'Corbeau was one of the Maquisards…'

'The rural French resistance.' Richard had heard of them obviously and seen many of the discreet dedications dotted around locally.

'The SS came looking for him and the others in August 1944, my father too. Valençay was torched.' Richard had never heard Madame Tablier talk about her family before. 'They got away. Some didn't though.' She rose from her seat, sniffed and then said, 'Well, all this won't get those windows cleaned, will it?' She left the room.

'Well, of course that doesn't mean he wasn't now unwell.' Lapierre was moved like the others, but he had a point. 'And, what is worse, if you'll forgive me, but because I showed an interest in the poor man, I have now been asked to be at the press conference later today! Not asked, told.' The others both looked at him wondering why this was such a problem. 'I was supposed to be in a fishing competition!' He looked back at the pair of them seeing if this personal devastation had left its mark. It hadn't. 'They want to make an announcement at this press conference, I don't know what. Well, I can only hope that it goes smoothly so I can get away quickly.' He paused, and took a sip of coffee. 'I hear they have a new press officer for this purpose.'

Richard spat his coffee out and started a coughing fit.

Chapter Eight

Richard drove slowly through the late summer countryside. It was his way to drive at a safe speed and not to
be hurried; partly his battered old 2CV wasn't capable of
much speed anyway unless it was going downhill, wherein
Richard kept his foot lightly on the brake, but it was just
how he took life. Safely. It had been Valérie's observation
that he drove how he lived, at a safe speed, at a safe distance,
taking in the view but rarely stopping to appreciate it. At
first it had annoyed her and she'd insisted on driving them
both everywhere in her very different, very sporty Renault
Alpine cabriolet. But after a while Richard had noticed
that she had begun to slow down at times too. Maybe even
to appreciate how Richard did things, and at the pace that
he did them. He hadn't voiced this observation, naturally;
he'd continue to enjoy the comforting thought without
the possibility of it being disproved.

This wasn't one of those times though.

'Richard, we really must hurry. We cannot be late for
the press conference; I want to see who will be there!'

Richard, feeling like he'd jumped involuntarily into
deep, shark-infested waters, was in even less of a hurry
than usual. 'Well, they can't start without me, I'm the

press officer!' He slowed down, approaching a not very tight bend.

Valérie smiled. 'Yes,' she said, a hint of satisfaction in her tone. 'That was very clever of you.'

'Oh, well you know…' He wasn't very good at modesty, false or otherwise, having rarely had the occasion to use it.

'What gave you the idea?'

'What idea?'

'To offer to be the press officer? What gave you that idea? It's brilliant!'

He changed gear. 'Well, partly it was a flash of brilliance, and partly I thought it would mean less night-time entanglement with that bloody peacock.' He looked at his heavily bandaged left forefinger, the one part of his hands that wasn't gripping the steering wheel.

'It was inspired, Richard, you have a real flair for this sort of thing I think.'

He shot her an unseen glance to see if she was joking, but of course she wasn't. 'Well, I just thought it would get us right to the heart of the production.' He was warming to his ever-so-slight deception. 'The thing about a press officer is it isn't what he, or she, says to the press. It's more about what he, or she, doesn't say to the press. That's what *we're* interested in.'

'And you think that you will be told these things?'

He thought about that, and the obvious answer was no. 'I don't know yet, I haven't started. Though I have to say that Friedman, the producer, or prodooser, is actually quite open, unguarded even.'

'Really?' Her eyes gleamed at the prospect of a weak link in the chain.

'Yes. Likes a drink too, preferably top-notch cognac. He told me that this is his last chance. He not only needs the film finished, but needs it to be a hit too.'

'To make money?'

'Yes, partly that. In the film business you don't always have to make a profit if the film wins awards. If it's worthy.'

'And, what do you think of this film so far, *The Master Servant*? Is it worthy?'

Richard thought about this for a second. 'Honestly,' he began, 'taking into account Amorette Arthur's objections, I think it needs to make money. I think it needs to make a lot of money.'

Valérie thought about this. 'I don't understand the film business. It seems to me that poor Lionel doesn't even like it either.' She bit her bottom lip in concentration. 'Could the death of Monsieur Corbeau be exploited for publicity, or even the stalker of Lionel, could that be exploited too?'

Richard drove cautiously around the roundabout leading into Valençay, always fearing that the 2CV would topple over. On the central island was the monument to the original creation of the SOE in the Second World War, the Special Operations Executive. It was the precursor to the SAS, which he knew little about other than David Niven and Ian Fleming had been involved. It was an interesting question that Valérie raised. 'I think the production is already *notorious*, because of what's happened to Lionel, and because of them moving out of Paris. So there's that. I don't know about Monsieur Corbeau, I suspect not. This will be a very small affair, this press conference, they'll announce that they'll dedicate the film to him and so on, give him a screen credit, but not much besides.' He sounded very much the expert. 'I suspect it will just be a few local journalists.' He slowed down at a zebra crossing. 'Sad really, after a life like that.' A military brass band crossed the road in front of him, carrying their gleaming instruments, ready to regroup on the other side of the road at the war memorial.

Richard looked slowly to his left and his heart sank. On the patch of ground in front of the cenotaph stood about two hundred people; some were obviously locals, but many, many more were not. There were some high-up military uniforms dotted about and, worse than that, television lights, platforms for cameras, reporters already doing pieces to camera for the national and international press. To show just how seriously the whole thing was being taken, the usually empty flagpoles were adorned with the Tricolore, the EU flag and various other heraldic excesses. Richard knew full well what that meant; if they put a flag up in rural France, this meant it was to be an 'event'. So it was to be a major press conference of which he, Richard Ainsworth, or more accurately for this event, Dr Richard Ainsworth, was ostensibly in charge. He made a decision, put his foot on the accelerator and forced the 2CV to go squealing against its will past the melee. He needed time to think.

'What are you doing?' Valérie asked in frustration.

'Erm, parking around the other side of the chateau. It'll be easier to get away.'

'To get away where?' she asked, not unreasonably.

'Anybloodywhere,' he muttered to himself, trying to get the thing to roar towards the chateau which was standing imperiously at the end of the road. He realised he had nowhere to go.

'Richard, where are we going? The press conference was back there.'

'I don't want to park there. I don't want anyone to see me in this car.'

'I thought you liked this car.'

'I love this car. But it has "Les Vignes – *chambre d'hôte*" plastered on the side and I want to look like a professional press officer, like I know what I'm doing. Not some has-been who's failed and has to take in paying guests.'

It was only partly true. Nothing would have pleased him more right now than to turn the car around, proudly display the advertising to the world's media, and go and enjoy being a has-been with his brood of hens. Nevertheless his statement had struck a chord with Valérie.

'Is that how you see yourself, a failure? A has-been?'

He slotted the car in a space next to the chateau and turned off the engine, and looked her seriously in the eye. 'A has-been, me? No.' He laughed. 'Madame d'Orçay, I'm a never-was!' He cranked open his car door. 'Now, shall we go to work?'

He got out of the car leaving her to sit there for a moment alone and deep in thought. Then, seemingly having made a decision, she followed him as he strode purposefully to the cenotaph.

'I wish I'd put a tie on,' he said, his stride slowing down as they crossed the road. 'I mean, it would look much more respectful. You're wearing a tie and I'm not.' It was true, Valérie was still going for the tweed suit look, but had swapped a roll-neck for a smart white shirt and black tie.

'Wear mine,' she said matter-of-factly.

'What will you wear instead though?'

'I have a brooch I can put on instead. Here.' She removed her tie, but didn't hand it over. Instead she stopped them both and faced him. She reached up and pulled up his collar, then swiftly tied a perfect Windsor knot before turning down his collar again. 'We are a good team, Richard, I think.' She looked at him, a very serious look in her eye and then they walked on in silence, she with her customary confidence and he with a rarely felt sensation: unaccustomed confidence.

'That's a nice brooch,' he said. It was actually a very ordinary brooch, showing an open book and some Roman numerals but he felt he ought to say something to try and look calm.

'Yes, it was a present.'

Friedman was there to meet them, glancing anxiously at his watch. 'Ah, Richard! I thought you weren't going to show. Hello, madame,' he added, smiling nervously at Valérie.

'Call me Valérie,' she said breezily.

He went to speak to Richard again, but couldn't take his gaze off Valérie, looking her up and down with a producer's eye. 'OK,' he said, still not looking at Richard, though Valérie was ignoring him and taking in the whole spectacle. 'OK, I've written down what I'd like you to say on our behalf about poor old er, Monsieur, um…'

'Corbeau,' Richard finished the sentence for him.

'Corbeau, that's right.' Finally he took his eyes off Valérie. 'We're going to give him a screen credit, but also a dedication to his life at the end of the film. He was a hero around here; I didn't know.'

'We only found out today,' Valérie interrupted.

'Also, they, the town brass, want to have a banquet in his honour tomorrow night after shooting. I don't want to really, but it wouldn't look good if we said no.' Friedman looked nervous about the whole thing.

In the background, the brass band started up with a rather unpractised rendition of 'La Marseillaise'; there were trumpets and tubas all in some sort of competition with each other so the effect wasn't quite the stirring anthem it usually was, more of a musical interpretation of a dog chasing its own tail. The band leader himself looked older than the man they were commemorating while the poor tuba player looked small enough to live inside his instrument. Richard made his way past them to the lectern just as the band ran out of steam and finished like stragglers at the end of a marathon. From where he stood on the podium, he could see most of the cast sitting, as if for a studio portrait, on the front row, though they were minus Dominic Burdett and the director of the film Sacha Vizard-Guy. The latter he noticed standing at the cenotaph monument itself, away from the others. Carefully, and first in French, he read out Friedman's prepared statement adding a few things that he felt were missing about how bereft the entire production 'family' felt. When he had finished explaining the end-of-film dedication to the old man, there was a murmur of appreciation and a smattering of polite, grateful applause.

'I want to thank you all for coming,' he said grandly, and then, warming to his role and getting slightly carried away with himself, added, 'Now, in order to do Monsieur Corbeau's memory justice we have a movie to make!' It wasn't that he had pitched the tone wrong so much as pitched it at all and so, with nothing of any great import to add, he leant closer into the microphone and said, 'He was a hundred and two!' This got a confused round of applause, but also got him out of a hole. 'Thank you, everyone,' he repeated and made to move off the stage.

'Excuse me!' came a voice from the crowd. 'I think we have a few questions to ask.' It was a French voice speaking English and it had a weary authority, like a yawning snake, which spelt trouble in Richard's book. He'd stopped halfway between the lectern and the stairs off the stage, and he comically pointed at himself as if he'd just been taken by surprise at his role. He walked slowly, reluctantly, back to the mic.

'Yes, sorry,' he said warily, clearing his throat, 'please go ahead.'

The same voice came back to him. 'Yves Crévin, Entertainment TV Channel.' Richard could make him out in the crowd, his face partially hidden by an enormous red sponge on his microphone with the letters ETVC! on it. 'It would appear that the untimely death of a war hero must be related to the stalking of Lionel Margaux. Would you care to comment?'

Any barrister worth their salt would have complained about 'leading questions' and any judge who wasn't asleep would have upheld the complaint immediately. Richard wanted to shout 'No, I bloody don't!' but instead noticed a smug looking Commissaire Lapierre standing just offstage.

'I'm not in a position to comment on that,' he began, pleased with himself. 'Monsieur Corbeau died of natural causes. He was a hundred and two. As to the other subject to which you refer, that is an ongoing police matter and

you should address all questions to Commissaire Lapierre.'
He pointed to the Commissaire who immediately lost his
smirk and replaced it with a look suggesting that if Richard
should be found going so much as 32kms in a 30km zone,
it would be the guillotine. 'But this isn't the time!' Richard
added hurriedly.

Richard answered a few more less-troublesome questions, deftly he felt, switching between English and French,
and sympathy and movie enthusiasm.

'Dr Ainsworth?' This time the question was not just in
English but with an English accent. 'Norman Barry, Paris
Correspondent, BBC World News.' Friedman, Richard
felt, really had gone all out on the press conference invites.
'Was it ever discussed how a war hero, Monsieur Corbeau,'
his pronunciation was perfect, 'came to be appearing in a
film about Talleyrand? As you'll know, Talleyrand, for some
in France, still represents treachery and self above nation?'

It was the kind of deep film historian question that Richard
had used to indulge in with colleagues over a few pints in
shady Soho pubs. It was not, however, something he wished
to discuss with a more informed journalist and in front of
live TV cameras. He had recently watched the famous film
about Talleyrand, *Le Diable boiteux*, the limping devil, and
it had wrestled with the same issues. Had Talleyrand saved
or betrayed France in the Napoleonic Wars?

He didn't know the answer and this wasn't the time or
place to be speculating, so instead he began stammering
some inadequate reply when he was drowned out by the
sound of an engine. It wasn't the deep engine of a motor
vehicle though, but the much whinier noise of light aircraft.
The crowd looked up as a small open cockpit biplane flew

just above their heads, buzzing them, almost tearing the flags from their poles. Everybody pointed upwards and there were excited gasps as they watched the plane turn around and swoop back for more. Cameras were pointed at the plane as it dived again, being skilfully handled, and reports were shouted into microphones by excited journalists. Who was the pilot? Why was he buzzing the press conference?

'It's Talleyrand himself!' shouted an excited onlooker with a pair of binoculars. 'Talleyrand is flying the plane!' Gasps went up from the crowd as they realised that Hollywood star Dominic Burdett was indeed flying the plane and in full Talleyrand costume. He turned again and this time threw petals out from the plane, not real petals, more like large confetti: blue, white and red confetti.

'Vive la France!' shouted Burdett, even his trained theatrical voice struggling to be heard over the engines. 'Vive la France!' he repeated, this time winning the battle as he swooped lower.

The crowd erupted in applause; the spectacle was pure Hollywood yet strangely appropriate for the occasion too. Flying away into the distance, all the journalists and their cameras now turned their attention back to the stage to interrogate the press officer about this unexpected and exciting development. Unfortunately for them the press officer had taken advantage of the situation and swiftly left the stage, where he was last seen wrestling with Ben-Hur Friedman for the possession of a hip flask.

Chapter Nine

It was Lionel who was standing in Richard's usual spot behind the breakfast bar this time, though unlike him she wasn't hiding. She was, in her words, preparing a 'simple pasta dish' because she needed to eat and then sleep before a big day on set tomorrow. Alain Petit had offered to chop the tomatoes for her, but she'd said no. This was how she learnt her lines she'd added, just doing mundane tasks and going over things in her head.

On the other side of the bar sat an array of people dotted about on the three separate tables. Madame Tablier and Alain were working on a broken piece of lighting equipment, muttering and shaking their heads like an old couple on holiday who'd stumbled onto a nudist beach by mistake. Commissaire Henri Lapierre sat on his own, leaning against a wall, a glass of wine in his hand. No one quite knew why he was there, though earlier on he'd told Richard and Valérie, mainly Valérie, that he was there because 'something is going on, even though it looks like nothing is going on, I think there is something going on.' He was now looking at them both across the other side of the room where they sat opposite each other. Valérie was preparing a vinaigrette for the salad; Passepartout at her side was sleeping on a chair, while Richard sat sipping at his wine, a hunted look on his face, mainly, he would have argued, because he was being hunted.

It isn't unusual in the modern age for a press officer to leave more questions than answers, obfuscation being very much the name of the game. Dominic Burdett's plane antics though required some explanation from a person in Richard's position so he had, wisely in his opinion, chosen to scarper. In his innocence of these things, he had assumed that Burdett himself would be the subject of any following press intrusion and had therefore been horrified to see, from a distance, that the press was already surrounding his car when he and Valérie had returned to it. Other arrangements had had to be made and within twenty minutes Martin – this time with a flushed Gennie – had arrived at the chateau in a siren-blaring ambulance and dropped them home.

Valérie had invited them to stay but they demurred. They had been 'in the middle of something' they said, and were keen to get back and pick up 'where they'd left off'. Richard, even now, a couple of hours later, felt nauseous at the very thought of what that meant and hoped, for the sakes of the medical reputation of the Follet Valley, that no one needed an urgent ambulance this evening or the help of a priapic first-aider in uniform. In very short order, of course, the press had simply looked up the address of 'Les Vignes' and a good number of them were camped out at the gate, though the crowd was thankfully thinning as Madame Tablier insisted on aggressively challenging them with a floor mop on the hour, every hour.

What was worse, in Richard's eyes, was that he had received a text from Clare. It had been their first communication in some weeks, neither of them having the energy to get on with anything as final, or as mundane, as a divorce. It was a simple one-line text, and it filled him with dread. 'Saw you on the Beeb tonight. VERY distinguished. May pop over at the weekend xxx.' Despite his obsession with golden age Hollywood heroes and the fact that he daydreamed about being one on a constant basis, he was not enjoying the attention. It was all very *North by Northwest* of course: he'd been buzzed by light aircraft and mistaken for something he wasn't; there was a femme fatale, though such was his confusion, he couldn't decide if that was Valérie, Clare, Lionel or even Madame Tablier. All he needed was his mother to turn up and not believe a word of it and someone to force alcohol down his throat to complete the Hitchcock full house. He was successfully managing the alcohol part on his own and the Commissaire was unknowingly playing the disbelieving mother role.

He finished another glass of wine, and Alain immediately appeared to top him up, Madame Tablier having once more gone to the gate to threaten members of the international press corps.

'It is totally absurd,' the Commissaire almost spat his words. 'I came here for the quiet life; many others come here for the quiet life. The Val de Follet, the Loire, is known for the quiet life.' He looked directly at Richard, almost pleadingly. 'Move, monsieur, please, I beg you, move to the Dordogne. I hear they like this kind of thing there.'

Richard felt this was a little unjust. It wasn't him who'd stolen an antique biplane, it wasn't him who had then parachuted through a priceless chateau skylight thereby leaving the unmanned aircraft to go careering into a nearby winery and destroying a year's worth of fermenting Valençay Sauvignon. And anyway, according to Friedman, the money men 'back home' were absolutely delighted by the coverage. 'Even if the movie stinks,' they'd apparently said, 'it's guaranteed a great opening weekend.' And Burdett was none the worse for wear. He had always done his own stunts and was practically unbreakable by all accounts, though how he squared flying a plane while being in character as early nineteenth-century Charles-Maurice de Talleyrand-Périgord, Napoleon's right-hand man, was anyone's guess.

Richard stood, slightly unsteadily, disturbing Passepartout in the process, who gave him a bored look before settling back down. 'Are you OK?' Valérie asked. She had been very quiet since their return and Richard had the feeling that something was bothering her, though he decided not to ask what until they were alone and he'd had more wine.

'Fine,' was the reply. 'But I need to consult with the gods,' he added dramatically and everyone, including the returning Madame Tablier, turned to watch him.

He went to the antique dresser by the wall and opened the middle drawer, pulling out a large book. It was his favourite book, his bible he called it: Halliwell's *Who's Who in the Movies*. It was the last one that was published, the 2006 update, had a young Daniel Craig on the cover, was well-worn and lovingly thumbed. Richard handled it carefully and returned to the table. Clare would have rolled her eyes at this, having long known that Richard in times of need and stress would usually dive into film encyclopaedias and bury himself in facts and figures that he knew by heart anyway. Valérie smiled at him instead. It was Passepartout who rolled his eyes.

'I want to look up what Halliwell says about Burdett,' he said.

'Isn't that book a little old though?' Lionel looked up from her food preparation. 'Why not use IMDB?' Even Valérie rolled her eyes at that one. 'Look,' the young actress continued. She wiped her hands and picked up her phone, while unknown to her Richard caught Valérie's eye, which was sympathetic. 'It's not working,' Lionel said, 'is the internet down?'

'No, my dear niece. That site is blocked at source; some hotels block pornography, Richard blocks IMDB.com. He sees it as the root of all evil.'

'Not all evil,' Richard tried to explain, 'but it certainly played a hefty role in making me a *former* film historian.'

'Oh, I see,' Lionel said hesitatingly, though it was clear that she didn't.

Richard flicked the pages of the book and came to the section on Burdett. 'OK,' he began. 'Born in 1958, he's older than I thought then. I mean his big breakthrough was playing a teenager and he must have been nearly thirty years old by then. Anyway, Halliwell calls him "an old-fashioned movie star, who can turn his hand to anything, sometimes even successfully."' He chuckled. 'Good old Halliwell.' He read on. 'It looks like he had a three-year break in the late 90s – this isn't my period of expertise – I wonder why?' He looked up from the book to realise that nobody else was listening. Only Lapierre seemed to be taking any notice at all and that was via a look of utter contempt. Richard carried on regardless. 'So he made a film called *My Brother's Wings* and then nothing for a bit... I need to cross reference this with Katz's *Film Encyclopaedia*...'

'*My Brother's Wings*?' Alain mused. 'Didn't a stuntman die on that film?'

Richard expected Valérie's ears to prick up at this information, but she still seemed elsewhere.

Richard flicked through a few more pages and reached for a couple of books. 'He's barely had a hit since, and almost always he's working with Friedman.'

'That's because no one else will employ him,' Alain said. 'He's either a drunk or a character.'

'He cannot stand to be himself,' Lionel said quietly before changing her tone completely. '*À table*!' she called breezily, signalling that dinner was ready. Alain pushed two tables together so that they could sit as a group, though the Commissaire still seemed unwilling to join them. His face brightened somewhat, however, as a beautiful, major international film star put a bowl of pasta and homemade sauce under his nose.

'*Merci*,' he said, a little embarrassed. 'This looks very good.'

Alain poured the wine while Madame Tablier went off to have one more late joust with any remaining journalists. Richard put his books down reluctantly and sat between Valérie and Lionel. The food smelt delicious and they all made grateful noises towards the chef, though Madame Tablier, before she'd disappeared again, had tutted at the amount of mess being made. 'Aunt,' the unstarlike Lionel said to Valérie, 'could you pass me the parmesan, please?'

Alain, who clearly took his wine duties very seriously indeed, asked if she wanted a top-up, but she declined. 'No, thank you,' she smiled, 'it's a big day tomorrow. I need to look and be at my best.'

'What is happening tomorrow, madame?' Lapierre asked, not knowing that he was dripping pasta sauce onto his tie while he did so.

'It's the big sex scene.' Lionel said it so matter-of-factly, so without nuance or edge that it could have been someone blithely reminding the room that they had a dentist appointment the next day. There was a brief moment where the only noise was cutlery against plate, then Lionel asked for some baguette which deftly punctured the tense atmosphere and which allowed Richard to explode into the coughing fit he was trying to suppress. Lionel slapped him on the back like a mother would a windy child, and Richard apologised.

'Sorry,' he spluttered. 'Must have gone down the wrong hole.' He turned bright red and was grateful at least that Martin and Gennie weren't there to make an appalling double entendre.

Valérie was still oddly silent and Richard, despite his Englishness antenna not always being attuned to these things, got the distinct impression that aunt and niece had already discussed the matter and were not entirely in agreement on the subject. Lapierre was wiping sauce off his tie and without looking at Lionel asked, 'How do you prepare for something like that, madame? It cannot be easy.'

Lionel sighed. 'They are not always easy, though they are less often than they used to be. This is not gratuitous, it's part of the story. Amorette said it's one of the few authentic historical episodes in the film!' She laughed a little nervously. 'Thankfully, we have a woman director too. Sacha is very aware of how awkward these things are. She even compared her role to mine, as a woman director in a man's world! Could I have some more baguette, please?' Richard passed the basket to her. 'The important thing,' she added seriously, 'is that you must trust each other as actors. Trust and respect are absolutely vital.'

The room went silent. 'And your partner in this, er, scene, you trust him?' Lapierre asked.

'My partner in this scene, monsieur, is Reed Turnbull.' Lapierre looked confused but a surreptitious shake of the head from Valérie told him to let it go.

'It is at least supposed to be his last day on set tomorrow.' Lionel sounded hopeful. 'This scene has been brought forward, so that he may leave early.'

The door opened and Madame Tablier huffed her way back in. 'Oh start without me why don't you?' she pulled back her chair and sat next to Alain. 'Well they've mostly gone for now, but they'll be back tomorrow they said. First thing. "Who is this Dr Ainsworth?" they kept saying. "We want to see Lionel Margaux." I hope you have an easy day lined up for tomorrow, missie, it'll be hell getting out of here.' She was met with silence. 'What?'

'I can do without that!' Lionel looked to Valérie for help, who looked at Richard to see if he had any ideas. And for once he did. 'Leave it to me,' he said coyly, and went off to make a phone call.

Chapter Ten

'You're lucky it's a clear morning,' Patrice Marnier said loudly as he turned up the gas. The flame grew larger, giving off an orange glow and plenty of heat. The large rainbow-coloured hot air balloon rose majestically off the ground drawing gasps of delight from the eclectic group in the basket. The tall Patrice wore a loose white shirt, had dark, straggly shoulder-length hair and a week's stubble and would have been any Hollywood producer's choice as the rescuer of a lady in distress. He looked like an off-duty musketeer and no one could take their eyes off him, except Richard who leant nonchalantly against the basket sipping a coffee with a very smug look on his face. Valérie was adding to his smugness by clearly being impressed with his innovation. She looked predictably beautiful, with a radiant smile and the breeze blowing through her hair, like it was a modelling shoot set-up; Lionel looked equally stunning, framed against the clouds, like a fragile angel; Alain, interestingly, looked slightly nervous and gripped the basket edge; Madame Tablier – and Richard couldn't work out why she was even there – looked unimpressed; and Passepartout looked absolutely terrified and had his snout buried in the crook of Valérie's arm.

'Thanks for coming at such short notice, Patrice,' Richard said, enjoying his literal moment in the sun.

'My pleasure!' Patrice replied, making some adjustments on the instruments and guiding the balloon high over the gate and the heads of furious waiting journalists. 'It's not every day I get to act as a taxi for Lionel Margaux.' He smiled at Lionel who was sensibly hiding in the middle of the basket to avoid long camera lenses.

'How lovely, monsieur, to be able to escape into the clouds when you feel like it,' she said, when they were clear.

Patrice smiled easily. 'Weather permitting, madame, weather permitting.'

'Please call me Lionel.'

He nodded. 'Patrice,' he replied.

Valérie coughed, dousing the atmosphere. 'How long will the journey take, Patrice?' she asked in a very business-like manner.

Patrice shrugged his shoulders, a simple gesture that basically said 'it will take as long as it takes,' and that travel by *montgolfier* wasn't subject to timetables or hurry.

'It can take all day as far as I'm concerned,' Lionel said quietly, thinking of the day that lay ahead.

The journey to Valençay was the stuff of dreams. The early autumn mist lay on the vineyards like wisps of candyfloss as it had in the days before, and deer gambolled ghostlike in the fields before seeking cover in the forests. The River Follet widened and narrowed, then widened again as it travelled through slowly awakening villages. At one point, Patrice lowered the balloon skilfully as they passed over a tiny hamlet.

'I'm not supposed to do this,' he said, 'but the customers like it.' The balloon was, to the amateur eye, dangerously low. 'Can you smell that?' he asked, breathing in the air deeply.

They could. Below them the chimney of a *boulangerie* was wafting its heavenly smell upwards, filling the basket. Even Lionel, who clearly by this point largely had her mind elsewhere, closed her eyes and took in a deep breath. Richard did too. The smell was so strong, you could almost taste a warm baguette.

'Patrice!' There was a cry from below and a rotund man in an apron came out from the back of the bakery. 'Throw down your rope!' Without answering Patrice did exactly that and the baker tied a smaller basket to the end. 'Bon appétit!' he shouted and saluted as he did so.

'*Merci*, my friend!' Patrice replied. 'I'll drop the basket back later!'

The balloon rose again, and Richard shared out an assortment of croissants and still warm baguette. It was the most memorable breakfast he'd ever had.

'This is wonderful, Richard,' Valérie said, standing next to him and looking down. 'So wonderful.' Richard made a mental note of her delight and wondered if he could get Patrice to give him some lessons so that he might take her up himself another time. Passepartout yapped in fear though, breaking his train of thought.

It took just over an hour to complete the journey, and only Alain and Passepartout had wanted it to end, but there was an agitated welcoming party waiting in the chateau grounds. Friedman was there inevitably and probably fretting over whether his insurance would cover his starlet being suspended in a basket high over the French countryside.

'Thank you, Patrice,' Richard said as they climbed out.

'My pleasure, Richard.' Then he looked at Lionel. 'Any time,' he said, smiling warmly.

'Thank you.' She smiled back. 'I wish I could go to work like that every day.' They shook hands a little stiffly, lingering on the gesture slightly longer than was the norm.

It was inevitably Valérie who interrupted them again as she badgered Lionel towards one of the waiting chateau golf buggies that would take them to their trailers and the set. Once there Richard watched as Lionel took a deep breath before nervously opening the door to her trailer. Before she could mount the steps, Valérie pushed past her and went in first, before quickly putting her head back out and asking Richard to give her a hand checking it over.

'Sorry, my dear,' she said to Lionel, smiling warmly as she did so, 'but it's better to be safe than sorry.'

Lionel shrugged and went to sit with Jennifer Davies who was on a bench enjoying the morning sun.

Richard stepped up into the trailer and Valérie immediately closed the door behind him. 'Look!' she hissed, pointing at Lionel's well-lit mirror. On the mirror, written in red lipstick was another message:

'Are you ready for this – whore?'

Richard raised his eyebrows. 'That's not very friendly, is it?' he said quietly.

She turned towards him to see if he was joking, making light of what she considered a dangerous development. She decided that he wasn't and that he was just being Richard, considering the wording and its implications in the way a sloth might peruse a leaf, so she said with some exasperation, 'You are so English at times!'

Richard was rather taken aback at this. 'What do you want me to say?' He sounded a little hurt. Maybe he was still in balloon-ride mode and over-relaxed, but it seemed a little harsh to turn on him. *He* hadn't written the message.

'What do you think of it?' Valérie asked, though it was clear she had a few ideas of her own.

'Well,' Richard began, thinking that he was, as usual, being tested. 'First, whoever wrote it has access to the shooting script, because I'm assuming it refers to the scene that's being shot today. That narrows it down to someone centrally involved in the production as the schedule was changed.' He was quite proud of this deduction, and looked at Valérie for approval. Valérie's brow was furrowed, and she nodded slowly, before tilting her head to one side.

'I admit I hadn't thought of that.' She sounded oddly unsure of herself.

'Oh.' Richard was as stunned by this revelation as Valérie.

'I was assuming that it referred to her as a person, in general. That whoever wrote it meant that they were about to strike!'

Richard re-read the short message. 'It might mean both,' he shrugged.

Valérie looked very worried. 'Richard, I don't like it. I'm very worried for Lionel.' They looked at each other via the mirror and through the scrawled message. Suddenly there was a knock at the door.

'Can I come in yet?' It was Lionel.

'Quick!' Valérie whispered. 'Clean it off!' She picked up a packet of make-up wipes and tossed them at Richard, who immediately set to work. He swiped through the message, smearing it and making it illegible. Lionel opened the door down the corridor of the trailer and Valérie went to greet her and steer her away from the make-up area.

'Is everything OK?' Lionel asked.

'Oh yes!' Valérie, Richard thought, and not for the first time, was such a bad liar. The way she said 'Oh yes!' was with such false, overwhelming enthusiasm that Lionel became immediately suspicious.

'Are you sure?' she asked nervously.

'Yes, sure.' Valérie toned it down a little. 'Richard spilt something so he's just cleaning up. He is so clumsy at times!' He couldn't help thinking that the woman had a bloody nerve. Then he heard them both chuckle. A rotten liar Valérie may be, but it was, apparently, entirely within the realms of believability that Richard was a cloddish oaf and incapable of being left alone.

'Well really!' he said under his breath, wiping the mirror completely clean. 'That's the last balloon ride I organise.'

'Have you cleaned it yet, Richard?' Valérie shrilled loudly.

'Yes!' he replied fractiously. 'Though I'm such a bumbling halfwit, who knows what I'll break next.' He laid the sarcasm on heavily hoping that Lionel was as immune to it as he knew Valérie to be. He went down the corridor to see them. 'All done,' he said morosely.

There was an awkward silence and it was clear that Lionel's thoughts once again were elsewhere. She didn't look nervous, so much as determined; like the shoot would be an obstacle she had to get over, something she had no enthusiasm for but an onerous task to be completed. It was clear too that Valérie was now even more unhappy with the situation. The thought that her beautiful niece was about to be laid bare in front of the cameras and pawed at by the boorish Reed Turnbull was clearly making her trigger finger itch, and Richard worried for her as much as he felt for Lionel.

'You know,' he said, trying to lighten the atmosphere. 'When they made *On Her Majesty's Secret Service*, Diana Rigg disliked George Lazenby so much that she ate garlic before every scene in which they kissed.'

'Do you have any garlic to hand, Richard?' Valérie asked acidly.

'No,' he replied, and was determined to keep his mouth shut from there on in.

That they all knew it was Lionel's job made it all the more difficult. Lionel was quietly preparing herself, Valérie was jumpy and as coiled as a mousetrap and Richard was, quite happily, far too English to want to discuss any of it. Lionel had made sure it was as historically justified as it could be and not just gratuitous nudity. Nor, and this had happened in the past, that the lead male actor would have a scene written into the script especially for his own delights. But no. She was Marie-Louise, Archduchess of Austria, Napoleon Bonaparte's second wife, the mother of his young son and twenty-two years his junior. Napoleon loved her, though not as much as he still loved the divorced Joséphine. A tender scene between them both just as Napoleon was beginning to have self-doubts seemed, on the face of it, natural. That didn't make it any easier.

The door to the trailer opened sharply and in jumped a grinning Reed Turnbull. In his hands he carried a bottle of champagne and two glasses. The grin didn't last long when he saw that Lionel wasn't alone. Even Passepartout, happily installed on a comfy chair, growled at the intruder.

'Ah,' he said, not bothering with any formalities. 'I thought you'd be alone.' Valérie walked slowly towards him and Richard again briefly wondered just how good Friedman's insurance policy was and if it included a 'lead actor swallowing a wine bottle' clause.

'She is not, Monsieur Turnbull. As you can see.'

Having watched Reed Turnbull the last few days Richard thought the man was utterly impervious to anything other than his own voice, but something in Valérie's tone got through his ego. In Richard's opinion, he'd have been wise to cross his legs. 'Not to worry,' he said backing out of the door. 'It's just a tradition I have before scenes like this,' he held up the champagne. 'It helps to, er, loosen...' He tailed off. 'See you on set, mademoiselle.' He looked around Valérie and had the nerve to wink at Lionel as he retreated quickly.

Valérie slammed the door shut. 'I love you, my dear niece, you know that. But I don't like your profession at all.'

Lionel smiled wanly and Richard kept his mouth shut. He wasn't all that keen on what Lionel was about to put herself through either, but it took some front for a bounty hunter and possible assassin to question the morals of someone else's day job.

There was another knock at the door and Valérie answered it this time, ready to showcase some of her 'self-defence' skills if it proved to be a returning Turnbull. It was the director, Sacha.

'Good morning,' she said, acknowledging everyone present. 'Lionel, we need to talk about this scene today.' Then she lowered her voice. 'I've made some changes.'

Chapter Eleven

For the first time that morning Richard sensed the true tension that Lionel was feeling, and it was clear that an irritable and protective Valérie, not always sensitive to a shift in mood, saw it too. Lionel's façade, her coolness, melted and there was a look of dread on her face.

'But I know this scene inside out now, Sacha. I have played it over and over in my mind. I am in complete control of it.' She sat down on a plush corner sofa, her hands in her lap, and she looked up pleadingly at the director. 'I need to be in control of it,' she said quietly.

Sacha sat down next to her and placed the newly typed version of the scene on Lionel's lap. 'Believe me, Lionel, I know that you do and I would not make any changes that would undermine you, none at all. I think if you read the amendments you will understand.' Sacha looked up at Richard and Valérie, though her eyes were partially hidden by the peak of her baseball cap, she seemed to be asking them for support. 'I think if we leave you to look at the script for a few minutes…' She stood up and went to the door, indicating the two of them should follow her out.

She closed the door quietly behind them as they waited by the steps. 'You are very close to her, yes?' It was less a question and more statement of fact.

'Yes,' Valérie replied for both of them.

'That's good.' Sacha nodded her head. 'Usually with a scene like this, a sex scene, I demand a closed set. Myself, the actors, camera and sound only. There is no need for a crowd. But I would like you two there please, for Lionel. She trusts you. Will you do that for her?'

'Of course,' Valérie said without hesitation, whereas Richard made some sort of vaguely encouraging noises and was already starting to blush at the prospect.

'Are you sure I…' he stammered.

'Don't be silly, Richard.' Valérie had no time for his Englishness this morning.

'Ah, right-o,' and he puffed out his reddening cheeks.

Sacha nodded at them and went off to prepare the set. Valérie stared at the trailer door, her jaw muscles tensed.

'You really are very close, aren't you?' Richard asked, trying to distract her a little.

'What? Oh. Yes, I am very fond of her. I have known her all her life.'

'I suppose you would as her aunt.'

'She's not really my niece. Her mother and I are close, very close, we worked together. She is almost more than family and I always look out for her.' She paused, and it was clear that she was finding the situation very difficult. 'It's not always easy to do because she is very famous. But it's my duty,' she added.

'She couldn't have a better protector, Valérie,' he awkwardly put his hand on her arm, 'but she's a grown woman. This is her decision.'

She turned towards him and smiled. 'I know,' she said softly. 'I know. Thank you, Richard.'

The door opened and Lionel emerged. She wore a silk dressing gown and, on her feet, something resembling hotel slippers. She also wore, as athletes might say, a game face. Concentrated, slightly cold, in the zone. But as Valérie asked how she was, there was a twinkle in her eye too. Richard would be the first to admit he couldn't read women, and even if he could read women he wouldn't admit to it for fear of someone testing him on the point. But if pushed he would say that Lionel was not only in complete control, as she had demanded, but that she had agreed with whatever changes Sacha had made, and agreed with them wholeheartedly. She looked, and there was only one word for it: keen.

Lionel led the way up the stairs to the set. For authenticity Sacha had commandeered one of the bedrooms on the first floor, which was ready for filming when they arrived. The set was dark; the lighting, such as it was, had been cleverly, strategically arranged to make it look like a shaft of moonlight was the only thing lighting the bed chamber. There were even shadowed bars across the light to mimic the effect of grilles across the fake light-created windows. It looked sultry and atmospheric, but not, Richard thought, as always reaching into cinema history, romantic. It looked moody and a little tense. Sacha had been true to her word; just Brian and Stella were on set for the camera, lighting and sound. Two solid, experienced professionals who knew how to be discreet in what could be a tense situation. They had encountered no one else en route to the set; Friedman, Samuel and the others were obviously staying clear.

Richard and Valérie hung back in the darkness and Richard could sense the nervousness that Valérie felt. It was one thing perhaps to watch someone close fake a scene like this on the screen but quite different to be there live as it were. He felt very uncomfortable himself. Lionel stood quietly waiting just a few yards away as Reed Turnbull bumptiously made his way onto the set reeking of expensive, masculine cologne.

'Right then,' he said enthusiastically, misreading the atmosphere entirely. 'Where do you want me?' The question of course should have been directed at Sacha who, as the director, was in charge. It wasn't though; it was directed with a creepy smirk at Lionel instead. Richard held Valérie's elbow as he felt her go rigid, and she looked up at him and nodded, almost apologetically.

'As we rehearsed please, Reed,' Sacha said forcefully. 'You make your speech as you walk towards Lionel. She is sitting naked on the bed. As you finish, you kneel and embrace her naked body. Places everyone.'

Lionel took a deep breath, stepped out of her slippers and handed her dressing gown to Valérie. In doing so she revealed that she was wearing what looked like a gossamer skin-colour bikini. It didn't hide her shapely figure, but rather made it look like she had been airbrushed for a prudish newspaper supplement. She walked silently to the bed, where it was Stella, rather than Brian, who positioned her to sit upright on the edge, facing the lighting rig, the fake window. Her face, shoulders and some of her midriff were lit but the shadows caused by the grilles hid her breasts. It was skilfully done and looked as artful as a painting.

'Very wise, my dear,' Reed said, referring to her 'costume', and either unable or unwilling to hide the edge in his voice. 'Very professional in these "Me Too" days.' He virtually spat the words 'me too'. 'Of course, it won't work for the close-ups.' He stood slightly to the side of the lights so as not to obscure them and Brian operated the camera that looked at Lionel from over his shoulder.

'OK,' Sacha called from behind her monitor. 'I want to do this in as few takes as is possible. We all know our words, we all know our movements. Roll sound. Roll camera. Marker.' She operated the clapperboard herself. 'And, action!'

'My darling,' Reed/Napoleon began, his tone pompous, not unlike Turnbull's own. 'You look too beautiful.' He walked slowly towards her, keeping artfully out of the light. 'I am your defeated soldier, a conquered, vanquished foe. I have triumphed over half of Europe, made grown men tremble with fear. Yet that is nothing to the spell you put me under.' He knelt before her and bowed his head. 'I am yours to do as you please. I beg you, though I am your emperor, take me as your prisoner.'

He bent down in front of his screen wife and opened his arms to begin the embrace.

'Cut!' shouted Sacha. 'Reed, you're in the light.'

'I don't think I was,' he responded irritably. He hadn't looked it in Richard's eyes either.

'Positions.' Sacha said, slightly aggressively. 'Roll sound. Roll camera. Marker. And… action!'

'My darling,' Turnbull began again. 'I am your…'

'I'm so sorry.' It was Lionel. 'But I think I'm going to sneeze. What is that smell?' She put her finger to her nose. 'No, it's gone away.'

'Still rolling. Positions.'

Turnbull went back to his starting position again, while Lionel just stared ahead of her. She looked like a marble statue.

'My darling, you look too beautiful.' Reed started to move forward again. 'I am your defeated soldier, a conquered, vanquished foe. I have triumphed over half of Europe, made grown men tremble with fear. Yet that is nothing to the spell you put me under.' He knelt before her and bowed his head. 'I am yours to do as you please. I beg you, though I am your emperor, take me as your prisoner.' He knelt once more, going for the embrace.

Lionel sneezed loudly. 'I am so sorry,' she said. 'Oh, I think I sneezed on your uniform Napoleon.'

Reed stood up quickly, clearly annoyed.

'Positions. Still rolling.'

'My darling, you look too beautiful. I am your defeated soldier, a conquered, vanquished foe. I have triumphed over…'

'Cut!'

'What now for Chrissakes?'

'You're rushing the moment, Reed, slow it down.'

'I'm trying to get it done before I get exiled,' he growled, going back to his mark.

'And, action.'

'My darling, you look too beautiful.' His tone was tender this time. 'I am your defeated soldier, a conquered, vanquished foe. I have triumphed over half of Europe, made grown men tremble with fear. Yet that is nothing to the spell you put me under. I am yours to do as you please. I beg you, though I am your emperor, take me as your prisoner.' Once more, he knelt.

'I am serious, can anyone else smell burning?' Lionel asked. 'Cut!'

This went on for some time, and each time there was something that Sacha, Lionel or, on a couple of occasions, Stella wasn't happy with. Almost every time the interruption occurred when Turnbull was about to embrace Lionel, and if she felt uncomfortable sitting naked on set, she didn't show it. It was Turnbull who was becoming seriously angry, unable to quite finish the scene and literally get his hands on his beautiful co-star.

'Action!' Sacha called for the umpteenth time.

'My darling, you look too beautiful. I am your defeated soldier, a conquered, vanquished foe. I have triumphed over half of Europe, made grown men tremble with fear. Yet that is nothing to the spell you put me under. I am yours to do as you please. I beg you, though I am your emperor, take me as your prisoner.' He knelt, by now a little creakily and probably expecting another interruption, which this time didn't come.

'I can and I will.' Lionel/Marie-Louise replied oddly, finally looking him in the eye. Reed/Napoleon stood and went for an embrace with the young, mostly naked actress.

Lionel stood up quickly and dodged the outstretched arms like a rugby winger, leaving Reed almost toppling over.

'Cut!' shouted Sacha.

'But, don't you want to see us actually hold each other?' the actor asked petulantly, standing and smoothing his uniform.

'We'll do the close-ups later, Reed.'

'Another take then?' Turnbull was feeling rushed. 'I don't think I got that quite right. Perhaps I should lay my head on her…'

'That was just fine. Brian?' Sacha snapped, looking up from her monitor.

'Great.'

'Stella?'

'Perfect.'

'Lionel?'

'I'm happy.'

Reed Turnbull began chuntering to himself.

'OK,' Sacha clapped her hands. 'We have a few minutes while we set up the same scene but from over the shoulder of Lionel.' Valérie put Lionel's dressing gown over her shoulders as she glanced at her script, all while Brian and Stella went quickly about their business. 'Reed?'

'Yes,' he snapped back.

'I have an idea for this shot.' Sacha sounded like she had just had an epiphany of sorts. 'It might not work, but I want to try it.' Turnbull sighed. 'If it works, we'll just need it the once. Then we can get on with the more intimate close-ups.'

'What do you want me to do?' he asked, for now willing to put up with a slight delay before what he obviously regarded as perks of the job.

'I'm going to keep the camera rolling, no matter what happens. I want you to improvise. Remember that you are not Napoleon at the height of his power, your influence is waning, you have suffered defeats. I want you to imagine that Lionel, sorry Marie-Louise, is another battle that must be won. An unexpected siege before the rout of the capital. I want to sense vulnerability and frustration.'

Reed smirked. 'Before the intimate close-ups?'

'Before the intimate close-ups.'

'He really is an odious little man.' Valérie didn't bother whispering, and she didn't care if Turnbull heard. It obviously didn't bother him either.

'OK!' Sacha clapped her hands again. 'Positions. Roll sound. Roll camera. Marker. And… action!'

Reed Turnbull started again. 'My darling, you look too beautiful.' He started to move forward once more, and it's fair to say that in Richard's eyes he didn't do 'vulnerability' with any great success, he looked more like a predator. 'I am your defeated soldier, a conquered, vanquished foe. I have triumphed over half of Europe, made grown men tremble with fear. Yet that is nothing to the spell you put me under.' Once more, he knelt before Lionel and bowed his head. 'I am yours to do as you please. I beg you, though I am your emperor, take me as your prisoner.' Again, he held out his arms to embrace the young actress, but she swayed away once more.

Lionel then looked down at him as before, but not as captured prey. 'I am to regard you as my conquest?'

Turnbull looked up. 'Defeated under your spell,' he replied, improvising.

'Yet I was *your* conquest, just as you defeated Austria, my home.'

'My lady,' Napoleon offered demurely, smiling at the memory.

'But Austria has risen again, has it not? It is no longer your defeated enemy.'

Turnbull's eyes flashed in anger. If it was improvisation, it was brilliant, but Richard suspected more that he'd cottoned on to how this was going to play out.

'You are still my conquest!' he said angrily.

'But I heard you, my husband. I heard you with our host the Prince de Talleyrand-Périgord. You described me as a womb. That you had "married a womb".'

'But I…'

'I was your conquest and you have the spoils of that victory, you have a son. You shall have no more.' She paused, and then, before Turnbull could say anything in response, she said coldly, 'I shall be yet another foreign land you have lost.'

From where Richard stood, he could see the monitor that Sacha was concentrating on. The camera had zoomed in on Turnbull's face, whose eyes were now blazing in rage.

'Do you know who I am?' he shouted. 'Do you, you a mere girl, think you can deny me?' It wasn't clear whether this was improvising as Napoleon or genuine anger as the actor Reed Turnbull.

'I can and I will,' Lionel said quietly.

'I will take…' Napoleon or Reed lunged forward.

'Cut!' shouted Sacha again, and Lionel moved swiftly off the bed and into her dressing gown, which Valérie was holding, standing with her back to Turnbull whose face was contorted in rage.

'Why wasn't I told of these changes?' he demanded. 'Why? Where's Friedman?'

Sacha walked calmly on to the now brightly lit set. 'Reed that was magnificent,' she said.

'What?' He barely acknowledged her, his eyes following Lionel.

'Remember, this is Napoleon at the end of his career.' Sacha took his arm, and led him away. 'He's a year away from exile and frustrated at his waning influence.'

'What are you talking about?' he spluttered.

'I am talking about frustration. You portrayed it to perfection.'

Turnbull paused for a second, staring at the director, and still no calmer. 'Where's Friedman?' he repeated menacingly, and took a small foil tab of pills out of his pocket, swallowing a couple. Sacha shrugged which made him even angrier as he stormed off the set.

Richard decided to follow him at a discreet distance and watched as Turnbull exited the chateau, kicking angrily at the door and, unfortunately for him, disturbing Clovis the peacock who had been sunning himself on the steps. The actor, looking for a victim and a target for his frustration, lashed out at the startled bird, which, all in one swift movement, not only smartly dodged the swinging boot, but managed a vicious peck at the once great emperor's hand.

'You'll pay for this!' Turnbull seethed, but the bird had flown.

Chapter Twelve

Richard sat in the darkness, the only light coming from his phone and the images of joy, as he saw them flickering across the small screen. He was sitting in the chicken coop watching *Singin' in the Rain*, something he had downloaded onto his mobile a while back just for situations like this when he needed a pick-me-up, a smile, a reminder of innocence and pure delight – in other words a fictional world. He watched as Donald O'Connor bounced off the walls making him laugh, as Gene Kelly wooed Debbie Reynolds, and as the three of them together, a force of nature, greeted the morning with nothing but optimism.

Optimism, he thought, *not one of my strong points*. The day on the film set had left him flat and he knew that Valérie felt the same. Even though the scene had been finished and with it Reed Turnbull's participation in the shoot, it had felt grubby, sleazy even, and he wanted to put the whole thing behind him. Turnbull would be leaving the next morning but Richard had no desire to go to a formal dinner this evening honouring Monsieur Corbeau or the production itself. Even if he suspected there may be the hint of a party atmosphere with the imminent departure of the despised Turnbull. Hence he was in the chicken coop, injecting real Hollywood verve into his blood system, sitting in his one and only formal suit hoping his beloved hens would do the decent thing and defecate on him so he couldn't go. They hadn't yet played their part; instead they sat quietly in their straw bed, murmuring contentedly, always happy in his company. Olivia de Havilland, Joan Crawford and Lana Turner – Richard's beloved symbols of old Hollywood, or relics, if you like. Ghosts some might say. But it was a world of glamour, finesse and élan. OK, it was true that in real life the three actresses between them had had assorted issues, like affairs, feuds, assault and battery, pornography, drug addiction, and so on, but you didn't hear about that, you heard only about the romance and the mystique and the glamour. You didn't hear about the underbelly, only the good things. Richard didn't want to hear about the underbelly. To him the world back then was literally black and white and he realised sadly, and not for the first time, that he'd been born about sixty years too late.

His only real connection with that world right now in fact was that he was trying to do a Greta Garbo; 'I want to be alone,' he said to himself, affecting a poor Swedish accent. He hoped at least that Valérie wouldn't find him. If Richard had a skill, it was an ability to shut things out, disappear for a while, hide. It was something he'd been perfecting for most of his adult life, with darkened, unlit screening rooms and dusty basement libraries providing the perfect escape. Unfortunately, and he was painfully aware of this, Valérie had her own particular set of skills, namely successfully hunting down those that either were, or felt, hunted.

The coop door opened and a resplendent Valérie stood there, a look of almost motherly disappointment on her face, mixed, he hoped, with a little sympathy. Doubtless to say, she looked fantastic in a flowing moss-green trouser suit which she was hitching up at the trouser to avoid any hen excreta from marring the ensemble. She sighed and smiled at him consolingly.

'I knew you would be here,' she said softly. 'We have to go.'

Richard looked at his screen; Debbie Reynolds was running out of the theatre. He knew how she felt. 'Must we though? I mean, can't we just let them get on with it, just for one evening?'

She shook her head. 'I do not actually want to go either, but someone is threatening my niece, and I want to make sure also that that odious little Turnbull man goes nowhere near her on his last night.'

He let out a deep breath. He knew she was right. 'Come on with the rain,' he said morosely, 'I've a smile on my face.'

'What are you talking about?' she said, moving off and leaving the door open for him to follow.

Within fifteen minutes, Valérie having driven, they were at L'Orangerie du Chateau, the impressive Georgian-windowed restaurant in the grounds of the chateau itself, and waiting in line to be shown to their seats. It was all very formal, like a wedding line and they waited with Jennifer Davies. She didn't want to be there either, so she was looking on the bright side.

'I'm not really in the mood for this,' she said to them both. 'My Tantriga Jyotidam insists that I should be fasting today and avoiding anything that could unbalance my chakras.' Both Richard and Valérie waited for the other to respond, neither having the faintest idea what the actress was on about.

'What's a tanty…' Richard started. 'Sorry. What did you say?'

'Tantriga Jyotidam,' Jennifer replied in a way that suggested he might be the very last person on earth not to have heard of it. 'It's tantric astrology,' she added, assuming that would help.

'Ah, right-o.' He decided not to pursue it.

'It's not like we can even now treat it as a celebration.' The actress's face changed dramatically to a look of disappointment, making Richard think she may have snapped a chakra.

'A celebration?' For her part Valérie looked confused. 'Of the life of Monsieur Corbeau, you mean?'

'Well,' Jennifer paused, 'that too, I suppose. No, it was supposed to be Reed's last day on set. The scene with poor Lionel this morning was brought forward by Sacha so that he would no longer be needed. We all thought he would be leaving tomorrow.'

'And he's not?' Richard was frustrated by this news. He had decided that Reed Turnbull was everything that was wrong with the world, and couldn't wait to see the back of him. The revelation that he was staying on would be bad news for everyone. He felt Valérie tensing up at the thought too.

'No. He's staying, he says.' Jennifer looked almost distraught. 'I hope he stays out of my way, but I doubt he will. He's evil, you know. I can sense these things.'

Richard, even without the advantage of spiritualistic auras or tantric calendars, felt much the same thing, as did Valérie who whispered, 'I think this means trouble, Richard,' and she gave him a worried look. He knew that under normal circumstances she would be excited by this sort of case development, but these were not normal circumstances.

They shuffled forward in the line where they were met by the Valençay dignitaries standing formally to greet them. On the table in front of them were two pictures of Monsieur Corbeau. The first had been taken during the war, where he wore the inevitable beret, his coat collar was turned up, a cigarette hung from his mouth and he had a rifle over his shoulder. The photo was slightly out of focus, yet Richard could still sense not just the courage, but the excitement, the danger acting like a drug as it did for Valérie. It was the same look on the photograph that sat next to it too, a much more recent portrait, in which the now old man was laughing heartily, his eyes watering. It underlined what Richard had said all along, namely that he just wasn't convinced that Monsieur Corbeau's death was in any way stress-related.

The mayor was a large grey-haired man in a dark suit wearing the blue, white and red sash of office. He had a practised sombre look on his face, but he was also unable to hide his fascination at meeting major stars, and was keeping the official photographer on his toes. Beside him was a smaller man who was making the introductions.

'Noel?' Richard asked agog, his sense of occasion falling away. 'What on earth are you doing here?'

Noel Mabit was, in Richard's eyes, a nemesis. Nobody knew quite what he did exactly, but if there was any sort of official ceremony in the Follet Valley, Noel Mabit would be there in some kind of weaselly, barely official capacity, acting purely as the grease on the bureaucratic gears. He had never made any attempt to hide his enmity towards Richard either, or his admiration for Valérie.

'Madame d'Orçay,' Noel Mabit oozed, 'how delightful to see you. You look *fantastique*.'

'Noel,' Valérie replied, also taken aback by his presence. 'How charming, thank you.'

'Monsieur Ainsworth,' Mabit said coldly, without looking Richard in the eye and with a tone in his voice like he was sipping corked wine. 'I'm not sure your name is on the list…'

'Look under doctor, press officer or head of security.' Richard wasn't one to throw his weight around, not previously having had any weight with which to do so, but the man got right up his nose.

'Ah, yes.' Mabit didn't bat an eyelid. 'You're here at the bottom.' He ticked his list then clicked his fingers *maître d'* style and Richard felt anger rising in him at the calculated rudeness of this jumped-up little oik. He didn't even want to be there. Valérie, sensing that he was about to explode, put her arm through his and led him away, following the waitress who was in classic, and clichéd, French waitress garb. The black dress with a white frilly collar, white frills on the sleeve and an equally frilly bonnet on her head was way over the top, and they smiled at each other at the absurdity of the costume.

'No other waitress is wearing this uniform,' Valérie whispered, and then it dawned on Richard why that was.

'Hello, Gennie,' he sighed heavily. 'Don't tell me, you needed an excuse for the uniform?'

Gennie and even Valérie giggled as Gennie showed them to their places. 'Well,' she said, smiling warmly, 'if you can't have a little fun at our time of life, when can you?

You both look lovely by the way. I love that colour on you, Valérie, brings out your eyes.'

To be fair it was also bringing out the eyes of every other man in the room Richard noticed, despite the attendance of major film star actresses.

'And I love what you are wearing,' Valérie replied innocently. 'It looks so classy.'

'Where's Martin?' Richard asked suspiciously. 'Out the back with the ambulance engine running presumably.'

'Oh no,' Gennie said. 'It's his night off.' Richard couldn't help looking relieved. 'He's in the kitchen dressed as a chef. Full hat and everything. René is quite jealous.'

Richard couldn't stop his mind from wandering to the potential kitchen hygiene issues should Martin and Gennie be overwhelmed by their current uniform fetish, but Valérie had other worries.

'René Dupont is doing the cooking?' She looked aghast. 'He is the *traiteur*?'

Richard was on the point of making some joke about *traiteur*, the French word for caterer, and traitor, which is what René was to France's culinary reputation, but he left it as Amorette Arthur was shown to the seat next to him. Gennie skipped off leaving Valérie looking white as a sheet at the prospect of the dinner to come.

'Good evening, madame,' Richard smiled as Amorette settled in.

'Good evening, monsieur, madame.' She didn't seem very sure of herself.

'Richard and Valérie,' he said, needlessly pointing to himself and then Valérie, as if there'd be some confusion on the issue.

'Amorette.' Again she smiled nervously. 'I didn't want to come!' It was obvious that she had been dying to tell someone.

'Why ever not?' Valérie had put René's future crimes away for the present and asked the question charmingly. 'You look delightful by the way. I love that dress and your hair, it suits you that way.'

Richard wondered what on earth had got into her. The dress was a simple black slightly above the knee affair and, frankly, Amorette Arthur's hair looked like it had yet to be done. He was no expert and he certainly wouldn't venture an opinion verbally, but the historian's blonde hair sat in a sort of bun on top of her head but looked like it was engaged in an ongoing civil war that was nowhere near conclusion. She looked like she had dressed in a hurry.

'Thank you, that's very kind,' she said, clearly not used to compliments. 'I've made the effort, but frankly, I'd rather have had a quiet night in. I'm rather tired of all this film-making stuff. I thought I had left it all behind.'

'The days are long, that's for sure,' Richard said, pouring wine for his two companions, and a larger one for himself.

'Also the egos,' Valérie added, puckering her lips as if sucking on a lemon. 'So many small people who think they're big.'

'It's not just that,' Amorette said, fretfully. 'I just wish they'd call it fiction and have done with it.' She drank some wine. 'You know that at first it was to be about the Second World War, this film, but then they changed their minds. I wish they hadn't. People still remember the war here; it's not so easy to ignore facts.'

'I didn't know that.' Richard raised his eyebrows and glanced at Valérie who at that moment was being introduced to the actor Gilbertine. He looked very dashing, wearing a chef's hat, a *toque blanche*, at a rakish angle but to Richard's eyes he was putting the buttons on his chef's whites under some serious pressure. French actors are a different breed, he thought, they like them to look like real men here, like they've always had a good meal. Valérie certainly seemed taken with him.

'So much is wrong, so much of it inaccurate!' Amorette Arthur continued, interrupting his thoughts. Clearly she'd been meaning to get all this off her chest. 'It's quite upsetting for a historian. I mean, Napoleon didn't travel with his mother, it's ridiculous. Some of the costumes and table decorations are woefully anachronistic. Where are the Spanish prisoners even? This is supposed to be the Treaty of Valençay 1813, the end of the Peninsular War, yet there's not a Spaniard to be seen.' She downed her drink and Richard refilled it. Valérie was chatting warmly to Gilbertine who was talking about the menu to come, pointing at it and the picture of Monsieur Corbeau which adorned it. It was as if by playing the role of Antonin Carême he had somehow developed his own culinary skills.

The meal passed pleasantly enough. René had surpassed himself with a *daube de boeuf*, probably going back to his experience of being a prisoner-cum-chef in various Paris prisons, cooking for larger numbers being his strength. On the high table, as it were, directly opposite Richard and Valérie, sat the mayor and next to him was Friedman. Meanwhile, Noel Mabit was flitting around the place annoying people like a wasp at a picnic. On the other side of the mayor sat Lionel, which seemed to be pleasing the dignitary greatly. To the right of Lionel was Burdett, who appeared to be slumped in his chair. Turnbull was next to him while Jennifer Davies was the other side of Friedman, with Sacha at her side, who was laughing for once while chatting to Samuel. It was noticeable that the women were being kept away from Reed Turnbull, presumably on Friedman's instructions. It really was such a shame he wasn't leaving in the morning. Brian Grace and Stella Gonzales were placed elsewhere around the open-square table plan, talking to local bigwigs and forcing a smile here and there, but fooling no one. Between courses, almost everyone got up to wander about. The cast and crew mingled, though not the two main male actors and the locals looked relieved not to have to fawn for a few minutes.

Gilbertine made his apologies to Valérie, saying he had work to do, straightening his ridiculous chef's hat as he did so.

'Enjoying yourself?' Richard asked a little stiffly.

Valérie puffed out her cheeks. 'Not really,' she replied. 'Do actors only ever talk about themselves? It's very tiring. No wonder Sacha looks so bored.' He looked across at the sullen director. She did indeed look bored, and she was fiddling endlessly with her menu, avoiding conversation. 'It must take a special kind of person to have to deal with actors and film people all day. I feel sorry for her.'

Gilbertine re-emerged from the kitchen carrying an enormous dish on which stood a magnificent *croquembouche*, the tall pyramid-like cone of profiteroles which was invented by Marie-Antonin Carême. It was held together by spun sugar and caramel and drew gasps from the diners. The actor placed the dessert in front of a frowning 'Napoleon' and a barely conscious 'Talleyrand', before bowing and accepting the applause of the crowd.

'Oi!' René had also come through the kitchen doors and was having none of this fawning, 'give credit where it's due.' Gilbertine stopped mid-bow. 'Ladies and gentlemen,' René said proudly, 'Madame Jeanine made the *croquembouche*.' Jeanine, the *boulangère* of Saint-Sauver and a friend to Richard and Valérie, appeared sheepishly from the kitchen door, nodding to the people in the room.

'Yes, bravo!' said a punctured Gilbertine. 'Bravo!' He stalked back to his seat, tearing off his hat.

'Oh I love profiteroles!' Amorette exclaimed and Richard poured some more wine. He was actually beginning to relax quite nicely, though not as nicely as Dominic Burdett was relaxing and he saw the actor get to his feet unsteadily. Richard thought he was going to look for the toilets and wondered if, in his capacity as security, he should follow. No, he concluded, he was going to take tonight off. These mostly dreadful people could look after themselves.

Burdett stood, swaying slightly, but instead of moving off, tapped his wine glass gently with his spoon. '*Mesdames et messieurs*,' he slurred, 'as Charles Périgord Sagan Talleyrand…' Richard heard Amorette tut loudly at the actor, who despite being fully immersed in his character had got his name wrong. Richard could have pointed out that the man was fully immersed in something else but let it go. 'We made a war picture once and,' he belched, 'it's a sad occasion when any child of France falls.'

Presumably at this point he was to embark on an early eighteenth-century inspired eulogy on Monsieur Corbeau but, alas, he too fell. Literally, back into his seat.

'Oh for Chrissakes.' Reed Turnbull now rose, wiping and washing his hands in the finger bowl, a nod to contemporary early nineteenth-century dining.

'Napoleon rescues Talleyrand. He is quite the man.' The historian to Richard's left was beginning to slur her words. To his right he noticed Valérie toying with the sharper elements of cutlery and hoped Turnbull's speech would be brief.

'We're obviously here to celebrate the life of old…' he pointed to the large photo portrait of Monsieur Corbeau, 'of, er, that guy. Well,' Reed Turnbull looked into the middle distance, 'my impression of the old man…'

At this point his face contorted in pain, he clutched at his chest and pitched forward taking the table with him. Well, thought Richard, if that's his impression of old Monsieur Corbeau, it was in very poor taste indeed.

Chapter Thirteen

Brian Grace had lit the set beautifully, the lighting subtle and low-key to reflect the mood of the players. There were soft, reflective shadows, a few fake candles too which were set to flicker as though in a draught and the natural light of the moon, coming through the shutterless windows, bounced off a strategically placed mirror. The set itself was divided into three areas and the players for the most part sat languidly awaiting their cues. There was the half dining table in the middle, its places still laid and where Jennifer, Sacha, Stella, Brian and Gilbertine were playing poker. Lionel lay on a day bed, a generic boudoir still 'dressed' in a tight corner of the room and Talleyrand was slumped in an armchair in his 'office' on the other side of the makeshift studio. He was resting a small bottle of water on his chest, while his left hand held a bottle of whiskey. Alain stood by the door, his arms folded, looking less like a wolf and more like a stuffed museum bear.

From afar it may have looked like the cinematic mock-up of a famous painting of Regency decadence, only this wasn't in the script. There were no lines to prepare and far heavier than the looming shadows, there was tension. Ben-Hur Friedman chewed on an unlit cigar and stared out of the window. He kept looking at his phone for updates, his nephew Samuel having gone with the ambulance. Amorette Arthur stood by the fake fire, an anxious look on her face, while Valérie sat on the edge of Lionel's day bed, occasionally glancing at Richard who couldn't keep still and was nervously checking on Talleyrand. If indeed it was Talleyrand. He was beginning to realise that a sober Dominic Burdett was Talleyrand and that a drunk Dominic Burdett was Dominic Burdett. He found it confusing enough; heaven knows what a muddle it was inside the actor's head. He'd acknowledged Valérie's glances with a sombre frown and guessed that she was now convinced, like himself, that Corbeau's death had not been natural causes.

The ambulance medic, who had been dressed in civvies because, she'd told him irritably, her 'uniform had gone missing', now had Richard down as a jinx. 'This is your second heart attack in three days, monsieur. I may invite you for dinner the next time my father-in-law is in town.' Valérie d'Orçay was not a fan of coincidence whereas her ex-husband, Commissaire Henri Lapierre, was and therefore had immediately put Turnbull's cardiac arrest down to stress even though, he'd said pointedly, frowning at Richard as he left with the ambulance, that 'he was not one hundred and two!'

Jennifer Davies threw down her cards. 'I can't stand this waiting,' she said, a touch too dramatically. 'Ben, is there any news yet?'

'No,' the usually ebullient producer replied quietly, and without turning from his vigil at the window. 'Samuel said he'd be in touch when he could.'

'Poor Reed!' Jennifer, to Richard's trained movie mind, was overplaying the scene. Everybody knew that she and Reed loathed each other.

'I did not know him well,' the young Gilbertine said, his sing-song English accent adding to a sense, perhaps a façade, of innocence. 'I met him for the first time on this film.'

'He *is* a great actor,' Jennifer said.

'Still is, madame, yes, as far as we know.' The young man held her hand offering solace while Friedman left his post and put his hand on Gilbertine's shoulder, grateful for what he no doubt regarded as familial support.

'I've known him for forty years,' Brian Grace said while studying his cards, his Australian accent stronger than Richard had remembered.

'And?' came Jennifer's question after a pause.

'And,' Brian drawled, placing two cards on the table. 'He was a great actor.' There was a slight smirk on his face as he said what was, on the face of it, a simple statement but one that left an awful lot unsaid, not least of which that he was assuming Turnbull was dead.

Stella picked up Brian's cards. 'I did not like him,' she said simply. 'He did not like women.'

'I don't know about that,' Sacha said, biting her nails while concentrating on her own cards. 'I think he liked women in his own way, so long as they did not say anything and did as they were told.'

Richard hadn't liked Reed Turnbull either but he was old-fashioned enough to feel a little sympathy for the man. He was, presumably at that moment, fighting for his life while his colleagues, Jennifer Davies aside, were declaring him dead and giving his character something of a shoeing.

'He was an important man!' shouted Burdett, as though in the throes of death himself. 'And I gave my life to serve him!' Ah, Richard thought, it was Talleyrand who spoke not Burdett; the actor must be sobering up.

'He wasn't an easy man to work with,' Lionel offered quietly, breaking the silence that followed Burdett's outburst.

'Ha! A challenge for a director for sure, certainly a woman director!' Sacha threw down her cards in triumph while Davies gave her an unsympathetic look.

'He was superb in *The Town That Never Slept*,' Richard said, 'well deserving of the Oscar I thought.' Nobody replied to this, though he noticed that Valérie had quietly sidled up to him.

'He was a chauvinist,' she whispered in his ear with such vehemence that he nearly ducked. 'He would have made a good Frenchman!' He'd never seen her quite this angry before; her usual cool diffidence in the face of danger was almost alarmingly frosty at times, but then family hadn't been involved in their previous adventures.

The door opened loudly and a tired looking Commissaire Lapierre appeared, a hangdog expression on his face, his shoulders slumped and inevitably the remains of dinner still on his shirt and tie. He walked in slowly, followed by Samuel who for once wasn't a ball of energy.

'*Mesdames et messieurs*,' said the Commissaire sombrely, 'I am afraid it is bad news. Mr Reed Turnbull died this evening in the hospital at Châteauroux. The medical team there did all they could for him, but in the end, I am sorry to say, his heart gave out.'

There was a brief silence. 'They were lucky to find it!' Jennifer Davies laughed, as swift a volte-face as Richard had ever seen from an actress.

'Jennifer…' Friedman pleaded quietly, clearly wanting to keep it in the family.

'You did not like him, madame?' Lapierre was on her immediately.

'No, I did not!' She couldn't help grinning either.

Burdett suddenly stood up, looking for every part like the famous diplomat Talleyrand. 'A woman will sometimes forgive the man who tries to seduce her…' he began, before losing his way, taking another swig of whiskey and slumping back down in the chair.

'…but never the man who misses the opportunity when offered.' Amorette finished the quote.

'You seemed quite sympathetic a moment ago?' It was Valérie who punched a hole through the ensuing awkward silence.

'A minute ago I thought he might still be alive!' Jennifer said caustically. 'But he's not, so I don't have to pretend that I feel any sympathy for him anymore.' She looked around the room, challenging someone to publicly agree with her.

'Like I said,' Brian Grace smiled, 'he was a great actor.'

Lapierre put his hands behind his back and walked slowly to the window. 'At the moment the official cause of death is myocardial infarction, heart attack. Naturally there will be an autopsy in the morning, but I don't envisage that will change anything.' He made a point of glaring at Richard and Valérie, making it very clear that he wanted no unofficial undermining of the official police line.

'We were not shooting in the morning anyway,' Sacha said, standing up from the table. 'We were to prepare the set in the morning for the afternoon scene. I think I will go to bed now,' she added. 'Goodnight, ladies and gentlemen.'

'That means an early start for us too.' Brian leant towards Stella as he spoke. 'Can someone give us a lift back to our digs?'

'I can do that,' Samuel said. He had noticeably kept his opinions of Reed Turnbull to himself. 'Where are you staying?'

'I can't remember the name… did you pick up a card Stella?' Stella shook her head. 'Anyway, our landlady was waitressing tonight, does that help?'

'Gennie. Martin and Gennie.' Valérie answered before Richard could make some inappropriate comment. 'The Commissaire has the address I believe.'

The Commissaire flushed. 'I think I could find it.'

'OK,' Samuel said, 'I'll get Dominic to bed in his trailer and keep an eye on him.'

'Thanks, Samuel. I'll go to bed myself. Oh, sorry. Jennifer, Gilbertine…' Friedman senior briefly forgot himself, 'Good night.'

Everybody started to get up from their places to make their way to their luxury trailers while the Friedmans attempted to shift a now snoring Burdett.

Valérie had her business head on, a very serious look on her face, and in her green trouser suit she looked like a general about to issue battle plans. Richard was still incongruously in his dinner suit and if he'd had the self-belief might have imagined himself as James Bond. Richard did not have the self-belief, even less so when Valérie was in 'orders-giving' mood.

'Alain,' Valérie said quietly, approaching the giant. 'I'd like you to take Lionel back to our place, please.'

Our place? This was probably the most important news of the evening as far as Richard was concerned. *Our place!*

'I think I would much rather stay here tonight,' Lionel said. 'I don't feel like travelling back.' Valérie made to interrupt, but Lionel gave her a strong look. 'I just want to be alone,' she added quietly, and pleasingly for Richard as she echoed Greta Garbo.

Valérie's jaw muscles tensed.

'Anyway, I do have a job to do as well you know,' Alain said gruffly, indicating the set.

'Yes, you do have a job to do.' Valérie turned on him. If she had no control over her niece, someone was going to get it. 'You must go back to our place and make sure that Passepartout is fed this evening, please.' Alain started to object, but Valérie raised her voice and hand. 'Not too much. He gets bilious after eleven pm.'

Alain didn't know quite what had happened to him but he'd suddenly gone from grouchy, intimidating behemoth to the lion in *The Wizard of Oz* and he skulked off to do as he was told. Lionel, looking utterly drained, kissed her aunt goodnight.

'Are we not going back then?' Richard asked, after it was just himself, Valérie and Lapierre remaining.

'No. I must stay with Lionel and I want to have a think about all of this, Richard.'

'Right,' he said, 'well you don't need me then really. I can…'

'Richard, I need you here. You help me think.'

'Oh, OK.' Richard puffed out his cheeks and caught Lapierre's eye as he did so. He was not getting a friendly look.

'Madame,' Lapierre said formally. 'I want to make it clear. It was very obviously natural causes. There is nothing for you to think about, only that you,' he looked at Richard as well, 'that you both are unlucky.' He concentrated on Richard. 'Very unlucky.'

'I do not believe this is bad luck, Henri. Maybe you think it is, but maybe that is what you would like. *I* do not believe it.' She emphasised the *I* before adding, 'Do we, Richard?'

'Eh?' Richard sparked into life. 'Oh, well, you know. Two heart attacks, looks a bit… you know? Odd.'

The others both looked at him. 'Odd?' Lapierre was practically snarling.

'Yes, exactly that,' Valérie stepped in. 'Odd. Two heart attacks are odd.' She seemed less convinced having repeated it. 'Monsieur Corbeau was old, we know, but Reed Turnbull was not.'

'Ah,' there was a glint in the Commissaire's eyes, 'but he had a heart condition and took regular medication for it!' He raised his finger in triumph. 'Madame, there is nothing I can do to stop your curiosity. I suppose I could have you locked up on some pretext, but I have known you a long time and I doubt it would help. I don't think the machinery of the French state could even begin to stop you. I will bid you both good night.' He went to the door and turned the handle. 'I will see you tomorrow when I will have confirmation.'

'Confirmation?' Valérie asked.

'Of natural causes, madame.' If he'd had a hat this would have been the time to put it on, but instead he left with his nose exultantly in the air, leaving Valérie with a look of doubt on her face and Richard with so many questions and points of order that he didn't know where to even begin.

Chapter Fourteen

They walked slowly around the perimeter of the chateau. Valérie was, for the most part, quiet, with the occasional glance back at the trailers, but mainly she was mulling things over, and every now and then firing rhetorical questions at Richard. He knew from experience that not only was Valérie aggressively averse to the idea of coincidences, it was also in her nature to provide alternative solutions immediately, no matter how outrageous they might be. And while Richard, in his more elevated moments, might consider it his role to temper her imagination, his mind was largely elsewhere, his senses occupied to the maximum, on guard for his nemesis, Clovis the peacock. It was like the film *Hell in the Pacific*, he thought, his senses distracted momentarily. Lee Marvin and Toshiro Mifune, enemies of war stranded on a deserted island, hunting each other down, wary of their safety and vulnerability. He couldn't decide if he was Marvin or Mifune; both of them were heroic in their nobility, protecting their physical bodies as well as representing their nations at war. Of course, he doubted that he and the peacock would ever reach the stage of grudging, necessary co-operation that developed in the film but…

'Richard!'

He realised that Valérie was sitting on a low backless bench some twenty metres away, while he had been carried off by daydreams. He turned back and sat down next to her, the moonlight washing everything a bluey-grey. She stayed silent, though fidgety at the same time.

'It's all go, isn't it?' he said after a while, admonishing himself for breaking the silence with the most asinine and typically English opening gambit possible.

'What is?' she replied irritably.

'Well… everything.'

'Going where?'

'Never mind. What's bothering you? You've barely said a word since Lapierre left.'

She weighed this up, and then sighed heavily, almost in defeat. 'What if you were right, Richard?'

'Is that what's upsetting you? That I might be right? Ha! Well I like that!' He paused and she let his indignation peter out, which it did quickly. 'Right about what?' he asked quietly.

'Poor Monsieur Corbeau,' she replied. 'That it wasn't natural causes after all.'

'Ah,' he said, sensing the inevitable direction in which this was heading. 'I didn't say that it wasn't natural causes, I said that I didn't think it was stress related.'

'So you do think it was natural causes?' Her eyes caught the moonlight and lasered in on him.

'That's what everyone else says. The medics, the police… everyone, even the autopsy. Which I would say is pretty definite.'

She nodded without taking her eyes off him. 'But you doubted it from the start, Richard.'

'Yes, I did. And I don't really know why, but I just had a feeling that he was stronger than people were giving him credit for. He didn't seem the kind to just keel over like that. I don't know why I thought that, think that. I just do.' He breathed in deeply. 'Why do you now think it wasn't natural causes? You must have had some doubts yourself at first or you wouldn't have bullied Lapierre into ordering an autopsy.'

'I didn't bully anyone!' She looked affronted by the suggestion, but Richard in response just raised his eyebrows and looked at her sceptically. 'Well,' she shrugged, 'maybe a little.'

'So,' he put his head back and gazed at the moon, 'why do you think it wasn't natural causes then?'

'Because you don't,' she said softly. 'And I trust your judgement.'

He tried to remain nonchalant but realised quickly that any further nonchalance would result in him falling backwards off the bench. Two things occurred to him: first, that Valérie didn't trust easily and second, that few people had ever previously trusted his judgement, nor even suspected he had any.

She grabbed his wrist tightly and said suddenly, 'Richard, I think you are right!' Her excitement was palpable and it acted like a drug on her, her eyes were wide and intense, her jaw rock hard, like her grip on his wrist. For his part Richard felt he should try and match her enthusiasm but he knew that the vein in his forehead would be standing out, a sure sign of nervousness and visible even at night. Was he right about Corbeau? Was it really not natural causes? Suddenly he wasn't as certain as he had been, and he hadn't even been all that certain anyway. It was just a vague feeling, but one that Valérie was now buying into. That was the thing about trust; it wasn't that Richard lacked confidence in his own instinct so much, but that when others showed any confidence in him at all he began to doubt their faculties rather than his own.

He tried, with difficulty, to control his voice. 'You think that Turnbull was murdered which means that Monsieur Corbeau was murdered too, is that it?'

'Yes!' She was almost ecstatic.

'I see,' he said, a little too stoically. It came across as though there was a touch of polite disappointment in his voice, like he'd just been informed that his rental car was automatic after specifically reserving a manual.

'Is that all you can say? *I see!*' By now she was used to his attempts at trying to rein her in, and though she wouldn't admit it to him, she was also aware that his role as fire blanket was what made them a good team. But equally there were other times when he was like a stodgy English sponge pudding, sitting heavily on the finer meal that had preceded it. This was one of those times. 'Richard, we have two murders here…'

'*Potentially* two murders…'

'Potentially two murders then, if you insist, and you are acting as if that is nothing to you.'

'Of course it's something to me,' he said, showing a touch of frustration. 'But we'll know more tomorrow when Lapierre has the post-mortem results on Turnbull.'

'We already know the results,' she said, shooting up off the bench. 'They were both murdered!'

'We don't know that for sure. It really could be coincidence. Turnbull had a heart condition and Monsieur Corbeau was…'

'Yes, yes, yes. A hundred and two. I know. So, have you changed your mind now?'

'Not necessarily,' he whined, 'we just need more information that's all. I mean, if two people die of starvation, it's not a coincidence if there's a famine, is it?' He had absolutely no idea of the point he was trying to make, and neither did Valérie. So, whether it was the dull common sense of his need for data or the lack of passion or excitement in his voice, or whether Valérie was tired after a long day, or even that she just needed some sort of emotional release to counteract his stolid, pragmatic nature, Richard couldn't be sure, but the effect was volcanic. She looked him square in the eye and howled in frustration, throwing her head back after a few seconds and continuing her exasperation at the moon.

'Sshh!' he hissed at her. 'Will you be quiet! You'll wake that bloody peacock!'

Whatever angry invective she was about to throw his way Richard would never find out, as back in the gloomy shadows of the chateau came a very similar cry to Valérie's, but this one tinged with physical pain and longer lasting.

'Now look what you've done!' He stood up, for once alert.

'That was not a peacock, Richard, *viens*!'

They raced back through the grounds, unsure of where the scream had come from, and they could see no obvious disturbance. The peacock itself was standing on a wall and looking decidedly unaffected by any potential shenanigans.

'Shall we split up?' Richard asked, though frankly it was the last thing he wanted to do.

'Yes, I think so.' Valérie was shining her torch into the areas where the chateau light couldn't reach. 'That was a man's scream, Richard. You go and look, I must check on Lionel.'

It made perfect sense, of course it did, and he didn't openly protest, but he knew he was probably getting the more dangerous mission. 'OK,' he said, this time his stiff upper lip catching the moment perfectly. 'Can I borrow your torch though?'

They separated, Valérie heading off towards the actors' trailers and Richard slowly approaching the chateau, trying not to make a sound on the gravel. The outside lights that lit the chateau domes and the majority of the outside provided long Gothic shadows in the courtyard and Richard swallowed nervously. The gravel crunched behind him as steady footsteps approached. He whirled round only to be confronted by the inquisitive Clovis, who stopped still in the light of the beam.

'For crying out loud, Clovis! You nearly gave *me* a bloody heart attack then. Now, shoo!' For once the bird did as he was told and stalked off proudly into the gloom. Richard turned back to the chateau and noticed that the main door was open. He approached it slowly and shone his torch into the hall and on to neat piles of film equipment. Silently, apart from the thunderous pounding of his heart, he stepped into the reception area and approached the welcoming desk that visitors had to pass by before viewing the rooms. On the wall were portraits, coats of arms and other assorted images, snippets of the chateau visit to come. His torch stopped on one image; it was the sculpture of an open book and had a different frame to the others and had been rather squeezed in, like a late addition. There was nothing else seemingly out of place so he was tempted to leave before he had the misfortune to find anything that was. Carefully walking backwards towards the door he noticed, to his left, a light coming from downstairs. His heart sank at his misfortune. *Just my luck*, he thought, *I'll have to bloody investigate that.*

The winding stone staircase that led down to the huge kitchens was normally well lit, but the light wasn't coming from there. It was coming from further away so he cautiously descended the steps hoping that it was nothing really or at worst Clovis had learnt how to switch the lights on. It was colder underground and the arched passageway which gave on to the kitchens looked particularly unwelcoming. He turned left first and inspected the old wine cellars. Now arranged with empty bottles, in Talleyrand's day they had been among the best-stocked cellars in France, the diplomat himself making a fortune buying and selling vintages. Some of the caves were sealed off with iron gates, but the largest one had public access, and was mocked up with fake dust to give off more of a wine cellar air. Richard felt something crunch beneath him and he shone the torch down at his feet. It was a broken wine bottle and instinctively he bent down to pick up a piece with the label on it, but he didn't see another shard behind and he yelped as a piece of glass re-opened the cut on his finger. He turned the torch off in case there was anyone else down here with him while he sucked on his bleeding finger, trying to stem the flow of blood.

Suddenly, regardless of whether he was alone or not, he turned the beam back on again and lit up his finger. It was a tiny cut, really not much, but that wasn't why he'd thrown caution to the wind and relit the light. He needed it to adorn his lightbulb moment. 'Eureka!' he whispered. 'A cut finger.' He must tell Valérie at once.

He knew there was another exit on this level, at the far end of the stone corridor and he walked quickly towards it, briefly shining his light into the two cavernous kitchens as he passed them. Nothing struck him as untoward so he scurried out of the door which was next to Ben-Hur Friedman's apartment. His thinking was that he could check on Friedman first and then go to meet Valérie at the trailers. Turning the corner he noticed there were no lights on in the producer's apartment, but the glass door was open there too. It was a warm evening yes, but for some reason Friedman didn't strike Richard as the kind who would trust natural ventilation; it wasn't *Californian*. Cautiously he approached the open door, pointing his now waning torch into the dark room.

'Mr Friedman?' he called, partly as a whisper, after all the man might just be asleep. 'Mr Friedman?' He went inside scanning his light haphazardly around the room. There was an open bottle of cognac on the desk and a glass which still had some cognac in it by the side. Richard didn't like the look of that at all; Friedman was definitely not the kind to abandon his expensive nightcap. There was no sign of him though, neither in the main room nor the bedroom, nor the bathroom. No signs of violence either, he concluded, though he had to admit that he didn't really know what to look for.

He went back outside into the gardens and decided to do a circuit over the small bridge. That's when he heard the groans. He shone his torch down into the disused moat and at first saw nothing. Then he heard the groans again.

It was Friedman lying on his back at the bottom of the steep incline, looking like an upturned tortoise. Slowly he began to sit up as Richard made his way carefully down the steep bank.

'What happened?' he asked urgently as the producer shook his head groggily.

'I'm not sure. Give me a minute, maybe two, but am I glad to see you!' he said eventually. There was blood on his temple.

'Did you fall?' Richard sat him upright, just as Samuel Friedman arrived at the scene too.

'I heard the scream,' the young man said. 'What happened, Unc, did you fall?'

'No.' The producer replied looking from one to the other, a look of hurt umbrage on his shadowed face. 'I was hit and then pushed!'

Samuel looked at Richard; there was serious concern on his face. 'Let's get him back up,' he said, standing.

It would have been difficult to climb up the bank in normal conditions, let alone try and carry the American producer as well, but in the end they managed it. Reaching the top, they all stood in a line, getting their breath back, Richard and Samuel each holding one of Friedman's arms. Richard's phone beeped and he briefly let go, so that Friedman buckled and nearly tumbled back down, Samuel catching him just in time.

'Sorry,' Richard said and looked at his phone. It was a message from Valérie. 'Come. Urgent.'

Chapter Fifteen

Richard didn't regard himself as unfit, in the same way that he couldn't say for sure whether or not he had the intellectual capacity to be an astrophysicist: a lack of testing meant the result was in doubt. He never did any exercise and so was never physically scrutinised in a way that would judge just how out of shape he might be. It felt now, however, as he leant heavily on a chair outside Lionel's trailer caravan, that the results were in and perhaps some form of gentle regular exercise might not be a bad thing. He felt like he'd been through a serious cardiovascular workout as it was, what with running around the place, clambering up and down almost vertical moat embankments, wrestling with peacocks and all that after quite a heavy dinner. But Valérie had said come right away, so he came right away. He stood up straight, dusted off his dinner jacket, ostentatiously adjusted his cufflinks, raised an eyebrow in traditional and laconic secret service fashion, even though no one was watching him, and then slumped back on the chair trying to make sure he'd got all of his breath back. He was not a little concerned that he might just fall for the current trend and have a cardiac arrest. Lapierre would love that, he thought; finally he'd get himself a death by natural causes.

He knocked gently on the trailer door and opened it slowly. The light was gloomy, with all the make-up mirror bulbs switched off and just a small bedside lamp on in the corner. His heart sank immediately when he saw Valérie holding the prostrate and apparently limp body of Lionel Margaux on the corner couch. He was shocked to see a look of anger and guilt on his friend's face, and he immediately felt the same.

'What's happened?' he whispered loudly.

'Look at the mirror,' she said quietly, not taking her eyes off her niece and stroking her hair.

He strode quickly down the corridor and did as he was told. On the mirror, written in bold red lipstick was another message:

NOW LOOK WHAT YOU'VE DONE.

On the table under the mirror was an open box of pills and Richard picked it up. It was Nitrazepam, which, he knew from when Clare still lived with him, was a brand of strong sleeping pills. Most of the packet was gone too. He shook his head sadly. The poor girl. Hemmed in and bullied by the fake world she lived in; he felt guilty that that was the same world, albeit of a different era, in which he – someone on the outside – found comfort and escape. 'The opposite to poor, doomed Lionel Margaux,' he muttered under his breath. And what of Valérie? Richard had never met anyone as apparently strong and as sure of themselves as Valérie d'Orçay, but this would be a terrible blow, it would hit her hard. He walked back to the couch and knelt by the two women.

'I'm so sorry, Valérie,' he said, his voice almost breaking with sadness. 'She must have been under a terrible strain.'

Valérie looked at him and in the gloomy light he saw that her brow was knitted in confusion, her eyes searching his for answers, answers that he couldn't give. He was right. It had hit her hard, very hard.

'Richard,' she said quietly, and he sensed that she was forcing her voice to sound stronger than it was.

'The poor, doomed girl,' he repeated, shaking his head in sorrow.

'Richard!' This time she hissed at him.

'You don't have to pretend to be strong, Valérie, sometimes it's good to let your emotions go, you know? It can be cathartic.' He went to hold her hand. She slapped his in return.

'Richard! What are you talking about?'

It was only now that he realised that he had completely misread her face. Any confusion or anger she had was directed at him. He made a quick mental note to never, ever try to read a woman's face again. He showed her the box of Nitrazepam. 'I… well, I thought that…'

Valérie's face softened and she smiled at him. 'She's just sleeping,' she said gently. 'Those pills are mine.'

'But I thought she was dead,' he stood up, embarrassed.

'No. I found her staring at the mirror. She looked exhausted and frightened…'

'Who wouldn't be?'

'Quite. So I convinced her to rest, and I gave her some of my sleeping tablets. It will do her good, I think.'

Richard tapped the box into the palm of his left hand. 'I didn't know you took these?' He tried to pose it as an innocent question.

'Sometimes,' she said, again stroking her niece's hair. 'Please don't take it as a comment on the quality of your beds, Richard.' As he'd now retired from trying to read women, he huffed some sort of neutral response instead. 'You know,' Valérie continued, an element of surprise or realisation in her voice, 'I have never had to take them while staying here.' She looked up at him and then started giggling. 'And Richard! An Englishman telling a French woman to "let her emotions go"! You are a sweet, dear man. Thank you.'

Richard cleared his throat and tried to remain calm. 'Anyway,' he decided a change of subject was called for, 'that message on the mirror there. What do you make of it?'

'Well, it's our stalker for sure.' Her manner had flipped completely as her anger again began to boil.

'On the face of it,' Richard began to pace, 'it seems to blame Lionel for Turnbull's death.'

'Yes, I agree. But that seems odd.' Valérie was thinking aloud. 'And I can't think of anyone who isn't pleased that he is dead.' She fell silent for a moment. 'Richard!' The ejaculation was so sudden it nearly knocked him off his feet. 'Perhaps our stalker is not from the film people?' The way she said it meant that she had already concluded that this was the case. 'I think I know who it is, Richard, and we have to be very careful.'

'Who?' He stopped pacing.

'Lionel's father.' There was anger in her voice. 'Or, more accurately step-father, Armand Duvert. Her natural father died before she knew him. Duvert is a nasty man, violent, but capable of great charm and so deception too.'

'And your friend, Lionel's mother, she fell for this Duvert fellow?'

Valérie sighed. 'She did, many did. He was very handsome.'

Richard sat down opposite her, still toying with the pill box. 'But why would he be stalking her? I thought stalkers were more, you know, sexual, if you see what I mean?'

'Not always. I think they are obsessives.'

'I still don't understand why you'd stalk your own daughter though, even step-daughter.' Richard, as the father of a grown-up daughter himself felt disgusted at the thought of it.

'When Lionel was old enough, she was told about her real father. She had asked and we didn't think it right to keep it from her any longer. She had never been too close to her step-father, and this killed their relationship for good.'

'I see. And he didn't take kindly to the rejection? The swine!'

Valérie smiled at the effrontery he felt on Lionel's behalf. 'Quite,' she said enigmatically. 'Lionel is an extremely good judge of people. She decided to have no more to do with him after he and her mother divorced.'

'And he took it badly?'

'It would appear so. He probably needs money.'

They sat in silence for a moment.

'But,' Richard was thinking aloud. 'That means that either this Duvert killed Corbeau and Turnbull to eventually somehow frame Lionel, or they did die of natural causes and he's taking advantage of that to drive her mad?'

'I don't like…' she began.

'…coincidences.' Richard finished the sentence. 'I know.'

'He may have killed Corbeau and Turnbull, not to frame Lionel, but as you say, to drive her mad. But we don't even know that they *were* murdered.'

'Ah!' Richard stood quickly, and banged his head on a ceiling light. 'I'd forgotten in all the excitement. I think I know how they were poisoned!' He hissed the last word in case anyone, though it seemed unlikely, was listening. He held up his finger which had the small cut on it.

'You've cut your finger again?' There was no emotion in her voice, it was more like she'd been forced into playing charades and wasn't joining in properly.

'Remind me not to come to you for sympathy,' he said. 'No. You see, Corbeau had a cut finger. He showed me, said he was going to the doctor to have it dressed.'

'OK.' She sounded dubious.

'And Turnbull was bitten on the hand by Clovis!'

'Remind me, who is Clovis?'

'The peacock.'

'The peacock. I see.'

He opened his arms wide as if begging. 'I don't think you do. Both victims had a cut finger. Both victims played Napoleon. What does Napoleon do? He puts his right arm inside his tunic. I think that's how they were poisoned.'

She stared at him for a full ten seconds, then started nodding slowly. Richard, who was briefly back in the business of trying to read women, knew that this was either because she saw merit in his arguments or that she thought he'd completely flipped his cog. Her nodding speeded up; she was siding with him.

'Richard,' she whispered as Lionel stirred momentarily. 'Brilliant!'

He sat down feeling very smug with himself. 'Ah, well, you know…'

'How did you cut your finger, Richard, was it this Clovis?'

'Eh? Ah, no!' He stood up again. 'The door to the chateau was open and I went in…'

'Well done, Richard, you are very brave.'

'Yes, of course it's my job.' She smiled at him again. 'Anyway, there was a light on downstairs, where the kitchens are, so I went down and I was checking out the wine cellar…'

'And you were attacked?' Her anger shot up again like a water geyser.

'No! No, not at all, not me anyway.'

'Someone else was attacked?'

'Yes,' he replied impatiently, 'I'm coming to that. I trod on some broken glass. A couple of the bottles in the old wine cellar had been dislodged and had smashed on the floor. Stupidly I tried to pick some of the glass up and re-opened the cut on my finger. That's what made me think of Corbeau and Turnbull.' He sat down again, satisfied with his work.

Valérie stopped stroking Lionel's head for a moment. 'So who was attacked then?' she asked.

'Friedman.' He realised he was getting almost as animated as she usually did.

'But by whom?' Her eyes were wide with the excitement of it all.

'Unfortunately he didn't see who it was. He says he was hit from behind and pushed down into the old moat.

Which makes sense because whoever was in the wine cellar left by the door near Friedman's apartment.'

Valérie took a moment to take this all in but before she could respond there was a knock at the door and the younger Friedman, Samuel, let himself in.

'Oh gee,' he said, surprised. 'I didn't know if you were still here. I'm just checking everyone's OK.'

'We are fine, thank you,' Valérie said quietly. 'How's your uncle?'

'Oh, he's sleeping. Which is good, because usually he's up most of the night worrying. He'll be…' He caught sight of Lionel's mirror. 'What's this?' he asked worriedly. Valérie quickly caught Richard's eye and he knew she was trying to get him to understand something urgently. He wasn't entirely sure what, but he was going to have to take a guess.

'Oh that?' he stammered. 'That's erm… motivation.' Samuel didn't look like he was falling for it.

'Motivation?' he replied sceptically.

'Yes, motivation.' Richard decided that pompous umbrage was the way out of this. 'I would have thought you'd know that being an AD. Madame Margaux, in her role as Marie-Louise of Austria, has doubts about how she is treating her husband. She is torn,' he was warming to his task, 'between love of country and love of the man she, er, loves. It is a dangerous game she's playing, so she asks herself, "What have I done?" It is a testament to Madame Margaux's professionalism and integrity as an artiste.'

Samuel sat down at the mirror; he looked defeated by Richard's onslaught. 'Have you ever done any acting yourself, sir?' he asked quietly.

'The theatre is in my blood,' he replied, overdoing it by a country mile.

'It has been a very long day for you, Samuel.' Valérie extricated herself from the still sleeping Lionel and approached the two men.

'It sure has,' the young man said, removing his glasses and rubbing his eyes. 'First Reed, then my uncle. This is my first movie. I hope they're not all like this.'

'How was it at the hospital? It cannot have been very nice for you.' Valérie gave him a small bottle of water which he took gratefully.

'Pretty rough.' He twisted the cap off the bottle and took a swig. 'It was obvious as hell that Reed wasn't going to come through it. The man's had a heart condition for years – angina, high blood pressure. He smokes, he drinks. Well, he used to anyway. It's a wonder he lived this long. They were taking blood tests while he was still breathing. I mean, why do that? Let the guy go.'

'He must have been on a lot of medication,' Richard probed.

'I'll say; the guy was a walking drugstore. One of my jobs, every Sunday, was to lay out his drugs for the week. You know in one of those days-of-the-week pill folders. He was on half a dozen pills before breakfast, and that's only the ones I knew about.'

'You think he took more?' Valérie asked.

'I've no proof,' Samuel said, holding his hands up innocently, 'I only arranged his official meds. But I think he had a few unofficial ones going on too, the more recreational kind shall we say. Uncle always said he could be a liability.'

136

'So why employ him then? He was a liability and no one else liked him. Why have him around?' Valérie sounded indignant.

'Well, ma'am, the truth is my uncle is a romantic. None of these people have done good work for years and he wanted to get the team back together, one last job. Even Jennifer Davies, though that was more Sacha's, erm Madame Vizard-Guy's idea. She knew that she and Reed would be poison for each other, but she felt sorry for her. You know she's doing make-up and wardrobe too while we're here? It's how she started, how her and Reed first got together. Rumour is, she got pregnant, he paid for an abortion and then she discovered she had acting ambitions. My uncle has put everything on the line to get these people and himself back on top. Put up what's left of his grandaddy's art collection as collateral.'

'And someone is trying to stop it you think?' It was Richard who asked.

Samuel shook his head. 'I didn't say that. Natural causes is the official line. Sacha and my uncle are sticking to that.'

Valérie scoffed at the suggestion. 'No one really believes that!'

The ensuing silence was broken by her phone announcing a text message, which she read with very obvious agitation. She put the phone down and grabbed Samuel's arm. 'Well, you are doing a very good job, Samuel. I think you need some rest now, we can keep an eye on things.' She opened the door, and practically pushed him out. She slammed the door shut behind him.

'What's up?' Richard asked.

Her eyes were wild with a mixture of excitement and vindication. 'That was a text from the Commissaire!' She held up her phone in a gesture of triumph. 'Reed Turnbull *was* poisoned.'

Chapter Sixteen

The sun shone magnificently on the chateau the next morning, its dignity and serenity restored after the events of the previous night. An autumn haze hung in the air that would be burnt away by lunchtime as the sun climbed higher. It was a morning where all things felt possible and despite neither Richard nor Valérie getting much sleep, they felt vindicated, Richard especially, by Lapierre's text. Of course, it wasn't *good* news as such, Reed Turnbull was an odious individual but he was still dead. However, the fact that he had been poisoned as Richard and Valérie had suspected was, all things considered, the kind of confidence boost Richard needed.

The two of them walked through the parterre box-plant garden towards René's breakfast van. The skeleton crew, which consisted of Brian, Stella, Alain Petit and, surprisingly to Richard considering he was her employer, Madame Tablier, were busy assembling equipment. The acting talent had been given the morning off so there was an unhurried atmosphere, one more relaxed than previously. Commissaire Henri Lapierre was waiting for them, a tiny Styrofoam cup of espresso in his hand, and it was plain to see even from a distance that his body language was very far from self-reproach: it was actually quite bullish.

'He looks pretty full of himself for a man on the cusp of an apology,' Richard said quietly.

'I know that look,' Valérie replied, through a false smile. 'He's up to something.' Passepartout, who had been returned to her earlier that morning, gave a low throaty growl which Valérie did nothing to discourage.

'Ah,' the Commissaire greeted them like old friends, his arms stretched wide. 'If it is not Sherlock Holmes and Doctor Watson!'

The alarm bells in Richard's head were never far from full pelt at the best of times; they were now giving off like it was a royal wedding.

'You are ever so smug today Henri. It is most unpleasant.' Valérie wasn't hanging around, as usual choosing attack over subtlety and patience.

'*Moi*, smug?' The man replied, a false and wide-eyed innocence giving way to an unpleasant little chuckle. 'Over the years, madame, I have had so very few victories in life. I am a hard-working servant of the people. If I do well, nobody says thank you. If I err, the world, it falls on me. It is the lot of the humble policeman, I do not complain…'

'Oh stop it, you silly man!' Valérie punctured his pomposity like a balloon, the man visibly deflating before them. Richard almost felt sorry for him. Almost. 'You sent me a message last night to say that Turnbull had been poisoned. That is what we told you would be the case, didn't we, Richard?'

'Yes, I…'

'So,' she continued, Richard's support for the moment not really needed. 'You insisted that it was natural causes, poison suggests that it was murder. So why are you looking so smug? It doesn't suit you; you haven't had the practice!'

Richard was relieved he wasn't needed if that was her line of attack.

Lapierre wiped the inevitable crumbs from his tatty moustache; he wasn't, by the looks of it, quite done yet. 'Shall we settle for misadventure, *mes amis*?' He looked from one to the other, hoping for a reaction. Valérie looked like she might just beat the man to a pulp and hang the consequences, so Richard decided to step in.

'Two espressos please, René,' he said, putting himself physically between the former married couple. 'Commissaire?'

'I have mine, thank you, *monsieur*.' The way he said the word monsieur was as though he didn't feel Richard had quite earned the title. It was dismissive at best, and the way he then took a victory slurp of his steaming hot coffee added to the man's nasty air of superiority. Air that quickly evaporated, however, as the coffee was far too hot for slurping causing the Commissaire to turn puce and spit the liquid down his shirt front.

'Poor Henri,' Valérie said, giving her tiny dog a hug to illustrate just how far down the pecking order ex-husbands were. 'Now, stop being so silly, clean yourself up and tell us what you know, please.'

For the moment humbled, the Commissaire led them to a table outside the Orangerie restaurant where they'd eaten just the night before, though it felt like days ago, so much had happened since. Sitting down at the table Richard decided he'd had enough of being sidelined by these warring exes: it was, after all, his suspicions of foul play that had led them to this point.

'When you say misadventure, Commissaire, do you mean the poison was self-inflicted?'

The question caught Lapierre slightly off guard, having hitherto considered Richard not only the junior partner in the investigating double act but, like him, beneath Passepartout in terms of seniority and priority.

'Yes, monsieur.' This time there was a little more respect shown.

'Pfft!' Valérie gave it the full pursing of lips and shrugging of shoulders that only French women have perfected, and which Richard sensed was either in the genes or taught at school. 'I do not believe that that man would commit suicide. There was no *humilité* in that man, none at all.' She was becoming quite angry. 'Richard! Tell him about the fingers.'

'Ah, right. Well…'

The Commissaire, having gone from cat-with-the-cream to hangdog, didn't look happy to be receiving new information, especially information that might undermine his own conclusions. He looked even less convinced when Valérie held up Richard's cut finger, a minor injury at best, with the purposeful look in her eye of an avenging mother going after a school bully.

'See?' she said, before Richard could explain. It was fair to say that the Commissaire did not see, he did not see at all; what he did do was throw Richard a sympathetic glance for once. It was only a brief flicker but it had 'I feel your pain' written through it like a stick of rock.

'What am I looking at?' he asked, his voice so weary it barely made it to the end of the question.

'The cut!' She held up his finger again.

'Are you suggesting he may bleed to death?'

'Argh! You always were impossible, Henri. So closed. Monsieur Corbeau and Reed Turnbull both had injured fingers.' Again Lapierre tried to catch Richard's eye, possibly as one last plea for help. 'We think that that is how they were poisoned.'

Lapierre sighed. 'Have you been poisoned, monsieur?'

'No,' Richard admitted.

'Not yet,' Valérie added, which put the wind up her partner somewhat. Richard hadn't considered that possibility at all.

'But, madame, Valérie,' the Commissaire was trying to be patient, trying to appeal to a calmer side which Richard, though he had known Valérie only a fraction of the time, could have told him was a futile exercise.

'Do not Valérie me,' was the predictable response. 'It strikes me that both men were murdered and poisoned somehow through a cut in their finger.' She leant back in victory, took a deep breath and added, 'Probably a nerve agent. Ricin, Novichok, something like that. A substance that acts quickly and overloads the respiratory system. Probably Ricin as it is difficult to trace in a post-mortem.'

It was Richard's turn to spit out his coffee and quickly drop his cup too. This was all news to him. All he had done was notice a physical coincidence, he hadn't really thought beyond that, whereas Valérie was in the realm of Cold War assassination. Lapierre looked from one to another and then, again as if appealing for some sanity, at Passepartout.

'I bow to your expertise in this field,' he said coldly, 'but Reed Turnbull did not die of Ricin, Novichok or exploding cigars. Nor did that damned peacock dip his beak in digitalis in his role as covert assassin.' He was trying to stay calm. 'Monsieur Turnbull died of heart failure...'

'It was you who...' Valérie started to interrupt, but the Commissaire raised his voice to talk over her.

'...brought on by a massive overdose of sildenafil.' This time he took a more conservative victory sip, but it was nevertheless a victory sip.

'I don't know this sildenafil,' Valérie said quietly, almost talking to herself.

'And you, monsieur, do you know this sildenafil?' Something in the question suggested that Richard should indeed have heard of the substance, but he shook his head. 'Maybe you would know it more by its common name?' Again Richard indicated the negative. 'It is Viagra, monsieur, Viagra.'

Bloody cheek, was Richard's first thought. His male pride was not often dusted off for public consumption, but there were limits.

'Viagra?' Valérie was sceptical. 'Through his finger?'

'Hardly, madame, no.' Again he turned to Richard. 'You did not know that Viagra could kill?'

'Of course he didn't!' Valérie laughed, her mind elsewhere. 'He may not have your issues, Henri.'

It wasn't in Valérie's nature to be so cutting, and it wasn't a comment made with any real venomous intentions at all, but to describe these words as a blow to Commissaire Henri Lapierre would be understating it. The man looked like he'd been run over before his soul was then extracted and given a further thrashing.

'*May* not,' he spoke quietly, clinging to the one positive he saw in Valérie's undiplomatic candour.

Richard had often retreated from his own domestic showdowns and certainly felt uncomfortable being present at this one. The interaction raised a number of questions, but mostly his thoughts were once again dominated by how unlikely a pairing these two had been. Valérie had told him that they had met at police training college, but it still seemed implausible. The stolid future policeman and the glamorous future bounty hunter. They appeared to have absolutely nothing in common at all and yet here they were publicly discussing their sexual history. Or rather, Valérie was publicly commenting on their sexual history and the Commissaire was being humiliated.

Richard decided to get the conversation back on track. 'If Turnbull died of heart failure brought on by Viagra, does that mean he was... you know...?'

'Brilliant, Richard! Of course! But who with?'

Lapierre was evidently relieved the conversation had moved on. 'We do not know the answer to that yet,' he said, restoring his official tone. 'I'm not sure that it matters. Any *médecin legiste* will conclude that it is accidental death, or misadventure. Certainly not murder.'

'Pfft!' Valérie said again, thoroughly unconvinced. Richard agreed with the Commissaire though. 'You still must be interested in who he needed Viagra for?'

'For what purpose, to gossip?' He was getting angry now.

'To do your job, Henri!'

Again, Richard felt the need to intervene. 'Did the post-mortem show that Reed had, erm, well, you know... I mean recently that is?'

'That is a very good point, Richard. Had he had sex?' Valérie thumped the table.

'I am still waiting for the full results of the post-mortem,' the Commissaire said sheepishly.

'Then how do you know about the Viagra?' Richard asked reasonably.

'I insisted that blood tests were taken immediately at the hospital, while the heart still had some activity.'

'Very good, Henri,' Valérie conceded, to which he nodded courteously in reply.

'I also asked Monsieur Friedman, Samuel that is, what he knew of Monsieur Turnbull's health. The result is not in doubt. Monsieur Turnbull was taking medication for angina and for blood pressure; apparently the nitrates in these medicines clash with sildenafil in Viagra and can cause heart failure. He was also a smoker. It is a cocktail for disaster, but not for murder.'

Valérie for once looked beaten. 'Death by vanity,' she said quietly, before suddenly perking up. 'But we still have the full results to come!'

'Indeed,' the man sighed so heavily it seemed all life force had left him. 'I have little doubt in the outcome, however.'

'What makes you so sure?' Her question was quite dismissive and he ignored it.

'If I were you,' he turned to Richard, 'I would keep my next press conference as short and as vague as possible, monsieur.' *Oh Lord*, Richard thought, *I hadn't considered another press conference.*

'Henri Lapierre.' Valérie wasn't letting this go. 'I ask again, what makes you so sure that it was the heart and blood pressure medications mixed with Viagra that caused his death?'

'Because, madame,' the Commissaire sounded defeated, 'I take heart and blood pressure medications and I heed the warnings.'

Richard saw it now and he decided to sip his coffee quietly and not catch anyone's eye.

Chapter Seventeen

Leaving the Commissaire to 'tie up a very few loose ends' as he stressed it, Richard and Valérie walked without speaking back to René's breakfast van. They were both silently, but in their own way, mulling over the conversation with the intransigent policeman. Valérie was shaking her head constantly, refusing to let go of her own conclusions. Richard felt the same, but was acting less demonstrably. His logic was that whichever way you looked at it, one death by natural causes and one by misadventure still meant two deaths in just a few days. Both men had suffered cuts on their fingers too, though that didn't seem to mean much to the authorities; also, both men had been playing Napoleon as well. Richard wasn't one for unnecessary upheaval but the coincidence was too convenient, even for him, just too pat.

He stopped walking, reaching for Valérie's elbow as he did so. She stopped too and looked at him expectantly. 'No,' he muttered, and shook his head, as if in regret at what he was about to say. 'I don't buy it.'

She smiled at him sympathetically. 'I'm sure that you don't need to, Richard. Alas it was never Henri's forte.'

He narrowed his eyes, trying to understand her meaning before the penny dropped. 'What? No! No, not that.' He felt his cheeks reddening and then double reddening at the very thought of blushing. He was now blushing squared. 'I mean I don't buy the coincidence thing! Not the other thing. I've never bought that.'

She giggled at the misunderstanding and he managed, impossibly, to blush some more. 'I'm so sorry, Richard,' she said, then her face suddenly went very serious. 'And no,' she continued, 'I do not buy it either.'

Richard took a deep breath. He was about to ask a question that he already knew the answer to but which, for the first time in their relationship, he wasn't dreading. 'So,' his jaw was rock hard and he spoke through gritted teeth, 'what do we do? Neither of us believes this is all coincidence, but there's no evidence to suggest the opposite. Just a hunch.'

She pursed her lips. Her brow was furrowed too, the very picture of serious thought, before she then gave him the most Gallic of shrugs. 'Do you know what I think, Richard? I don't think you are helping at all!'

He might, under ordinary circumstances, have been rendered stunned and hurt by this bolt from the blue. Instead, he just nodded in resignation. *Just when you think you have a handle on the woman...* was his first thought, followed swiftly by righteous indignation and a desire to be very un-English about the whole thing and let his stiff upper lip take part in some emotional and probably salty invective.

'What the...' he began, before she gently put her hand to his mouth as she saw him about to lose control.

'I am not used to being agreed with, Richard, not by anyone and not by you.' She smiled at him warmly. 'I am not as silly as you think, you know. *Normalement,* you are my leash, you keep me in check. Sometimes I even just say things or have ideas just to see that side of you. That is why we are a good team. But now, if we do both agree that this is not coincidence, that there is a murderer and more, that Lionel,' she paused, 'that my niece is threatened... I will need your help. Not only to catch a killer...' she paused, '...but to stop me from killing that person.'

She lowered her hand from his mouth, and her eyes urgently searched his face for a reaction. It was the first tacit admission that she could, and probably even did, kill for a living. And though he had suspected it all along, this had broken through a wall in their partnership; he didn't know whether to be flattered or scared, so he decided to mix the two.

'Well, erm... I think two deaths is enough really, don't you? We don't want you getting arrested, you know, just as we are...'

'Exactly, Richard!' she laughed, and he was grateful for the interruption. 'Now,' she said over her shoulder as she moved off. 'Why do we not think it was coincidence?'

Richard smiled to himself. The wall had been quickly patched up and he felt a slight relief at that under the circumstances.

'Napoleon,' he said firmly. 'I don't know how they really died. And I really, really do hope it's not some kind of nerve agent,' he added stiffly, as if someone had put too much milk in his tea. She failed to suppress a giggle at his words. 'Look,' he said. 'Yes, I know that sounded terribly English, but I'm actually not at all used to discussing methods of assassination!'

'I am sorry,' she said, though it was clear she still found him funny.

'Right. As I say, Napoleon. That's why it's not coincidence for me. They were both playing Napoleon. Nobody, at least I can think of nobody, had a reason to dislike Monsieur Corbeau, and certainly not to kill him. Whereas...' he tailed off, gathering his thoughts.

'Whereas?' Valérie prompted.

'Whereas it seems everyone disliked Reed Turnbull.'

'Enough to kill him, you think?'

'Well, yes. Unless he really did die because, you know, he just wanted too much.' Richard was seriously running short of euphemisms for Viagra use, to the extent that he was beginning to hope a nerve agent might soon be revealed to be the culprit to save him any further bother. Valérie stared at him for a second, trying to work out what he meant. Then one of her lightning quick smiles flashed up.

'Brilliant, Richard!' she beamed, as usual her extreme excitement dancing like fire in her eyes. Something which pleased him and unnerved him in equal measure.

'Ah, Richard, and er...' It was a subdued Ben-Hur Friedman that greeted them as they neared the refreshment van.

'Valérie.' Valérie nodded formally.

'Valérie, right.' He seemed to be conducting some kind of meeting with the crew and the actors present, who were all seated and which included Jennifer Davies, Gilbertine and Lionel, though worryingly, given recent events, no Dominic Burdett. Samuel was there too, as was Amorette Arthur. Brian Grace and Stella Gonzales were sat at a separate table while Sacha Vizard-Guy stood next to her producer. She looked almost as worried as Friedman, though she didn't have a bandage around her head.

'How's the head?' Richard asked, his upbeat approach at odds with the mood of the group.

'Not good and getting worse,' was the morose response. 'We're having a meeting, trying to decide if we should pull the whole thing. You know, because of Reed's... well.'

'Murder!' wailed Jennifer Davies. 'We all feel it!' She looked around for support but no one was prepared to catch her eye. It was Valérie who spoke next.

'There is no reason to cancel your film,' she said loudly. 'Reed Turnbull was poisoned by himself.'

'Suicide?' Friedman had a look on his face that suggested that was worse than murder in terms of the box office.

'No,' Richard stepped in confidently. 'Reed Turnbull was on a number of medications for heart trouble and high blood pressure. Unfortunately he mixed them with... er... with something else. And the result was...'

'Monsieur Turnbull took too much Viagra.' Valérie said as if it were a press announcement. 'Combined with his other drugs, this caused heart failure.' She caught Richard's eye to let him know what she was trying to do.

There was a stunned silence that followed the news and drinks were stopped halfway to people's mouths. 'Viagra?' Friedman's day was getting worse with every new development and he put his hand to his scalp, accidentally dislodging his bandage.

Richard and Valérie scanned the gathered faces, trying to gauge any reaction. Most just looked stunned though Brian Grace was trying to suppress an obvious smirk, Gilbertine looked confused and Sacha was nodding as if she'd suspected as much all along.

'Well he never needed it with me!' cried Jennifer Davies, clearly trying to rule herself out as a suspect. 'Reed had a lot of problems, but that wasn't one of them, let me tell you!' *Please don't*, thought Richard. 'He was a bastard, but that guy could have drilled for oil!' She looked around defiantly allowing Brian Grace to finally release his smirk, Gilbertine to look surprisingly uncomfortable and Richard to silently conclude that Jennifer Davies' calming chakras and tantric vibes had obviously taken the day off.

'Jennifer, I don't think…' Friedman began.

'What? You don't think he'd want to hear that? Really? He'd want it on his tombstone, Ben.' She sat back in her seat, emotion now getting the better of her. 'The only thing Reed ever needed to take in the sack was a gag.' She looked around again. 'He was a talker,' she explained. 'Practically gave speeches all night. Not that he often stayed around all night. No, no wait a minute… that was Dominic. I'm afraid my past is a bit vague.' She beamed to the world, as though accepting a prize. 'I'm all about the future now,' she added, sounding rather as if she were trying to convince herself.

Richard knew nothing whatsoever about hysterical, damaged women other than he knew one when he saw one, and Jennifer Davies was clearly upset and couldn't stop her-self from talking. She may have come to dislike Turnbull intensely, but they also had a great deal of history and Richard felt a bit sorry for her. The other two on Davies' table weren't taking it well either. Amorette Arthur was shaking her head silently in disbelief and Lionel, not for the first time, looked like she'd had enough of the whole thing.

Nobody knew how to follow this so Richard decided to quickly change the subject. 'Do you still think you have to shut down production, Mr Friedman?' he asked, trying to refocus the group.

The producer shook his head. 'I don't know, I don't know. I think Reed would want it to go on.' There was a murmur of approval. 'All of his scenes were in the can already.'

'There were some pick-ups we were going to do,' Sacha added, thinking aloud. She had remained quiet throughout, but there was a sense of relief that production looked like it might continue. This was her big opportunity after all; there might not be another. 'But we can use a double for any over the shoulder shots.'

Richard leant into Valérie. 'I don't think there'll be many takers for that,' he whispered. 'Quite literally a poisoned chalice.'

'They are all really quite ruthless,' she replied and he wondered if she counted her niece in that.

'OK,' Friedman suddenly came to life with a zest of enthusiasm that was right out of the Hollywood cliché manual. He even tore off what remained of his bandage. 'We go ahead!' The mood of the camp was largely lifted, apart from Lionel and Amorette, neither of whom looked keen. 'And,' Friedman added grandly, 'we start back tomorrow and we do it for Reed!' If he was expecting cheers at this point and hats to be tossed up into the air, he was mistaken. What he got were polite nods and a rather embarrassed silence broken by a visibly furious Madame Tablier and Alain Petit marching into the centre of the group.

'You two,' the fierce woman pointed a spanner in Richard and Valérie's direction. 'You call yourselves security? Well someone has stolen my bloody motorbike!'

Richard and Valérie looked at each other in confusion while Ben-Hur Friedman groaned at yet another disaster. 'Madame,' he was addressing Madame Tablier, 'could I talk to you for a minute, maybe two?'

Before she had time to grant him an interview, however, a loud roar erupted as Madame Tablier's motorbike came speeding ridiculously out of the gift shop entrance to the chateau, scattering Clovis into the bushes as it did so. The bike did a couple of laps of the parterre garden, skidding around the edges as it went, pushed full throttle by a be-wigged Dominic Burdett and his helmeted passenger whose long blonde hair flowed behind.

The bike skidded to a halt in the middle of the group and Amorette Arthur, historian and self-appointed custodian of the majestic history of the Chateau de Valençay finally snapped.

'What the hell do you think you are doing?' she screamed, standing up as she did so.

'Madame,' Burdett replied calmly. 'I am Charles-Maurice de Talleyrand-Périgord, Prince de Bénévent, and Minister for Foreign Affairs under Emperor Napoleon Bonaparte and as such,' he stepped off the bike, 'I own this joint.'

'This is not right!' she screamed again. 'None of this is right!' She burst into tears and ran off towards the chateau and presumably her apartment.

Everybody, except Richard, watched her go. He was concentrating on the motorbike, a look of impending

155

doom on his face which turned immediately to defeat as the pillion rider dismounted, removed her helmet and freely shook her long blonde hair.

'Hello, Richard.' Clare Ainsworth beamed innocently. 'Fancy meeting you here!'

Chapter Eighteen

'Did you know she was coming?' Valérie was at Richard's shoulder and the tone of her question had a touch of diffidence about it, almost too diffident, forced even. None of which Richard actually noticed as most of his mental faculties were currently dealing with the rank injustices of the universe. Not that he disliked Clare at all, far from it, but she had a habit of turning up at awkward times and appearing to check up on him, like a supervisor at a work station. Their marriage was over, they both recognised that; they were both a little relieved too, even though they still managed to get on with each other. But Richard knew that Clare was still being territorial while at the same time making sure his field remained fallow. Dominic Burdett gallantly helped her dismount.

Valérie coughed. 'Richard,' she repeated, 'did you know that she was coming?' This time the tone was less jaunty, more acidic.

'What? Oh, yes I suppose so. She did mention it.'

'I see.'

Richard came out of his trance of self-pity. 'She saw me on the news. I didn't ask her to come out here. Why would I?'

'It is none of my business,' she said icily.

This was all getting too much for Richard Ainsworth. On the one hand, and in better moments, he might have been flattered to inspire jealousy – flattered and disbelieving. But on the other hand he got the distinct impression that neither woman actually wanted him, they just didn't want the other woman to actually get him.

'Typical,' he said to himself.

'I'm sorry?' Valérie had become stiffly formal.

'Typical that she would turn up now when we have so much to do together.' He tried to look for her reaction from the corner of his eye; she seemed to relax slightly.

'We still have our jobs to do, Richard,' she smiled at him. 'No distractions.'

'No distractions,' he smiled back.

Clare came over from the motorbike leaving a quite vacant Burdett hovering between reality and his imagined eighteenth-century grandeur. He appeared quite lost.

'Ah Valérie! How lovely, you're here too! We're all back together again then.'

'*Bonjour*, Clare, you look so well. Have you lost weight?'

Unseasoned Valérie observers may well have concluded that the comment was unusually arch, if not downright catty, for Valérie, but Richard knew differently. It was simply a factual statement. If she had put on weight, Valérie would have pointed that out too but Clare did indeed look in very good shape, she had lost weight and she was confident enough to recognise a genuine compliment when she heard one. 'That is so kind, Valérie, and I love your outfit. Not many women can pull off the masculine look.'

Clare on the other hand… thought Richard.

Dr Zhivago was his next thought, giving himself some side. Omar Sharif as the eponymous doctor torn between his two loves, Julie Christie and Geraldine Chaplin. He let his mind wander briefly but became aware that they were both now staring at him, knowing he had drifted off.

'Sorry,' he said quietly.

The two women approached each other, overly keen, in Richard's view, like two wrestlers determined to show pre-bout bravado, then they did the very Parisian 'mwah-mwah' cheek kiss that had so much distance between them Lionel's trailer might have been parked there.

An awkward silence followed which Richard knew better than to try and fill. 'Well,' Valérie said at last. 'It seems that we all now have the day off. I shall go and organise transport to take us home.'

'Home?' Clare raised an eyebrow at Richard as Valérie left.

'Erm, I guess it is her home, sort of.' He didn't like the look in Clare's eye. 'Well, not really. Obviously.' The look in Clare's eye wasn't going anywhere. 'Do you remember the film *Separate Tables*?' he asked desperately. 'It's about a boarding house but people live there permanently, so it's a kind of home… to them.'

'Richard.'

'David Niven won the Academy Award.'

'Richard!' Clare snapped. 'Stop gibbering.'

'Yes.' He looked to the ground.

'It doesn't matter to me in the slightest. It's not my home even if I do still own half of it. Anyway,' her mood brightened significantly, putting Richard on high alert.

'I'm here to help you out. I saw you on the television and about the only decent thing about your appearance was your tie.' She looped her arm through his and walked him through the garden. Everybody else had gone to get their gear together, relishing a day off away from the claustrophobia of the film set. 'We need to go shopping, in my opinion,' Clare was saying. 'Have we time to get to Paris before your next appearance, do you think? If not, Tours will have to do, I suppose.'

Richard didn't hear the end of the sentence, what he heard inside his head was the long scream of a man falling off a cliff. He had briefly forgotten about the inevitable second press conference. What on earth was he supposed to say about Reed Turnbull's death? Assuming he was allowed to tell the truth, his knowledge of the whys and the wherefores surrounding the nitty-gritty of the man's demise was limited at best. The journalists at the last press conference had been aggressive enough, and they were film experts like him. Suppose this time it was a collection of Pulitzer Prize-winning erectile dysfunction hacks?

'Ah, Dominic, dear. Is everything OK?' Clare asked, an easy informality existing between them already, Richard noticed. Burdett was still standing by the motorbike, unable to leave until Madame Tablier had given it a thorough inspection for damage. She was going over it like a police trooper in a stop and search, a look of angry disappointment on her face that so far everything seemed in perfect order.

'I don't care who you think you are,' she was saying to a dozy Burdett, 'you don't touch my motorbike.' She looked at Clare with a stony face. Nothing surprised Madame

Tablier, everything just got added to a list of half-expected irritations. That her motorbike had been briefly stolen by a major Hollywood superstar but had been returned with the ex-ish wife of her employer on the back and had appeared through the doors of a gift shop, didn't fill her with the wonder that it might otherwise have done. She looked Clare up and down and tutted loudly. She kicked off the bike stand and wheeled it away.

'And *bonjour* to you too, Madame Tablier.' Clare smirked as the older woman moved off, her painted leather jacket showing a winking Johnny Hallyday as she disappeared. 'She's still as warm as ever then!' Richard was becoming increasingly unnerved by just how good a mood Clare was in. From experience, he knew it did not bode well.

'Samuel has already arranged for a limousine to take us all back,' a returning Valérie said. 'He is very efficient.'

'Do you get the same treatment from Madame Tablier, Valérie?' Clare asked innocently.

'Treatment?' Valérie looked confused. If she did get the same treatment, and everybody did, she simply hadn't noticed. 'No. I don't think so.'

Clare's smile slipped briefly.

'A limousine, Madame d'Orçay?' Richard was looking for a distraction and overplayed his hand. 'I mean, there are, what, only five of us going back?'

'That's what Samuel said, Richard,' she replied, emphasising his name. 'And there will be eight of us, including Passepartout.'

'Right-o.' Richard decided to spend the intervening few minutes looking at his feet, leaving the big beasts to weigh each other up.

'Did somebody order a limousine?' a grinning Martin Thompson stood at the door of the gift shop. He was wearing a smart grey suit, a chauffeur's cap and dark sunglasses and looked every inch the classic limousine driver. For once Richard resisted the urge to let his heart sink at Martin's arrival on the scene; this time it was a welcome distraction. You knew where you stood with Martin. There was no hidden agenda, no games – mental ones anyway – just as straight as a die, bona fide, you-get-what-you-see pervert and sometimes, he had to admit, that can come as a welcome relief. Gennie appeared at his side, dressed exactly the same way and Richard's heart, which would normally now be somewhere around ankle level, soared at the solidity of it all.

'Hello, Clare!' Gennie said, taking her glasses off. 'I didn't know you were back. You look lovely! Doesn't she, Martin, doesn't she look lovely?'

'Rather!' Martin gave a throaty reply.

'And you two look dressed for action!' Clare exclaimed. 'Is this a new venture?'

'It is!' Gennie was practically jumping with excitement. 'You know how Martin likes to tinker…' Martin opened his mouth to say something. '…not now Martin. Well, he's been playing with this old thing for years and we thought, why not?'

Martin proudly balanced on his tiptoes. 'I mentioned it to young Friedman last night on the way to the hospital, when he wasn't on the phone to the States anyway. And he rang up half an hour ago. "Let's go, old girl," I said.' He turned to the large red gates at the end of the parterre garden and there, gleaming in the sunlight, was a large black limousine. Its windows were darkened and the back door opened to reveal white leather seating and a gaudy purple light on a glass drinks cabinet. 'A 1978 Lincoln Continental, does about forty metres to the gallon, but fully stocked with the local stuff!'

'And you've bought this for your sideline business then?' Richard was only trying to be polite.

'Sideline? Oh, you mean the *Introductions* Agency?' Gennie emphasised the word introductions making it sound like an underground club in 1970s Soho. 'Do you know what, we hadn't thought of that, had we, Martin?'

'No! Bloody good idea though. You can borrow it if you want!'

Richard's stomach did a backflip.

The Thompsons led the way to the behemoth of a vehicle. The film people were used to the spectacle obviously, but Clare and even Valérie looked impressed. Richard was still slightly stunned. Brian, Stella and Lionel got in first, followed by Clare and Valérie, who held Passepartout tightly. Alain Petit squeezed in with difficulty at the end.

'Can I come too?' Jennifer Davies ran up to join the group. 'This place gives me the creeps, can I stay with you tonight?' she asked Richard directly, and he noticed both Valérie and Clare looked unimpressed with the actress's obvious flirting technique.

'Well, erm... I... the thing is...'

'I can sleep on the sofa downstairs,' Alain offered helpfully. 'You can have my room.'

'Yes, but...' Richard stammered.

'Nonsense!' It was Gennie who intervened and spoke to Alain. 'We have space at our place, come back with us.'

Richard noticed the reaction of Brian and Stella and it suggested that Alain Petit may very well be a warrior of a man, but he was about to experience a whole new ballgame. Jennifer Davies gave profuse thanks to the big man and sat beside him. Richard was about to follow, but was halted by Valérie.

'Richard,' she said, an air of practised distraction about her as she stroked her tiny dog. 'Why don't you ride in the front? You could ask Martin about Viagra.'

Chapter Nineteen

It was probably the longest short journey of Richard's life. Sitting on the bench seat in the front of a stretch limousine between two uniformed chauffeurs, the male party of which did his best to break the Guinness World Record for the number of Viagra double entendres in a twenty-minute period, was just about more than he could bear. It started badly and got progressively worse.

'Viagra, eh?' Martin croaked, sliding on to the seat beside him. 'Trying to keep up with both your women, that it?'

Before Richard had a chance to disabuse him of any ménage à trois notions, the arch voice of a distinctly unimpressed Clare came over the limousine communications system. 'Perhaps it might be wise to turn your microphone off, Martin,' she said, as though she had a mouth full of drawing pins.

'Ah.' Martin did as he was told, while Gennie giggled. 'Sorry, old man. Still,' he had at least the good grace to look at Richard apologetically, 'breaks the ice, eh?'

Martin's subsequent performance was in some ways impressive, but mostly it was dispiriting. Richard had never been one for the traditional British nudge-nudge, wink-

wink, saucy postcard style of humour, it all seemed rather childish to him and lacked finesse, but this was worse. This was like a torture scenario: Richard the front seat hostage in a relentless, cruel game of smut-deluge monopoly.

Amid the onslaught Gennie added some facts, for instance that Viagra can increase the life of potted flowers or that buying the drug saves the lives of endangered species as desperate men aren't in Africa scrabbling around for rhino horn and the like, but all in all Richard felt like he was in a bawdy take on the aversion therapy scene from *A Clockwork Orange*. He was desperate to change the subject, not just because it was a tsunami of 1970s teatime sitcom faux-vulgarity but because he knew full well that Clare, thanks to Valérie's guilelessness, would later want to talk about it too and to know precisely what was going on. Why was Richard interested in Viagra, for instance? Clare and Richard had never been very good at conversations like that.

The final nail in the coffin for Richard was a rather lacklustre attempt – Martin was by this point running merely on fumes – to equate Reed Turnbull's death with fifteenth-century executions. It was something along the lines of being well hung, drawn and quartered and at that point he just sort of deflated, a spent force like a marathon runner who has hit 'the wall'.

'It's a serious business is Viagra,' Gennie said, as always the childish innocence of her appearance at odds with what Richard knew about her. 'We had a friend who didn't want his wife to know that he was taking the stuff. He used to grind out the tablets and put the powder in empty vitamin capsules.'

Martin winced at the memory. 'That's right, only his wife had done the same. Didn't want to hurt his feelings and all that. Poor fella was in hospital for a week. Touch and go.' He paused, wondering if that constituted yet another innuendo, but decided it didn't. 'I can get you some if you don't fancy going to the doctor?' As always Martin was as affable as it was possible to be and yet still made Richard feel uncomfortable. His brief feeling of warmth towards the man's solidity and consistency had waned significantly.

'It's not for me,' he said. 'It was Reed Turnbull last night. The police say he died of an overdose of the stuff. Apparently it reacted with his other medications, heart and blood pressure.'

'Yes, that is a dangerous mix,' Gennie said seriously. 'The doctors always warn against that.'

'Still, what a way to go, eh?' Martin just couldn't help himself. 'It's the undertakers I feel sorry for.' Richard and Gennie looked at him curiously. 'It's not going to be easy getting the coffin lid on.'

Eventually they arrived back at Richard's *chambre d'hôte*; there were still a few journalists hanging around the gate, the news of Turnbull not yet out, but those that remained had been cowed into submissiveness by Madame Tablier who stood on sentry duty, pitchfork at the ready, threatening to turn them all into colanders. Martin glided the limousine through the gates skilfully and parked up. There was no need to play the chauffeur and open the rear doors as Lionel was already out, and gasping for air. 'Sorry,' she said unnecessarily, clutching at her chest, 'I find these things really quite claustrophobic. Give me a balloon anytime.'

She looked too fragile for this business Richard thought. He was always one for defending the glamour and élan of Hollywood and cinema in general, but he knew how brutal it was. How it was capable of chewing people up and spitting them out and it had to be said that Lionel looked like she no longer had the stomach for the fight. Jennifer Davies staggered awkwardly out of the car behind her. It was hard not to compare the two. If Jennifer was Lionel's future, it might not be worth the effort and he could see Valérie protectively having the same thoughts. Clare, however, looked to the manor born and rose gracefully out of the car, a look on her face suggesting that she was half-expecting flashbulbs to go off.

It suddenly struck Richard that with everything going on they had yet to get to the bottom, or frankly even the top, of how his estranged wife should turn up at the Chateau de Valençay riding pillion on Madame Tablier's motorbike hugging a major Hollywood film star. As usual, it was all getting a bit much.

'Aperitif, anyone?' he asked a little too enthusiastically. He knew that enthusiasm wasn't his strong point, but he could mix a decent drink and he could certainly do with one.

'We'll have to pass, old man,' Martin said, disappointment in his voice. 'I've got a shift on the ambulance tonight. And the way you lot are going,' he chuckled, 'it might be a busy one!'

'Oh, Martin!' Gennie admonished him. 'Anyway we've got to set up Alain, is it? We have to set him up with a room.' They all made their tired goodbyes before Martin smoothly took the limousine back out of the gates.

It was then that the full horror of Richard's immediate predicament dawned on him. They all stood just outside the doors to the salon, a Passepartout-clutching Valérie, a frowning Clare, Lionel, Jennifer, Madame Tablier and Richard. He felt like a dead rabbit at snake-feeding time at the zoo. The aperitifs would be large.

'What a charming place you have,' Jennifer Davies gushed, as always slightly overplaying her role. 'It has such good vibes.'

'Yes, thank you,' Clare replied stiffly before opening the salon door. She looked from Valérie to the two actresses, and then to Richard. 'Right then,' she said, 'Viagra. Richard what's going on?'

They all followed her indoors, Richard hanging back to the end, while Madame Tablier apparently tutted at being left out of the Viagra investigation line-up.

'I don't know who you are,' it was Jennifer who addressed Clare, a hint of aggression in her voice, 'but as you're obviously close to Dominic you must know what's going on. He tells everybody everything when he's asleep.'

'I wouldn't know that, my dear,' Clare replied frostily. 'I only met Mr Burdett today. My husband's car broke down – not for the first time.' She gave Richard a filthy look. 'And a man in a wig came by on a motorcycle. Of course I recognised him.'

'Your husband?' Davies said the word husband as though it were a mythical beast, rarely seen outside of fantasy fiction. Clare pointed at Richard, who gave a weak smile. 'So who are you?' she asked Valérie.

'Business partner,' was the impatient reply. 'And Lionel is my client.'

'Business partner? Right!' Davies laughed. 'You guys have more action going on than a film set!'

'And I'm just a nobody, I suppose,' Madame Tablier said over her shoulder as she went to the stairs. 'I'll get your room ready then. That's what nobodies do…'

Clare shook her head. 'Extraordinary woman,' she muttered. 'Richard, where are those drinks?'

'Ah, right-o. I'll go and get some…'

'And don't go disappearing with your ladies, we need to talk.'

'What ladies?' Davies asked. 'He has more ladies?'

'His hens dear. He's really not as exciting as you seem to think he is. Are you, Richard?'

'Oh no. Oh lord, no.' Richard was more than happy to come clean on that score, and slunk out of the door in search of some nerve-settling cold drinks. He lingered a while in the cellar hoping that in his absence, gaps would have been filled in, Is dotted and Ts crossed, but one look at the various faces on his return told a very different story. It looked like a freeze-frame from the warring tribes in *West Side Story*.

'I'll get the glasses then,' he said, affecting an air of irritation. 'Does everyone like champagne? Of course, we do.'

'I don't,' Jennifer said, 'sorry I don't drink anymore.' She looked around the group, a look of needless apology on her tired face.

'You do not need to apologise, madame,' Valérie said warmly. 'I think I will not have a glass either. I want my head to be clear.' She looked at Richard and if there was a suggestion that he should possibly follow suit, it wasn't strong enough to have that effect. Quite the opposite in fact.

'Well I need a drink,' Richard said, avoiding her eye. 'It's been a long few days in the security business.' He popped the cork and poured out some glasses, while Valérie found some juice for herself and Jennifer.

'You, Richard? You are in the security business?' Clare laughed, but it sounded more like a horse being shocked into fear.

'We are,' Valérie retorted putting a swift end to Clare's braying.

'And how is it going?' Clare asked, prompting a silence so pregnant it might have been having triplets.

'We have two deaths,' Jennifer said. 'So far.'

'Well, yes,' Richard interrupted. 'Statistically. But one was an old man…'

'He was a hundred and two,' Valérie helped. 'Natural causes.'

'And the second was accidental…'

'Reed Turnbull,' Jennifer offered dramatically, causing Clare's eyes to open widely.

'He mixed his heart meds with his Viagra drugs,' Richard sounded unconvinced. 'Accidental.'

It was Lionel who first held out her glass for a refill. She had been quiet since they had returned and looked as pale as ever.

'Like I said,' Jennifer carried on. 'He never needed that stuff with me.'

'Yes but you have not had an affair for years!' The younger actress was losing patience with the older.

'It was last week, honey!' Jennifer downed her juice like it was bourbon whiskey. 'Old habits die hard. No offence.' She took a deep breath. 'And don't think you're better than me *young* lady, 'cos if you stick around long enough, I'm your future.'

'Your room's ready.'

Madame Tablier's timing was perfect and Jennifer replied with an unctuously sweet, 'Why thank you.' At the foot of the stairs, she turned back to the room. 'Like I say, Reed never needed any of that stuff, not with me. And anyway, it wasn't me banging him before dinner last night. I was with the much younger Gilbertine, much, much younger.' She disappeared up the stairs.

'I don't like her,' Madame Tablier said, approaching the others. 'Any of that left for me?'

'You know what?' Richard sounded wistful. 'She seems to have developed a successful sideline in ruling herself out of things that she wasn't necessarily ruled in for.'

'She's lying though,' Lionel said, almost in a whisper. The look on Valérie's face suggested she was about to hear some uncomfortable revelations from her niece. 'I have known Gilbertine since we were twelve; we were both at drama school together. He would never have been with Jennifer.'

'Younger men do occasionally go for older women, I'll have you know!' Clare felt compelled to defend her generation.

'Yes, madame, but Jennifer is not his type.' Lionel sounded very certain.

'Gay is he?' Madame Tablier asked and, tired of waiting for someone to pour her a drink reached for the bottle herself.

'It could even have been Gilbertine with Turnbull then?' Richard was developing a nasty habit of thinking aloud, which invariably led to people listening to what one said. 'You just never know, do you?'

Valérie gripped his hand. 'Brilliant, Richard! It must not be ruled out.'

Clare was more sarcastic. 'Yes. Brilliant, Richard,' she said, arching a beautifully plucked eyebrow. 'I do hope you can keep this up.'

Chapter Twenty

'So where's my car then?' Richard handed Clare a *tisane* and sat down opposite her on the terrace. The others had gone to bed, all except for Valérie who couldn't rest and was walking Passepartout in the garden.

'Your car? Oh, it's not far from here. Don't worry, Richard, I don't think anyone will steal it.' They both sipped their drinks. 'You really are having a high old time, aren't you?' she said, without looking at him.

It could potentially have been a trap but Richard knew when Clare was laying traps and this wasn't one of those times. 'It's certainly busy,' he replied, staying wary nonetheless.

'Lucky you.' She smiled warmly at him. 'I really am very happy for you, you know.'

'Thank you,' he smiled back. 'Is that why you came, to check up on me?'

She pretended to pick some fluff off her lap. 'Oh, I don't know…' She stopped. 'Maybe it was. I was bored. I was rather hoping you'd be bored too, then I saw you at that press conference thing on the television and realised it was quite the opposite. Don't worry, I'm not here to tread on anyone's toes. I do have some bank stuff to do as well.'

'I don't like the idea of you being bored,' he said, 'it's not you.' He was trying not to commit himself to either sympathy or vanity. 'I thought you were keeping busy?'

'Oh, I am! Terribly busy. Charity stuff here, theatre trips there and so on. Bridge nights. But I don't have the level of excitement you have!'

'Be careful what you want?' he asked sympathetically.

'I suppose. But then, you! Richard Ainsworth, the great adventurer! Who would have thought that?' They both laughed.

'It doesn't always fit easily,' he admitted.

'No, I'll bet. But you are having the time of your life, aren't you?' There was a sadness in her eyes. He didn't want to say yes, not to Clare, but he knew that he was. 'Is it dangerous, Richard?'

He laughed. 'Do you think I'd be doing it if it was?'

'Because Valérie seems very tense. I hope that's not down to me…'

'No,' he replied, perhaps a little too quickly. 'It's because Lionel Margaux is her niece. So she's very stressed obviously.'

Clare was quiet for a second. 'Her niece. That would explain it then.' She took another sip. 'But working on a Hollywood film, Richard! It's what you always wanted.'

He looked at her, and nodded slowly. 'Be careful what you want.'

'Ah. Has reality met the dream?' She leant forward, the solar light catching her eyes which were full of concern.

'I'm afraid it has. Nobody likes each other for a start. There's no glamour, no… no.'

'No Grace Kelly? No James Stewart?'

'I know. I'm a dreamer, I always have been and I know that the Hollywood world I thought existed anyway was just a thin façade. I do know that. But there's something I can't put my finger on here. They don't like each other, they hate each other even. Yet they need each other; for this film at least, they need each other. Like some ragtag group on a mission, hoping for a pot of gold at the end.'

Clare laughed. 'That's my Richard. Which film did you go to at the end there? No, don't tell me. Greed, betrayal… *The Man Who Would Be King*?'

Richard smiled and raised his eyebrows in a plea of innocence before wilting. 'Same director,' he said. 'Different era. *The Treasure of the Sierra Madre*.' Clare smiled back as Valérie sat down next to her and put Passepartout between them.

'Richard, I have a question to ask.' Valérie's intensity was the exact opposite of Clare's laid-back demeanour. Clare with her shoeless feet up on the rattan furniture and Valérie, sitting hunched, rubbing her hands together as though trying to start a fire with a stick. Two very beautiful women, he allowed himself the brief thought before *The Treasure of the Sierra Madre* came back again to pour water on any potential ardour. What was it the old man said in the film? 'I wouldn't talk, or even think about women. T'ain't good for your health.' Walter Huston, he reeled off to himself internally, Best Actor in a Supporting Role… he heard fingers being clicked.

'Richard! Hello? Valérie asked a question.'

'Ah, yes. I was just mulling it over.' He broke off. 'What was it again?' They both tutted at him.

'I asked the question, why would anyone want to sabotage a film? What is there to gain by doing so?' She gave him an earnest look.

Clare stood up. 'I'll leave you two to it,' she said, yawning. 'It's been quite the day.' She picked up her shawl. 'And it looks like you've both hit upon the same idea too. Greed and betrayal,' she said, sashaying down the path. 'Greed and betrayal.'

'You have thought the same thing too?' Valérie asked, once Clare was out of sight.

'Sort of,' he said, not confident enough to consider it an idea or even a hunch as yet. 'Just that this family, as Ben-Hur Friedman would have it, is collapsing in on itself. I'm trying to work out why a bunch of people who obviously don't like each other much, would agree to work with each other.'

'For money?'

'Of course, but are they really that short of it though? I don't know.' He tapped the table in front of him. 'You think someone might be deliberately sabotaging the film itself then?'

'I don't know, it's just a thought.' She didn't seem to have much faith in it any longer. 'I think I would want to, if it were me,' she added. 'These people are horrible. I do not understand your fascination with this world at all.' She looked at him for an explanation.

'I'm fascinated with the end product,' he offered a half-truth, rather than go over the same ground again. 'They're not all bad. I do think Lionel is different to the others.' It sounded like a vain attempt to cheer her up, but he did mean it. 'I did mean it,' he added, making it sound even more like a vain attempt to cheer her up.

'I hope you're right. I think you are.'

'In my opinion, and as you know I'm an extremely good judge of women,' he regretted the joke but persevered, 'I don't think her heart is in this world, that world.'

She looked deep and seriously into his eyes, hoping for immediate confirmation that he was right.

'I hope so,' she said softly. 'Maybe you're a better judge of women than you think.' Inside Richard's head a hat was tossed into the air. 'Well, maybe not women, but people,' she continued. The hat landed in a puddle, but he wasn't to be outdone yet.

'I think it's a good thing for Lionel to be working with these people,' he started, then on immediately seeing the fire ignite in Valérie's eyes, he continued rapidly. 'Let me finish. Like I say, I don't think her heart is in this, not just this film, but this industry, this world as we've said. She shrinks from it, even something as banal as a limousine. She's almost developed an allergy to it all. I booked her the balloon again for tomorrow morning, she seems to like that.'

She smiled gratefully at him. 'Thank you,' she said. 'I'll go with her as well.'

'You can trust Patrice Marnier.' Richard hoped that was true. He hardly knew the man.

Valérie thought about this. 'Nevertheless,' she said firmly. 'Madame Jennifer Davies really could be her future, like she said.'

'Oh, in theory, yes. I didn't think that was an insult by Jennifer by the way.' Valérie snorted in derision. 'No really. I think it was a genuine warning.'

'A warning delivered like an insult.'

'Well, possibly. I think she overacts every scene she's in, on or off camera. But I feel sorry for her. She's the product of a pretty hard life.'

'So you think that it is she who is sabotaging the production? A bonfire of ex-lovers and men who have manipulated her?'

'I didn't say that. It's possible, if Corbeau was an accident or a rehearsal. And if it was some contraption in the costume...' He shrugged. 'But she says she wasn't with Turnbull. And maybe her alibi with Gilbertine is solid after all.'

In the candlelight he could see Valérie's jaw muscles working overtime as she thought all this through in her usual intense fashion.

'Revenge isn't the only reason for sabotage,' he said eventually, and began searching through the labyrinth of his film knowledge mind looking for examples. 'The locals sabotaged the set of *Doctor Doolittle* because a dam the producers had erected was ruining their duck pond.' Valérie shook her head. 'No, me neither. Ah, there's *Ghost in the Noonday Sun*. The star was Peter Sellers and he hated the script so he sacked the producers on the first day.'

'Can you do that?' she asked, confusion on her face.

'No, well maybe if you're Peter Sellers you can.' He noticed the vacant look on her face that had descended like a roller blind. 'You don't know who Peter Sellers is, do you?' He sighed in disappointment.

'Does it matter?' she asked.

'Yes, it does to me. He was Inspector Clouseau. He was also... oh, look, never mind. He then called in a friend to rewrite the script. Apparently it was worse than the original. On top of that, Peter Sellers faked a heart attack so he could sneak off and have lunch with Princess Margaret.'

Valérie did not look impressed. 'Richard, this is no time for jokes.'

'I'm not joking! It's true. He didn't want to make the film, so he set about ruining it.' He nodded slowly. 'But Reed Turnbull hasn't faked a heart attack, he definitely had one.'

'But someone may have faked one for him?' Her eyes widened in the candlelight.

'You mean someone gave him the Viagra that killed him?'

'He might not have known that what he was taking was Viagra.'

Richard stroked his chin. 'What does our Commissaire say about the drugs? I assume he searched Reed Turnbull's trailer?'

'Yes,' she sounded crushed already. 'Everything was as it should be. Bottles and packets clearly marked, each one with number of doses per day. There was a Viagra bottle, which he shouldn't have had but we know he was a vain man, perhaps he thought it worth the risk.'

'There is another thought,' Richard said slowly, thinking the idea through as he did so. 'Let's say he knew how ill he was. He knew what the Viagra with the other drugs would do. He had finished with the film; perhaps he'd had enough of everything else too. So…' He shook his head in disbelief at his own theory.

'So…' Valérie prompted earnestly.

'So he committed suicide to doom the film.'

They sat in silence again, trying to put the meat on the bones of this latest idea. *Where does that leave old man Corbeau?* was Richard's main doubt.

'I do not think he would do that,' Valérie said eventually. 'If he were to do that, he was the kind of person who would try to incriminate someone else. Even if he were not around to see it.'

Richard could see the logic in that argument for sure. 'I suppose everyone's incriminated in a way.'

'I thought there would be more evidence in the pills,' she said, throwing her hands in the air.

Richard slapped his forehead. 'There may be!' he exclaimed, annoyed at how slow he had been. 'Lapierre was looking in the wrong place. Samuel Friedman prepared all of Reed's pills, every week. I doubt Lapierre looked in Samuel's caravan.'

She grabbed his arm. 'Oh, Richard, that is brilliant!'

They sat quietly for a few moments, almost worn out by the brain-storming session.

A small shadow crossed the candlelight on the low table in front of them, followed immediately by a tentative, throaty *bwark*. 'Olivia,' Richard softened his voice like a concerned parent whose child has had a nightmare. 'Can't you sleep, what's the matter?' He picked her up gently, placing her on his lap and stroking her head soothingly until she was almost purring like a cat.

'This world really isn't for you either is it, Richard?' Valérie smiled warmly. 'I like that.'

Chapter Twenty-One

Richard had plucked off Clare's handwritten note, pinned to the lapel of the suit hanging outside his cinema room cum bedroom. 'This is the best I could find,' it said. 'Off to Tours today to buy a new one. Presumably there'll be more deaths to tell the world's press about.'

He'd smiled at her usual heavy-handed sense of humour, a smile that had lasted until he took a further look at the suit. They had chosen it together a few years earlier, just after the move to France, having been invited to an expat divorcee wedding, the first of many. He couldn't remember who this particular couple were, only that he and Clare hadn't stayed at the wedding long and the couple hadn't stayed together much longer than that. The suit just wasn't him, it never had been. It was a bit flashy, a bit smarmy. But he was wearing it anyway, along with a floral patterned shirt that Clare had also picked out, and he felt less like a press officer and more like some dance-floor-skirting cruise ship lothario.

He'd been up early to put Lionel and Valérie in the hot air balloon with Patrice, and then watch it rise majestically into the early morning light. It was clear that a bond was beginning to form between the two younger people; Lionel was literally lifted by the romance and freedom of the experience and Patrice was aware of the effect it was having on her and couldn't suppress his pride. This was despite a much more wary Valérie watching them closely from a corner of the basket, a look on her face like a widowed Italian chaperone. All she needed was the black dress and a veil. She had handed Passepartout to Richard without giving any instructions, which meant that she trusted him implicitly and which in turn gave him confidence, confidence he badly needed for his second stint in front of the world's press.

Martin and Gennie had arrived in the absurd limousine not long after. Alain, Brian and Stella were already in the back sipping coffee and Jennifer appeared with her own hip flask of cucumber and spinach juice. 'Good for the skin,' she'd said through a cloudy mask of heavy make-up. Richard had joined them clumsily with Passepartout in his arms, his suit clashing with the leather upholstery and issuing an awkward squeak as he slid into place.

'Feeling a bit stiff this morning, old man?' Martin had oozed, before getting a well-deserved elbow in the ribs from Gennie.

The journey was relatively quiet, Alain constantly check-ing and re-checking his tool belt, like a paratrooper, while Brian and Stella pored over some printed storyboards, and talked angles and lighting. Jennifer sipped her juice and read her script.

At one point Gennie's voice came over the tannoy system. 'Good morning, everyone,' she began needlessly like an air hostess. 'Do you mind if I open the sunroof cover?'

Nobody objected; in fact some natural light would be most welcome in Richard's opinion. The dark windows and nightclub lighting interior of the limousine was disorientating in the early morning, but slowly light was revealed as the sunroof cover mechanically pulled back. The reason for Gennie's desire to open up to the skies some became apparent as Patrice's rainbow-coloured hot air balloon hung silently above them.

'That would make a great shot,' Brian smiled before getting back to their notes. Stella lingered on the image a little longer, also smiling warmly.

'We should tell Sacha about that, she may want to use it,' she said.

'Hmm.' Brian wasn't convinced. 'That's if our great director recovers enough to ever get out of bed.' His sarcasm ruined the moment as the limousine left the balloon behind and Gennie closed the roof again.

'Did you say Sacha is ill?' Richard asked innocently.

Stella nodded sympathetically. 'She messaged me late last night. She has a stomach bug, she says, a *gastro*. She thinks it might be food poisoning.'

Richard didn't like the sound of that one bit. I mean, it wasn't entirely implausible when René Dupont was doing the catering, but it still sounded a bit suspicious. He placed Passepartout on the seat next to him and texted to Valérie that they needed to talk, though he didn't expect a reply immediately. His phone rang a few seconds later, it was Valérie.

'How on earth do you get a signal up there?' was his immediate response.

'Patrice,' Valérie shouted, so that the entire limousine crowd heard her, 'is a very clever man. He has a cellphone aerial on the balloon. It's good for business, he says, for social media posts from customers.'

'That's good,' Richard spoke much more quietly.

'I cannot hear you, Richard!'

'Well the entire car can hear you!' This time he raised his voice. What was meant to have been a discreet passing of perhaps vital information was now being broadcast, literally, by satellite.

'Oh,' Valérie said, and rang off.

He texted her the news and his own phone pinged about a minute later. 'Sacha is ill?' Valérie's text began. 'Food poisoning? She bites her nails.'

He understood the inference immediately and as soon as Martin had parked up at the chateau he had a quiet word. 'How much medical training do you actually have?' he asked mutedly, careful not to be overheard.

'Well, all the basics obviously,' Martin replied proudly. 'Kiss of life, Heimlich manoeuvre, forehead stroking, that sort of thing.'

'Do you think you would recognise food poisoning?'

Martin gave him an odd look. In the last few months Martin had begun to realise that there was a lot more to the mild-mannered Richard Ainsworth than he'd previously let on. 'Something up, old man?' he asked, matching Richard's hushed tones and slowly removing his chauffeur's leather gloves.

'We have a suspected food poisoning with our director, Sacha Vizard-Guy. Would you take a look?'

'Of course,' Martin's response was stiff with duty, 'lead on. Gennie, darling, give the seats a wipe would you? Won't be long.'

Richard, still holding Passepartout, led Martin to the small group of caravans arranged in a circle in the chateau grounds and separate from the larger 'star' trailers. It looked like a circus village, but was temporary home to Sacha, Samuel, René's recently moved refreshments van and separate make-up and wardrobe units. There was also Alain's equipment area, which looked more like a tinker's shed. From this area Richard looked back some fifty yards or so, towards the Orangerie restaurant directly in front of him. A raised stage had been built, with microphone set up and seating for about fifty journalists in front of the stage. The place was beginning to fill up too; lights and cameras fired into life. Richard and Passepartout both gulped.

'Which caravan is it, old man?' Martin was thankfully being quite businesslike, taking his medical duties seriously and Richard guided him to a plush, medium-sized caravan at the edge of the circle. Richard knocked on the door gently.

'Madame?' he asked gently, but there was no answer. 'Madame Vizard-Guy? It's Richard Ainsworth.' He looked at Martin. 'Security,' he added shyly. There were some vague noises from inside and Richard decided that if indeed he was 'Security', he needed to act a little more forcefully. First, however, he decided to knock again, but the result was the same. 'OK,' he said more loudly, 'I think we need to check.'

He opened the door and ushered a nervous Martin in first. All the blinds were drawn so the interior was gloomy, but the outline of Sacha was easily distinguishable in the half-light, lying on the bed under a messy pile of thin sheets. She wasn't moving and Richard couldn't make out any breathing either, so for once decided to take swift action. He rushed over to the bed and with his one free hand, shook the woman's shoulder in panic. At first nothing happened, then Sacha woke with a scream. Richard responded with a scream of his own, and for a few seconds the two screamed in each other's faces almost in competition to see who was the more frightened. It turned out to be Richard.

'What are you doing?' Sacha asked, not unreasonably, before breaking into a violent coughing fit.

'I'm sorry,' Richard stammered, 'I thought you were dead!' He was still incongruously holding a startled Passe-partout, who he placed gently on a chair.

Sacha sat up with difficulty. 'Who's this?' she asked weakly, noticing Martin for the first time.

'Martin Thompson. Healthcare professional.' Martin was acting rather coy.

'You look like a chauffeur,' Sacha said sceptically, before coughing again.

'He's, erm, he's undercover.' Under other circumstances Richard might have been rather pleased with this speedy subterfuge, but a second more violent coughing fit from Sacha left him no time. Even less so when she leapt out of bed, ran to the toilet and was violently and loudly sick. A few minutes later she flopped back into her bed.

'I'll get you some water,' Martin said and went to the kitchenette area looking for a glass.

Richard carefully replaced the covers over a shivering Sacha. 'How long have you felt like this?' he asked softly, putting his hand on her forehead to check for her temperature. She seemed warm to him, but he never had been a good judge of these things.

'Last night, quite late,' was her weak response.

'Did you eat anything?'

'Nothing. I had the same as everyone else at lunch.' She retched again as Martin returned with a glass of water.

'You had no dinner?' Martin confirmed and Sacha shook her head. That ruled out René at least, which was something.

'We were working late.' She coughed again.

'We?' Richard asked quickly, but before Sacha could reply the caravan door was wrenched open and Valérie rushed in.

'What has happened?' she demanded, a worried and slightly angry look on her face. Sacha, Richard and Martin all made to reply at once, such was the force of Valérie's question and the immediacy with which she had taken charge, but before anyone could say anything coherent Valérie fired out another question. 'Where's Passepartout?' she asked urgently. Then she saw Passepartout on the chair in the corner, giving himself a good clean. Valérie relaxed. 'OK,' she said taking a deep breath. 'Now, what has happened?'

Sacha groaned and retched again, before taking another gulp of water. 'Don't talk too much,' Martin warned, 'you need to let your stomach settle. I'll go and call a doctor…'

'No, don't. It's fine,' Sacha said with difficulty, 'it's just a bug. I sometimes get them when I am stressed. Ben has enough problems for now, please don't.'

Martin looked at Valérie for guidance and she shook her head. 'OK,' Martin agreed, 'but if there's no improvement later then we should get someone in.' He put his chauffeur's cap back on. 'I'll leave you to it,' he said with a formal flourish and did exactly that.

Valérie waited for Martin to close the door behind him before turning back to Sacha. 'Well, madame?' she asked, and Richard noticed a total lack of sympathy in her voice.

Sacha seemed to notice it to. 'We were in the chateau kitchens until quite late,' she began. 'Ben, Gilbertine and myself. Gilbertine wants to build up his part.' She coughed violently. 'He's been learning Marie-Antonin Carême's cooking techniques and wanted to show us his *croquembouche*, you know, that profiterole pyramid.'

'Another method actor?' Richard couldn't help but tut at the thought.

'It was very sickly, too sweet; I didn't have very much.' She ran her fingers through her hair and both Richard and Valérie noticed how red her fingertips were, bitten raw almost to the cuticles. It was an image completely at odds with the confident, in-control figure that she cut on set and with the actors.

Valérie sighed and took Richard aside. 'You must go to this press conference,' she said, and his heart sank at the thought. 'I will stay here for a while to make that sure she improves. I don't like it.'

'I don't like it either,' Richard agreed. 'Do you think she's been poisoned?'

Valérie shrugged. 'I do not know,' she said. 'But if she has been poisoned, then our murderer has made a very serious mistake.'

Richard didn't get it. 'In what way?' he asked.

'He has not killed her.' Richard still didn't get it, but nodded in serious agreement anyway. 'I will ask Henri to make sure the kitchens are sealed off but profiteroles are surely the easiest thing to poison.'

It wasn't a question, it was a statement of fact, but Richard didn't see how she was so sure. 'How do you mean?' he asked, as if just seeking clarification.

'It's obvious. When you bite into a profiterole, you do not know for sure what's inside. The outside, the choux pastry, hides whatever is within.'

'It sounds a bit like this whole thing,' he said morosely.

She looked at him for a second and smiled. 'Anyway, I need to get into Samuel Friedman's caravan.'

'But it's too open in the daylight, surely?' he reasoned.

'I agree.' Valérie tapped her lips with a finger. 'We need a distraction,' she said, before pointing that finger at Richard.

Chapter Twenty-Two

Backstage, Richard went to straighten his tie, then remembered he didn't have one on. Catching his reflection in the window of the Orangerie restaurant he immediately hit upon the problem with the outfit Clare had chosen for him. It was just too slick and Richard didn't do slick. In fact, if pressed, he'd confess to a carefully cultivated air of vaguely competent befuddlement; that way if you made a mistake people weren't too disappointed and if you somehow managed to score a win, they were surprised, considered it a fluke and didn't push for a repeat performance. In character terms he was more Clouseau than Marlowe, and he was more than happy with that.

'So, doc, ready for a repeat performance?' Ben-Hur Friedman appeared and put his arm around Richard's shoulders, the unlit cigar in his right hand. Despite the upbeat greeting, he looked tired and even a little defeated. Richard saw that behind the thick-rimmed glasses the eyes were sunken and red, and the hand that held the cigar was visibly shaking. The production and everything that was going wrong with it was taking its toll on the producer. It might even have floored a lesser man, but Friedman, as Richard well knew, was old school, steeped in the history of Hollywood at its peak. He was going to see this through to the bitter end at whatever personal cost, be that financial, physical or emotional.

'Has Talleyrand got the plane ready in case I run out of things to say?' Richard joked, and for a second regretted it as the humour flew over Friedman's head and landed somewhere in the chateau grounds beyond.

'Ha! I like it!' he said eventually, though he clearly didn't. 'I've got Samuel nursemaiding Dominic on set somewhere, going through his lines. We should be safe from any drama.'

Pity, thought Richard, *I could do with a way out.*

'You know that Sacha's ill?' It was meant as a rhetorical question, Richard not suspecting for one minute that Friedman wasn't aware of developments, but he was wrong.

'What? What do you mean she's ill?' He removed his arm from Richard's shoulder as if Richard was contagious with something too.

'It looks like food poisoning. Valérie's with her now.'

'Christ!' He produced a handkerchief and wiped his brow. 'Why me?'

'I don't think it's too serious, just one of those things, you know?'

Friedman took a big, deep breath. 'OK, look don't say anything to those guys, got it? They're vultures.' He shook his head. 'Just stick to the script,' he added, then flashed a smile and in a perfect Ronald Reagan accent said, 'Do it for The Gipper!'

'Ha,' Richard laughed. 'Ronald Reagan in *Knute Rockne, All American*, 1948! Your impersonations are extraordinary.'

'Well, I grew up around these guys,' Friedman said modestly. 'Sundays we always had Mitchum, Lancaster, Curtis, you name it, come for a cookout.'

Richard sighed. His 'Sundays were watching his mum do the ironing while guessing the values on *The Antiques Roadshow*. Friedman sloped off and then it hit Richard what he'd said, 'Stick to the script.'

Ah, thought Richard, *what script would that be then?*

He took a deep breath of his own and climbed the stairs up to the hastily prepared stage. Tapping the microphone, he re-introduced himself to the awaiting journalists and was immediately engulfed by a wave of cold indifference. They had collectively put on a 'Not you again' face and Richard's brittle confidence fell apart and lay like smashed crockery at his feet.

For a few minutes or so he thought he handled things pretty well. Never well enough for any confidence to start seeping back into his veins, but well enough to be getting away with it at least. He waxed lyrical with platitudes such as 'what Reed would have wanted', 'true professional', 'one of the modern greats', 'ill for some time', 'the show must go on', etc. and was drifting towards an underwhelming conclusion of 'he wouldn't have wanted to go any other way', when something caught his eye in the distance.

From his vantage point on the stage, and over the heads of the bored press corps, he saw Valérie emerge from Sacha's caravan. He could see that she didn't have Passepartout with her either, which meant one thing – she was up to something. Richard drifted on in his speech, vaguely skirting around the issue of 'complex individual' when he noticed something else too. Valérie had made her way stealthily to the right-hand end of Sacha's small trailer, while at the other end, and not visible to Valérie was Commissaire Lapierre. He also looked like he was up to something but fortunately he hadn't noticed Valérie yet.

Richard lost sight of his partner as she moved behind the caravan, while Lapierre comically made his way to the front. Within seconds they had swapped positions at either end, still unaware of each other's presence. 'He wouldn't have wanted it another way,' he intoned as Valérie made her way, still unseen by the Commissaire, towards Samuel's caravan twenty or so metres away.

'You said that already!' said a rather belligerent New Yorker on the front row of the press conference.

'Sorry, what?' Richard had difficulty tearing his eyes away from the pantomime that was happening beyond his immediate audience.

'I said, you said that already!' the man repeated. 'We get it! The show must go on, but I have a question!'

He suddenly had Richard's undivided, terrified attention. 'We won't be answering questions until the results of the inquiry are in,' he said. He'd seen plenty of squirming politicians use this line and it was the first thing that came into his head.

'What inquiry? I thought this was natural causes.' The journalist was practically dripping with scepticism.

Richard still had half an eye on Valérie as she approached Samuel's caravan. He saw her remove her skeleton key wallet from her pocket and slip inside, just as Commissaire Lapierre did the same with Sacha's trailer.

'Are you suggesting,' this time it was a female French journalist eager not to be outdone by the aggression of the New Yorker, 'that Monsieur Turnbull did not die of natural causes?'

'No.' Richard decided to go for flat denial tinged with mock outrage but she wasn't having any of it.

'That he may have been poisoned like Napoleon himself!' She finished with a flourish as though reaching a successful '*J'accuse!*' conclusion in a particularly keen game of Cluedo.

'I didn't know Napoleon had been poisoned!' he replied honestly. 'Was he?'

'That is the rumour,' the French journalist said haughtily. In Richard's book it all seemed a little late for speculation about the death of the real Napoleon Bonaparte, but his thoughts were interrupted by the sight of Commissaire Lapierre emerging from Sacha's digs with an unimpressed Passepartout in his arms.

'It is true, there are suspicions that Napoleon was poisoned.' From nowhere a pale looking Amorette Arthur had emerged and Richard wondered if historians were governed by instinct and could smell historical controversy in the air like lions with blood. Or was that sharks?

'And who are you?' the New Yorker asked, as if Amorette might be so insignificant she may not even have a name.

'Amorette Arthur,' she replied weakly. 'I am historical advisor on this film, and historian in residence at the Chateau de Valençay.'

'Amorette Arthur!' This time it was the French journalist and she snapped her fingers in recognition. 'You used to be on television – what was it?'

'*Notre pays historique,*' Amorette said quietly.

'*Notre pays historique!* That's right. Sacked for violent misconduct, I remember.'

Something snapped in Amorette. 'It was self-defence!' she shouted, obviously used to hearing the accusation.

'Yeah, yeah, whatever.' New York was at it again. 'What's this about Napoleon and are you suggesting Reed Turnbull was poisoned too?' An excited murmur went through the throng but far worse than that, Richard saw Commissaire Lapierre make his way slowly towards Samuel's cabin.

'Napoleon's body was exhumed in 1840,' a calmer Amorette began. 'Nineteen years after his death, but thanks to a process of arsenic mummification his body had not decomposed to any great extent. The suggestion therefore was that he was killed by arsenic poisoning.'

The journalists talked quickly among themselves, while Richard wanted to be anywhere but onstage in front of them. He wondered what Lapierre would do when he found Valérie in Samuel's caravan. He would arrest her for sure.

'Listen, lady,' the New Yorker would have exasperatedly tipped his hat back if he'd been wearing one. 'Are you saying that Reed Turnbull died of arsenic poisoning because someone actually believed he *was* Napoleon.'

'Wallpaper,' was the enigmatic and frankly inadequate response from the historian and while Richard was frantic in his fear for Valérie's position he also saw Ben-Hur Friedman at the side of the stage putting his finger across his throat, indicating that Richard should wind this debacle the hell up and quickly.

'Wallpaper?'

'It's unlikely that Napoleon was assassinated, but that his wallpaper was poisonous.' Amorette suddenly sounded like an enthusiastic teacher. 'In the early nineteenth century, arsenic was used in pigments on wallpaper. In a warm, damp room, such as Napoleon's bedroom in exile, it would give off toxic fumes.'

'Is she for real?' the newspaperman from New York was losing patience.

'Reed Turnbull knew all this,' she continued. 'He had done a lot of research on his character and on the chateau itself, not just the Napoleonic period but the Second World War as well when the Louvre Museum hid priceless artefacts here.' Richard noticed for the first time that Amorette Arthur was swaying as she spoke, almost like she was playing charades and imitating the action of rowing. The poor woman, presumably as a result of grief for Reed, was as tight as a banker's braces.

'Yes, but what has this got to do with Monsieur Turnbull's death?' It was now a race between the two prominent journalists to see who would explode in frustration first.

The door slowly opened to Samuel's caravan.

'I think, ladies and gentlemen, that that will do for now.' Friedman had had enough. 'We have a picture to finish!'

'Was Reed Turnbull poisoned?' shouted New York.

'Of course he was not poisoned!' the French journalist shouted back. 'It would have been found out in the post-mortem!'

'I don't know, lady, seems like the French here don't know what they're doing!'

'How dare you!' she shot back. 'Our health service is far better than yours!'

'It doesn't need to be any good, nobody lives long enough to get better!'

'Ladies and gentlemen, please!' Friedman shouted into the microphone.

'Reed Turnbull didn't need to take Viagra!' Amorette shouted tearfully as she grabbed the microphone, immediately securing everyone's attention other than Richard's.

Commissaire Lapierre, Passepartout still in his arms, stood on the steps of Samuel's caravan and shook his head. He looked defeated and Richard let out a huge sigh of relief.

'Were you and Monsieur Reed lovers, Madame Arthur?' It was typically the French journalist who asked this question and while doing so the crowd had swelled. Everybody from the cast and crew was now there as well.

'Yes, yes we were.' Amorette Arthur's reply was simple and quietly put.

'I got it!' shouted New York. 'Reed Turnbull Poisoned! So Says Film's Hysterical Advisor!' There was some laughter in the press corps, and Friedman put his arms around a sobbing Amorette and led her gently off the stage giving Richard a filthy look as he did so. Still with one eye on the caravans beyond, the reluctant, and hopefully temporary press officer, now had to face the press alone. He opened his mouth to speak.

'Don't tell me!' the New York man shouted again. 'It's what he would have wanted!' And the press corps laughed again, even the French journalist who still seemed piqued at the suggestion of French health service incompetence, broke into a smile.

A dazed and confused Richard put his hands in his pockets, banged his head on the microphone and then slowly descended the stairs. It dawned on him that he should find Valérie and preferably before the Commissaire did, so he quickened his pace and jumped the last few remaining steps, turned the corner smartly and ran straight into Valérie d'Orçay.

'Well done, Richard!' she said, her eyes as wide as they could physically get and still remain socketed. 'That was a brilliant distraction!'

Richard felt like falling to the floor, adopting the foetal position and remaining that way for some considerable time. 'If it really is a nerve agent,' he whimpered instead, 'I'll be fine. I don't have any nerves left.'

Chapter Twenty-Three

Valérie moved quickly, the concentration rigid on her face and her eyes cold like a predator. She brought her arms up quickly and snapped back her assailant's own arms which had been gripping her jacket lapels. Now open to attack, she spread two fingers and poked her would-be attacker in the eyes. He staggered back, temporarily blinded.

'Bloody hell!' Richard whined, as he walked into a wall. 'You're supposed to be coaching me, not putting me out of action completely!'

A contrite Valérie tried to put a consoling arm around his shoulder, but Richard flinched away expecting further beatings. 'I am so sorry, Richard, I am not trained to hold back. That is not how the Krav Maga technique works.'

Up until half an hour ago Richard hadn't considered the possibility that he would welcome a return to straight-forward security and detection services, but he had been forced to admit that was where he was at. Clare had watched the whole press conference debacle on television and had driven immediately back to Tours to return the two suits that she'd bought. 'I don't think you'll be needing these, Richard,' she'd said with heavy disappointment. Valérie, however, thought it all very revealing and now had a plan of action, though that action as far as Richard could tell was to give him a thumping.

'What is Krav Maga anyway?' he asked, rubbing his weeping eyes.

'It is a system of self-defence that is taught by the Israeli secret service. A mixture of other forms of self-defence, developed mainly for women because the size of your attacker doesn't matter. Are you OK?'

'I can't see,' he replied quickly. 'And I think poking a fellow in the eye is a little underhand frankly.'

'Perhaps there is an English self-defence technique where I politely ask my attacker to stop and we discuss our next move over a cup of tea – would you prefer that?'

Richard had never heard Valérie attempt sarcasm before and for a first attempt it was a very cutting effort, making him feel contrite. 'I'm sorry,' he said, 'you're right. I wouldn't make much of an attacker, would I?'

'That is not something to be sorry for,' she said seriously, then relaxed a little. 'You need to learn from my moves, Richard, this is for when *you* are attacked.'

'I *am* being attacked,' he groaned, but he knew she was right. Her plan was to have as many operatives on site tonight after dark as possible. All cast and crew were staying in situ ahead of an early start the next day and she had a hunch that things were coming to a head. The operatives would just be extra eyes and ears; she'd roped in Martin and Gennie, René Dupont, Madame Tablier, even Clare. But for some reason she felt Richard might be a target and was now giving him a few painful lessons in how to protect himself. For his part Richard wondered if Israeli self-defence techniques worked on peacocks.

'It gets the adrenalin flowing, yes?' Valérie said, bouncing on her feet ready to attack again. 'It helps to think.'

'Is this how you managed to avoid Lapierre in Samuel's caravan?' he asked, standing, hopefully, out of arms reach. 'Did you blind him before he could see you?'

'I told you,' she relaxed from her Tigger antics. 'I got into Samuel's bed, pulled the covers up and started to snore.'

He shook his head in wonderment; she really was the most astonishing woman. 'I'm surprised Passepartout didn't recognise you though.'

'Ha! Henri with his cheap attempt at bait!' She lashed out with a leg, narrowly avoiding Richard's knee. 'My Passepartout is too well trained for that.' Passepartout was asleep on the sofa beside them, his right leg twitching as he dreamt.

'And you got Turnbull's pills before Lapierre too, very clever.' He took another step back as Valérie started bouncing again. He walked over to the large dining table and looked once more at the medical debris that lay on a table mat. It looked like a drug dealer's lab: open capsules some containing white powder and some containing blue. It was just as Gennie had suggested: Viagra had been substituted into Turnbull's medication with lethal effect. 'So we know how Turnbull was killed, ground-up Viagra in his angina capsules, but why? And it doesn't look good for Samuel, does it? I mean, he just doesn't seem the type.'

'I agree that I don't see his motive; also, anyone could have had access to his caravan, and he obviously told Henri that he prepared Reed Turnbull's medication.'

Richard stroked his chin. 'Samuel reminds me of Charlie Chan's number one son: very enthusiastic and would do anything for "pop".'

'I have no idea what you're talking about, Richard.'

'Not many would,' he admitted. 'Let's look at motive instead,' he said, avoiding another swinging leg.

'OK, but we must train at the same time. It helps me think.' She turned her back on him and adjusted the elasticated waistband on her grey sweatpants.

'Well, what do we know about Reed Turnbull?' Richard began to pace the room. 'Major star, dies of heart failure which is the result of deliberate poisoning. Was having an affair with Amorette Arthur and possibly Jennifer Davies; genuinely loathed by many and has known them all for ages, in fact since *The Sidewalk Romantics*, which he made with Friedman senior, Brian Grace, Davies herself and Dominic Burdett, twenty-five years ago.'

Richard temporarily forgot where he was and paced a little too close to Valérie, who crouched down and then swung her right leg around, knocking both of Richard's legs from under him. He hit the ground with a thud.

'O-O-D-A,' Valérie said simply. 'Observe, Orient, Decide, Act. Sorry.'

Richard held the small of his back as she helped him up. 'Maybe Turnbull *has* done this deliberately, just as a kind of revenge?'

'Hmm, I think he would want to be witness to it.' Valérie started bouncing again.

'I think you're right. OK, next. Sacha Vizard-Guy. It appears that an attempt has been made on her now; again though, why? I don't get it. She's written the film and is directing it. She even changed the story to suit Friedman's desire for a costume film. So she wouldn't sabotage anything, nor can I see who she's in the way of. And why didn't Friedman or Gilbertine have food poisoning? That doesn't make sense to me.'

'I agree and Henri swears that there was no poisonous substance found in the kitchens, but do we trust that a thorough search was made?' She swung out an elbow aggressively. 'So what about Monsieur Friedman?' Valérie asked, skirting close to a wary Richard.

'Again, he needs this picture to be a success. He wants to be a major player again and sees this as that opportunity. There is no sane reason why he would sabotage it. But then there's Dominic Burdett.'

He turned quickly to face her, an idea coming into his head. It was something he immediately regretted as Valérie brought her knee up swiftly in the direction of his unprotected groin. Her knee stopped no more than a centimetre from that most sensitive of areas but he doubled up nonetheless, an instinctive move, his face contorted in expected pain.

'Sometimes,' she said brightly and stepping back, 'it is just the anticipation of pain that can buy you time if you are attacked. What about Dominic Burdett?'

Richard didn't move from his position and his voice was strained as though a direct hit had actually been scored. 'He and Turnbull have invested in Friedman's pictures before, maybe they did with this one? They're both listed as Executive Producers.' He struggled to stand. 'Plus I'm not sure how sane he is? If he's sober he's an early nineteenth-century French diplomat and if he's drunk he's a mess. And talking of a mess,' he added, backing away.

'Poor Amorette Arthur.' Valérie nodded.

'Yes. Poor Amorette Arthur. Well, we know that she was sacked from her television job for violent conduct…'

'Self-defence.' Valérie said strongly.

'Yes. Self-defence, though I'm beginning to think there's a fine line between the two. They are the oddest couple, were the oddest couple I should say, her and Reed Turnbull.'

Valérie had walked a good couple of metres away from Richard and he was able to breathe a sigh of relief at the distance now between them. 'I do not know much about films, Richard, but if Reed Turnbull was the great star, he must have had some charisma, some attraction.'

'I suppose so, yes. When you put it like that.' He turned to look out of the window, so didn't notice Valérie perform a perfect forward roll which left her inches away from him. She bounced up and aimed an elbow at his Adam's apple, again stopping just short. He gulped and stood stock still, afraid to move. 'Also,' she added, 'Turnbull took a great interest in the history of Valençay itself.'

'Good point,' he said stiffly. 'Up until then, she's probably just been ignored.'

'But he was such a cruel man, I think. He has made a wreck of Jennifer Davies.'

Richard sighed. 'Not just Turnbull I suspect,' he said quietly. 'The whole system.'

'Really? You think so.'

'Unfortunately, yes. Hollywood wants women when they're young and glamorous but doesn't know what to do with them when they're older. There're only so many roles where you can win an Oscar with a prosthetic nose.'

Valérie gave him a confused look. 'Never mind. Again though, this was her big comeback, so why would she ruin it?'

'It's her big comeback but also the perfect setting for revenge perhaps?'

'Yes, there is that I suppose.' Richard walked to the opposite side of the room and weighed up carefully what he was about to say next. 'Then there's Lionel…'

He half expected a load of Ninja Valéries to descend from the ceiling and cut him to ribbons, but thankfully that didn't happen. Valérie walked to the window and looked out. He could just see her reflection and the pain on her face.

'Her stepfather is a violent man,' she said quietly. 'It wasn't easy for her growing up and her mother did not want her to become an actress.'

Richard walked gingerly towards his partner, approaching from an angle rather than directly from behind and crouching down to avoid a blow to the head as he did so. 'For what it's worth,' his voice was calm and steady, 'I think she's ready to give it all up anyway.'

'But she *could* be sabotaging the film to make certain, is that what you think?'

'I think it's something we have to consider. For instance, the stalker? It could be her stepfather, or it could be her imagination?' Valérie whirled round to face him and he hit the ground deliberately as she did so, an instinct of self-preservation taking over just in time. She looked down at him and though he was potentially in a very vulnerable position he had momentarily gained the element of surprise. The look of anger on her face dissipated immediately.

'You are learning very quickly, Richard!' She stepped over him. 'So who does that leave us?'

Richard stood up stiffly. 'Gilbertine, who we know is Jennifer Davies' alibi for something we don't know about, only that he can't be because he's gay. It's all a bit vague with him.'

'Except that he takes his role as Marie-Antonin Carême very seriously and has set himself up in the kitchen in the chateau.'

'Where Sacha says that she was poisoned.'

'And where you followed someone sneaking about at night.' They both sighed in unison at the vagueness of Gilbertine's details. 'We need to keep a closer eye on him, I think,' Valérie said eventually.

'So that leaves Brian Grace and Stella Gonzales then.' Richard began to pace the room again. 'Brian Grace directed the film *The Sidewalk Romantics*. Friedman produced it; Turnbull, Burdett and Davies were in it. It was a disaster; maybe he blames them for that, so is wrecking this one?'

'It is possible, yes, that makes sense.' Valérie had her arms loosely folded and was toying with her brooch which was pinned to her shirt collar.

'And Stella, what do you think of her?' Richard asked, having no information himself.

'She is very serious but also generous.' Valérie knew as little as he did then, he concluded from that. 'She gave me this brooch on our first day, which was a nice gesture I thought.'

Richard stepped forward to take a closer look. It was the same image he had seen on the wall of the chateau. 'I know this image!' he said excitedly and leant forward to touch it.

It was, after everything he had supposedly learnt that morning, an imbecilic, naive thing to do. Valérie instinctively grabbed his arm, twisted it around his back, whirled an astonished Richard around like a gymnastic ribbon before sending him rolling across the rug and into a crumpled heap in the doorway. It took him a moment or two to adjust to the position and rather than immediately get up, he decided to stay put hoping he was now out of harm's way. He opened his eyes tentatively and found himself looking up at a distinctly unimpressed Clare.

'Yes, well let's be honest, Richard, you probably deserved it,' she said, stepping over him with disdain.

Chapter Twenty-Four

Valérie d'Orçay stood on the fourth step of the stairs leading to the press conference stage and addressed her troops. It wasn't exactly General Patton addressing the 3rd Army, or rather George C. Scott as General Patton addressing the 3rd Army which was how Richard saw it, but she was definitely in command. If she had felt the need to exhort her forces with a film quote along the lines of 'we're going to cut out their living guts and use them to grease the tread of our tanks', Richard felt there would have been few dissenters. There she stood, shining her torch up under her chin so that she looked almost spectral, assigning duties like she was the famous general himself.

'Now, René,' she said, and he all but snapped to attention. 'I want you to cover the area where your van is. That's Sacha, Samuel, make-up, wardrobe, etc. Brian Grace and Stella are also onsite there, as is Alain Petit. Everybody is in bed ready for a very early start. I want to know if anyone leaves their accommodation.'

'I get it,' came the serious reply. 'And if they do?'

'You have your talkie-walkie?'

'Yes.'

'Then let me know immediately but as discreetly as possible. I won't be far away. Same goes for you, Martin and Gennie, at the gift shop entrance and the restaurant. I like your outfits by the way, nice and dark.'

As far as Richard could tell all they had done was swap their peaked chauffeur caps for woollen beanie hats, and they looked like extras from *The Guns of Navarone*. Martin saluted and Gennie giggled, which was a mistake.

'This is not a laughing matter, Gennie. Please take your duties seriously.' Valérie peered at them through her torchlight.

'Sorry, old girl,' Martin grumbled.

'Madame Tablier, I want you to take the courtyard and arches on the South Gallery. That way you can see the keep and the chateau door as well, but please be discreet. Stay in the shadows.'

For some reason Madame Tablier always had to have some form of implement with her. So as well as muttering something about Napoleon, she was leaning wearily on what looked like a garden hoe in the same manner a longbow archer may have done with his bow if feeling that Henry V was going on a bit. She tutted, showing a little dissent which was her way, but Valérie wisely chose to ignore it.

'Clare, I want you to stay near me where the big trailers are. Between us we'll have Dominic Burdett, Jennifer Davies, Gilbertine and my... er... Lionel Margaux. But I'll be doing the rounds, so you may be on your own at times.'

'That's fine, Valérie,' Clare said, her voice alert, with a hint of excitement in it for good measure. Richard was feeling a little intimidated if he were honest. Both Valérie and Clare had on the same outfits: black ski pants, boots and tight-fitting black roll-neck sweaters. Valérie wasn't wearing any headgear but Clare had a thick black headband on and her blonde hair in a ponytail. He was reminded of one of those 1960s sub-James Bond spy capers where the assassins were always incredibly attractive women, *Deadlier than the Male* that was one. Elke Sommer, 1966 if he remembered correctly, or was it 1967? He became vaguely aware of another voice.

'Richard, are you listening?' Valérie sounded exasperated at his obvious lack of attention and he also noticed Clare smirking like the teacher's pet.

'Of course I am!' he tried to sound insulted, but failed. 'You want me, er… where was it again?'

'I want you to patrol inside!' She really had lost patience with him, and he cast his eyes to the ground, ignoring Clare's smirk. 'You know the inside better than anyone, but please don't touch anything in the kitchens, just in case. I trust you to be discreet, Richard.'

She'd thrown the dog a bone, as it were, and out of the corner of his eye he saw the snigger drain from Clare's face to be replaced by something approaching jealousy.

'Shall we synchronise watches?' Martin hissed.

Valérie had turned off her torch but now switched it back on again. 'Why?' she asked.

Martin shrugged. 'I don't know really. I just thought that was the form.'

'I don't think there's any need.' Valérie seemed irritated by the question and turned her torch off again. 'OK, everyone. Stay in touch and good luck.'

Martin and Gennie held hands and moved off as though they were eloping; René lit a cigarette, smoothed his hands on his filthy apron and returned to his refreshments van. Madame Tablier put her hoe on her shoulder as though it were a rifle and marched towards her sentry post, while Clare and Valérie, looking for all the world like they were on a modelling photoshoot, walked quietly towards the actors' trailers.

Richard cautiously moved off too and within ten minutes he was sitting at a harpsichord in the music room on the ground floor of the chateau. From his vantage point he could look along two corridors, see some of the courtyard and also spy on the trailer area, ready to respond should the need arise. He felt pretty sure, however, that if a situation did arise and that between them Valérie and Clare couldn't cope with it, it was highly doubtful he'd be much use either.

Apart from waiting and keeping his eyes open, he wasn't entirely sure what he was looking out for. Valérie had had one of her hunches and felt that with everyone being onsite together, something might occur. But beyond that she had been pretty vague. For his part Richard couldn't work it all out. He was fairly certain that Reed Turnbull had been murdered, a lethal concoction of drugs doing for him, but he couldn't work out who would actually gain by sabotaging the whole film in such a violent way. It had to be something in the past and Richard made a mental note to scour Halliwell's books again for more information on *The Sidewalk Romantics* when he got home. If, of course, it was even called that in the UK. He rolled his eyes and muttered to himself, 'What an idiot I've been! Of course, sidewalk, pavement!' He felt like texting Valérie but decided not to disturb her, out there in the shadows of the trailers, hidden in the dark.

Clare, he noticed, was not so hidden in the dark. Her blonde ponytail was always going to be an issue in the moonlight and Richard could see it occasionally bobbing about in the gloaming. He hoped it wouldn't pose a danger for her and he was glad that Valérie was there too to look out for her. Then, a few minutes later, he was reminded that Clare Ainsworth did not need looking after at all, not one iota.

Richard didn't see himself as the jealous type, and both he and Clare knew their marriage was over. They had recently settled into a sort of post-relationship comfort, almost like brother and sister, fond of each other, looking out for the other's best interests and competitive too in a way. But something stirred in him as he looked out across the moat valley and saw his wife in an embrace with Hollywood legend, Dominic Burdett. Clare was being playful and coquettish while he, as ever in a powdered wig and state dress, had his arms around her, attempting to kiss her neck. She put her arms around the man's waist, almost physically lifting him off the ground, and in a reversal of wedding night etiquette carried him over the threshold of his trailer. The door closed behind them.

'It is none of my business,' Richard told himself through clenched teeth, and in total opposition to how he actually felt. 'None of my bloody business.' He kept watching the trailer door for any further signs of activity, but there were none. All that happened was that the light inside went dark and Richard suddenly became aware of a noise close by, but then realised it was him grinding his teeth.

There was another noise though, and he heard it again. It sounded like footsteps on stairs but he couldn't make out where exactly it was coming from and he felt very out of his depth. Once again, Richard Ainsworth, *Doctor* Richard Ainsworth, had to remind himself that he wasn't an undercover 1940s film noir gumshoe. He was a film historian who ran a posh B&B and who, if he had any skills at all, had a remarkable ability to hide from the world and everybody in it. So why – he was now warming to his sense of injustice – was he sitting in the shadows of a frankly creepy French chateau, listening out for footsteps and signs of nocturnal activity when there was quite clearly a murderer on the loose? And why, to cap it all, was his ex-wife getting all the fun while he was potentially on the cusp of being assassinated?

He stood up quietly and peered down the corridor towards the chateau reception area. It was the best lit of his viewpoints as the moonlight was streaming in through the large windows. He couldn't see how anyone could approach him from that angle and not be seen. To his right was a much smaller corridor, darker but still with enough outside light to see clearly that no one was there. Nor could anyone get into the music room from the outside as, although it was ostensibly the ground floor, there was a sheer drop outside the window into the old moat.

He heard the footsteps again. They were cautious, moving slowly, aware that he was there perhaps and ready to spring. He gulped and felt that the noise it made was so loud it sounded like an artillery gun. He looked again down the corridors, peering beyond the shadows, but though the footsteps continued, he saw no one. In his fear he knocked over a museum notice off the harpsichord and bent down to pick it up. It was an explanation of the music room: who used it, the age of the instruments and that hidden in the recess behind him was a secret staircase that led directly to the bedroom of the Spanish prisoner king on the floor above. This vital titbit of information came just too late to save him, as from behind a large curtain a figure leapt at him and knocked him flying across the room, banging his head on the floor.

Remembering some of the moves that Valérie had taught him he quickly got to his feet; his assailant now had their back to the windows and was silhouetted against the moonlit sky. He couldn't make out who it was as they'd adopted the same uniform as Valérie and Clare, black being the in thing this season clearly. They also wore a balaclava, so all he saw were the eyes catching the shards of light from outside. He raised his arms like a wrestler about to grapple and immediately got a poke in the eyes for his trouble, sinking to his knees he knew he should have seen that coming, but as he went down he grabbed at his attacker's clothing and removed a metal button from the jacket. Whoever it was then jumped over him and ran down the corridor towards the courtyard.

Pocketing the button, Richard went after them gingerly, his eyes still stinging. The figure turned right and into the gardens, past Friedman's apartment and towards the trailer area. He ran in the same direction, but lost sight of whoever it was in the dark. The next thing he knew he was sent flying again as one of the Chateau de Valençay golf buggies whirred at him out of the bushes, knocking him out of the way. He got back to his feet just as Valérie and Clare came running over to him, but before they could say anything Richard reached for one of his favourite film quotes, 'I am mad as hell,' he said, 'and I'm not going to take it anymore!'

He ran to the nearest golf cart and jumped on, starting it up in the same motion. In his mind he had willed the vehicle into life and roared off in pursuit of his attacker, but as car, or in this instance, golf buggy chases go, it was not high speed. He did have the advantage, however, of knowing the terrain better than whoever was in front of him and following a few judicious shortcuts he was soon just a few metres behind. He had no idea how long the charges lasted on golf buggies and it piqued him to think that possibly the most dramatic thing he had ever attempted in his life may just end with a whimper as they both ran out of battery.

He was not going to let that happen and pressed harder on the accelerator, gaining an advantage and finally coming alongside his opponent. But was it his opponent? Whoever had attacked Richard in the music room was not the driver of his rival golf buggy. The driver of his rival golf buggy was Dominic Burdett.

'What the bloody hell are you playing at, you maniac?' Richard shouted above the metallic din of the buggies.

Burdett's eyes flashed in anger. 'How dare you address me like that, sir? Do you not know to whom you speak?'

'Yes. You're Dominic Burdett and you're a bloody lunatic!' Richard felt a surge of anger, partly at the absurdity of it all and partly that his real attacker had got away and with no better idea in mind, he turned his buggy into Burdett's, ramming it from the side. Burdett retaliated in the same fashion and Richard narrowly avoided a large plane tree. He got back parallel with the actor and shouted across. 'Stop this nonsense, Burdett, just turn the thing off!'

'You'll never take me alive!' was the over-dramatic, frankly maniacal, response.

'Oh, for the love of…' Richard again steered his buggy at Burdett's and this time caught the actor off guard, sending him off the pathway and through the fence of the chateau's mini farm. Ducks, geese and hens were scattered as Burdett's buggy, now out of control, careered through the dozing animals. Clovis the peacock emerged angrily from the dark of his private shed, no doubt wondering what on earth was going on in his kingdom, but he quickly fled as the buggy went straight for him. It crashed into his shed, splintering wood and finally coming to rest as the coop collapsed around it.

Richard jumped off his buggy and felt a pain in his leg, the metal button he'd trousered digging into his thigh. He took it out and noticed for the first time that it wasn't a button, but a very familiar brooch.

'You, sir!' Burdett shouted, without dismounting or even turning around. 'What is the meaning of this?'

'Oh shut up!' Richard said, walking over to the man. 'You are an absolute…' His words dried up as he realised that Burdett wasn't addressing him at all. Instead he was directing his questions at the dead body of Amorette Arthur, sitting upright, her cold eyes open, and with what looked like chocolate smeared all over her face.

Chapter Twenty-Five

It was a horrific sight. Poor Amorette lying in Clovis's coop with her eyes open and her face smeared with chocolate suddenly brought home to Richard how dangerous this all was. Monsieur Corbeau was a very old man, Reed Turnbull a caricature whose theatrics made him seem not fully real. But Amorette Arthur seemed so innocent and not part of the set-up of the film at all, not part of the core group, an extra. She had certainly upset someone, however, and had paid the price for it with her life.

Dominic Burdett crawled from under the wreckage of his upturned buggy and saw Amorette's body properly for the first time. The struggle with reality suddenly contorted his features in horror and Richard went to grab him before he fell. He had no idea which Dominic Burdett he was dealing with – the sober method actor, so a nineteenth-century politician, or the drunk Hollywood star – and right now Richard was willing to bet that Burdett didn't know himself either. The actor struggled free of Richard's grasp and knelt next to the murdered historian. Tenderly he closed her eyes and removed his tunic to cover her up, as though to protect her from the chilly autumn night. Whether this was the action of Burdett or Talleyrand, who could tell? It didn't matter really, it was a touching moment and there were pitifully few of those about and Richard knelt next to him, putting his hand on his shoulder in solidarity.

The actor hung his head as if to pray and began mumbling some words which Richard couldn't quite hear. He leant in closer to do so.

'He has entered on a course to which there is no end,' Burdett said quietly and Richard concluded that he'd retreated into his Talleyrand character and was now quoting his script. 'This is worse than a crime,' he implored Richard, grabbing his lapels. 'It is a mistake.' Richard recognised it as one of Talleyrand's famous quotes, most of which were dotted around the chateau walls.

'What has happened?' An out-of-breath Valérie arrived and shone her torch on the two kneeling men, then she noticed Burdett's tunic on the covered body. 'Who is it?' she asked, unable to hide her fear and dread at the answer.

Richard stood. 'It's Amorette,' he said a little too coldly. 'You had better call the Commissaire.' Briefly he spotted relief cross her face that the victim wasn't Lionel, followed swiftly by guilt. She phoned Lapierre straight away.

A crowd soon gathered and Richard watched from the sidelines as Valérie and Ben-Hur Friedman carefully organised everyone. Jennifer Davies put her arms around Burdett and led him away while an ashen-faced Sacha, still frail from her bout of food poisoning, looked utterly distraught, and was being comforted by Samuel, who had his arms around her.

'I don't understand,' Friedman kept repeating, though he was far from the only one who couldn't fathom the reasoning behind this killing. Richard, rendered cynical by the events of the evening, wondered if they were distraught for the dead woman or for their precious production. Lionel Margaux arrived later than the others and looked terrified, her alabaster skin almost see-through as she shivered, in trauma as much as from the autumn evening. Clare led her away and back to her trailer, but not before giving Richard a look of serious concern. 'This isn't a game, is it, Richard?' it said. Stella, Brian and Alain Petit all arrived after the commotion spread, and helped Friedman to cordon off an area around the animal enclosure. They set up lights and speedily arranged things like it was an outdoor shoot. Their efficiency only added to Richard's dim view of the thing.

'Where's Gilbertine?' Friedman asked, trying to account for everyone.

'He'll be asleep,' Samuel replied, still with an arm around Sacha's shoulders. 'He took some sleeping pills earlier. I counted them out for him.' Richard turned his back on them both and spoke to Martin and Gennie on his radio, asking them to check on the actor then come to the mini farm with Madame Tablier.

'What are you doing, Richard?' Valérie asked quietly.

'I want everyone accounted for,' he replied, again coldly, and she looked at him for an explanation which didn't come as Commissaire Lapierre arrived with a team of officers.

He was shown silently to the body first, and then he commanded everyone to stand back and let his team do their job. His demeanour was different to how it had been. This wasn't the careworn Commissaire reluctantly going through the motions of an investigation, this was an officer of the law sickened but efficient. 'Can everyone make their way to the coffee area, please? Everyone. I shall be with you as soon as I can.' He pulled Richard and Valérie aside before they could leave. 'What is going on here?' he asked, not with an air of desperation as he might have done before, but with a stern will that told them he knew that they knew more than him.

'So I assume you think that this is another *coincidence* do you, Monsieur le Commissaire?' Valérie's use of the formal title spoke volumes and the question was unfair in Richard's eyes but emotions were running high.

'No, madame, I do not think this is a coincidence. I think this is murder and I think that you two have been withholding information from me.' Valérie went to interrupt but he talked over her. 'I am not saying that what you have kept hidden has led to this tragedy, but…'

'Don't you dare, Henri!' Valérie, almost always at boiling point anyway, erupted. 'You have had the same suspicions as we have, but we have done something about them.' This time it was the Commissaire who wanted to interrupt, but Richard could have told him it was a futile gesture. 'If you didn't have the same concerns as us, why did you go looking for Reed Turnbull's medication in Samuel Friedman's caravan?'

Commissaire Lapierre nodded, not so much in defeat as in resignation, then he held up his hands to signal a truce. 'Have it your way, both of you, but this has gone far enough now, so we must work together.' He looked from one to the other and received tacit, if not enthusiastic, agreement. 'So, tonight, how was the body discovered?'

It was Richard's turn to sigh as he tried to put in order, for himself as much as the Commissaire, the events of the evening just past. Valérie inevitably got there first. 'I positioned everyone where we could keep the whole place under surveillance...' she began, and listed the motley crew of 'operatives' as she called them and where they had been positioned.

The Commissaire, who was taking notes, looked up and repeated the word 'operatives' in a way that suggested he hadn't much confidence in the team. 'Operatives? A former felon, a cleaning woman, two sexually dubious hosts, and the third in your particular ménage à trois? This is your team?'

'Nothing would have got past the cordon we set up.' Valérie was stung by the implicit criticism.

'So, Madame Arthur was murdered before nightfall then? We will need to check on everyone's movements and we'll do that now I think.'

They walked off towards René's refreshments van, where the welcome steam of coffee was reflected in the powerful lights that had been set up by the team. Everyone was huddled together; Martin, Gennie and Madame Tablier had joined them with a groggy-looking Gilbertine in tow. As they walked Lapierre continued his questioning. 'How was the body actually discovered?' he asked. 'Did you go looking in the coop for *clues*?'

Richard, fatigued anyway by the evening's exertions, was getting equally tired with Lapierre's attitude. 'Dominic Burdett crashed one of the golf buggies into the thing.'

'How?' Lapierre stopped walking.

'I rammed his buggy with my buggy.'

'You rammed his buggy with your buggy?' The Commissaire was having trouble processing this information and trouble keeping his notes up to date.

'Yes.'

'Why?'

'Because I was chasing him.'

'Why were you chasing him?'

'Because I thought it was him who had attacked me.'

'You were attacked?' The Commissaire's pencil broke.

'Yes. In the music room.'

'In the music room?'

Richard felt Valérie's hand on his arm. Whether it was a sign of support or, the thought occurred to Richard, a warning not to reveal any more, he wasn't sure.

'Why were you attacked in the music room?'

'Because I forgot that there is a hidden staircase, and I had my back to it.'

'There is a hidden staircase?'

'Henri, is this getting us anywhere?' Valérie was acting like Richard's lawyer.

'I am trying to ascertain why Monsieur Ainsworth was attacked…'

'In the music room,' Richard added helpfully.

'At this juncture, monsieur, I am not sure that the location is all that important. Unless you were playing an instrument.'

Harsh, Richard thought.

'You say you thought Dominic Burdett had attacked you and that is why you gave chase, but now you think it was not him?'

Richard thought about this. 'Whoever attacked me,' he began slowly, 'was not wearing a tunic like the one Burdett wore. I am pretty sure of that.'

'You have evidence? It must have been dark.' The Commissaire's eyes narrowed.

'No.' Richard replied too quickly and the Commissaire looked from one to the other again. He shook his head and turned to address the group huddled in front of them instead.

'Ladies and gentlemen, while my team check the immediate area around the body, I want a full list of where everyone was tonight. First, when was Amorette Arthur last seen?'

At first, nobody seemed willing or capable of saying anything and it was left to René to break the silence. 'She came for a late coffee as I was packing up for the evening, about eightish,' he said in his usual defiant manner. 'She looked a bit down, but then she always did. "How do you like it?" I asked her and she reeled off some advertising slogan *"As black as the devil, hot as hell…"* I forget the rest.'

'*Pure as an angel, sweet as love*,' Sacha said quietly.

'That's it! What is it, Starbucks?'

'Charles-Maurice de Talleyrand-Périgord,' Dominic Burdett said, though without his usual pomp. 'It's one of his famous quotes. I think I know them all now.'

The silence returned.

'Did anyone see her after that?' The Commissaire looked around. 'No? Well, I'd say one of you did.' People shifted uncomfortably in their seats avoiding eye contact with the others, the Commissaire's implication not lost on them. 'I presume she then went back to her apartment at the gatehouse. I will check there shortly.'

'I was in my trailer all evening.' It was the usually more reticent Gilbertine who started things off. 'Samuel gave me a sleeping draught; the next thing I knew that lady was poking me in the chest.' He pointed at Madame Tablier, who confirmed the poking if nothing else.

'That's true,' Samuel said. 'I gave Gilbertine something to help him sleep, then went to find my uncle to see if he had anything else he wanted me to do.'

'And did he?' The Commissaire asked as Friedman senior didn't immediately back up Samuel's story.

'He wasn't there, but then I saw him walking Dominic around the gardens, so I assumed they were rehearsing or something.'

'And were you?' Valérie had had quite enough of sitting on the sidelines.

'Yes, thank you, madame.' The Commissaire was having none of it. He turned back to Friedman having dealt with her intervention. 'Well, and were you?'

'We talked about the production, whether it was right to carry on or not. Dominic is one of the producers and I wanted to know how he really felt.'

'And how did you really feel, Monsieur Burdett?'

Dominic Burdett puffed out his cheeks and shrugged. 'I'm afraid the early evening is something of a blur, dear boy.' Richard saw Friedman roll his eyes.

'That would figure,' he said. 'I had to hold him up for most of the time we walked.'

'I saw that from my trailer,' Jennifer interrupted. 'I'd been to check on Sacha – she was still a bit sick – then went back to my trailer to have a Zoom meditation with my Tirthankara, that's a Buddhist teacher. I saw them both; Dominic's knees went at one point and Ben held him up. You have amazing patience, Ben.'

Ben bowed his head in gratitude.

'I put him to bed at about ten-thirty,' Clare said. 'He was wandering about near the trailers and I think he mistook me for a *courtesan*.'

'Ah, apologies.' Burdett seemed wounded by his weakness.

'There is nothing to apologise for, Mr Burdett. I said no, you said fine and I put you to bed. You fell asleep almost immediately.'

'Thank you, dear lady.'

Richard blushed and felt guilty at doubting Clare earlier.

'Yet a half-hour later, you are crashing a golf buggy into a peacock coop.' The Commissaire wasn't finished. 'So how do you know he was asleep, madame.'

'Easy. He started talking in his sleep. I remember someone saying that's what he does. I mean he could have been pretending, but I don't see why?' Clare was losing patience with the questioning and that her word was being doubted.

'Talking?' The Commissaire sounded sceptical.

'Oh, Henri, do keep up!' Valérie said, also losing patience. 'What was he saying, Clare?'

'Oh, it just sounded like gibberish to me.'

'Gibberish?' Lapierre was lost by the English word.

'*Charabia*,' Richard added helpfully.

'Yes, well you would know!' was the Commissaire's truculent response. 'And you, madame?' He pointed at Lionel.

'I was in my trailer reading the script.' Lionel looked startled by the question, like she hadn't been paying attention.

'I can confirm that,' Valérie said in a tone that would brook no argument.

'I do not doubt that,' muttered the weary policeman. 'So, you three. Where were you?'

Brian, Stella and Alain were all seated at the same table and it was Brian who spoke first. 'We finished the set up for tomorrow in one of the upstairs rooms, then sat around talking and playing cards for an hour. I guess I was in bed at nine-forty-five. Stella was next door, I heard her music playing…'

'I heard that too,' Alain interrupted. 'Awful stuff,' he added.

Stella flushed angrily. 'That was Manuel de Falla!'

'It was loud, I know that!' Brian winked at her and she calmed down a bit.

The Commissaire tapped his teeth with his pencil. 'So, in theory you all have alibis but all of you were alone at some point in the evening also. So, none of you have alibis. This is absurd.' He seemed on the verge of genuine anger. 'You may all go back to bed for now. Obviously, no one is to leave. My officers are stationed everywhere. Tomorrow we will know more about this murder and I can pick apart your alibis more easily.' It was a sinister warning, not lost on anyone as they wearily sloped off. He turned to Valérie and whispered, 'Keep your people in place for now until I can get some reinforcements, please?' He nodded a curt goodnight, ignored Richard and stormed off back to the murder scene.

'Shall we all go back to our places then?' Clare asked, tired but definitely not bored with the whole thing. 'Is that wise?'

'Anybody'd be foolish to try something else tonight. This place'll be crawling with coppers soon.' René, his instincts betraying him, obviously wasn't comforted by the thought.

Silently everybody went back to their positions.

'You are very quiet, Richard.' Valérie spoke softly. 'It must have been a horrible thing to have discovered.'

Richard had stayed on the sidelines mostly, and had been trying not to let his own emotions show. As an Englishman it should have been a relatively easy thing to accomplish, but fatigue now had the better of him.

'No,' he said, attempting stoicism, 'it wasn't very pleasant. Nor was being attacked in the music room. I'd say that was worse.' He stopped walking and looked her in the eye.

'Worse?' she asked, confused.

'Yes, worse.' And he showed her the brooch he had torn off his attacker. It was Valérie's brooch.

Chapter Twenty-Six

'Richard...' Valérie looked stunned.

'No,' he interrupted. 'Let me speak. Look, I'm no good at being noble...' He stopped himself, just before he went into the full *Casablanca* 'hill of beans' speech and called her Ilsa. 'OK.' He took a deep breath and started again. 'I wish you'd told me, that's all.' Frankly, he'd hoped to produce something a little more dramatic than that, certainly something with more depth.

'You wish that I had told you what? I don't understand.'

'I've been doing some thinking, Valérie,' he said, as he started to pace around her. Ideally he'd have taken her in his arms, but he knew from painful experience that the most likely outcome of that kind of move was temporary blindness and a whack to the genitalia. He stopped moving and just shook his head. 'There is no stalker, is there? No violent stepfather lurking in the shadows?'

Valérie played with the brooch in her hands, then put it in her pocket. 'How long have you known?' she asked quietly, either in case someone overheard them or from a sense of guilt, Richard couldn't work out which, but he lowered his own voice too.

'I think since the last lot of messages on Lionel's mirror. I told Samuel it was a self-motivational tactic. I was playing for time, trying to cover up, but I was right, wasn't I?' Valérie didn't reply. 'All those warnings and messages on the mirror, they weren't aimed at Lionel Margaux, they were aimed at her character... what's she called...'

'Marie-Louise of Austria.'

'Marie-Louise of Austria, that's right.' He shook his head, still trying to work it all out. 'You, we, haven't been hired to protect Lionel from some madman on the loose. We've been hired to protect Lionel Margaux from Lionel Margaux and,' he paused, the revelation coming more slowly than he would have wished, 'to corroborate the theory of the stalker!' He clapped his hands, which was the sort of smug gesture he would usually detest.

'Yes, Richard.' If she was impressed with his intuition she was hiding it well.

'Lionel has had enough of all this, this...' he made a sweeping gesture with his arms that took in the trailers and the lighting and the rigs, '...all of this make-believe. She's had enough of the pretence. She wants out and your worry is that she will try anything to do that.' He stopped, suddenly realising where his thought process was taking him. 'Anything at all,' he added quietly. He turned to face Valérie and loosely, nervously even, held her arms. 'Why didn't you confide in me?' he asked. 'Why didn't you tell me how frightened you were for...' He paused again, and wondered whether or not to take the risk on his next guess.

'For Lionel?' She finished the sentence softly.

'For your daughter,' he replied, with a touch more confidence than he actually felt.

She looked into his eyes and almost imperceptibly shook her head, not in denial but in wonder. 'There is so much more to you, Richard, than you let people see,' she said softly. He knew he would have to remember the exact wording of that sentence for later on, just to work out how much of it actually was a compliment and how much was shock.

'I'm right though, aren't I?' he asked, his brief tide of confidence already beginning to recede.

She smiled at him. 'Yes, Richard. You are right. Lionel Margaux is my daughter.' Then a panic came across her face. 'But not even she knows that, Richard!'

'Blimey,' was his inadequate and frankly drama-deflating response.

They walked in silence for a while, away from the trailers and the lights, René's coffee wagon and the police cordon that was still brightly lit as forensics set to work on poor Amorette Arthur. They walked into the darkness of the night, up towards the deer park on the edge of the estate.

Eventually Richard broke the silence. 'Do you want to talk about it?' he asked.

In response, Valérie let out a breath so deep and long it was like the sighing of time, of history. He imagined it was the kind of thing that happened at the opening of a long-shut Egyptian tomb. 'Oh, Richard, I have wanted to talk about it for so long,' she said, the relief in her voice almost causing it to break. But that was all she said, so a few minutes later he had another go at it.

'I mean, you don't have to tell me anything,' he tried not to sound arch. 'But I'm here if you want to, anytime.'

He heard her give a slight giggle in the darkness. 'Richard, you are so beautifully English at times!' Again he wasn't entirely sure where the compliment, if indeed there was one, lay in that sentence. 'I am trying to remember so much of it myself, you see? Lionel's father was indeed a dangerous man, but magnetic, charismatic even, and I loved him while I hated myself for doing so. He knew he had a power over me, and I wasn't the only one. I just could not stay away.'

'Who was he?'

She paused, weighing up how much to tell him. Then she shrugged, decision made. 'You do not need to know his name, he is long gone. But he was an agent for the DGSE, the Direction générale de la Sécurité extérieure. Equivalent to your MI6. A James Bond,' she added with a derisive snort, but for the first time in their relationship showing that she had some semblance of film knowledge. This was dangerous territory for Richard; he knew he had to ignore the James Bond remark or his concentration would be shattered.

'How did you get away from him?' he asked, just in time.

'Ah,' Valérie said, and he saw her eyes flash in the moonlight. 'I met his wife.'

'Right. Awkward. She warned you off, did she?'

'Yes, she did. But not how you think.' She sighed again. 'His wife is an amazing woman, a great woman and now a close friend. But I saw the damage that he had done to her, that I had done to her also, and I knew that was not for me.'

'But you were pregnant with Lionel by now?'

'Yes. That is when it became more complicated.'

'I'll bet. So you had Lionel and…' He didn't know how to finish the sentence, so he hoped Valérie would do it for him.

'And her father never knew,' she said, a note of triumph in her voice.

'He never knew about Lionel?'

'He never knew that she was my daughter.'

Richard tried to work out what she meant by that, but eventually had to admit defeat. 'Nope, I don't get it.'

She stopped walking and put her hand on his arm gently. 'I told his wife that I was pregnant. She was, let's say, in a position to help me.'

'Oh.' He had no idea what else to offer.

'Not like that! She was my superior when I was also at the DGSE; she was also her husband's superior.'

'I didn't know you were in the DGSE?' He looked about him, in case it was still a secret.

'You never asked,' she replied matter-of-factly.

'Well honestly, it's not the kind of question… never mind. So, what happened?'

'His wife, my boss if you like, his boss too, arranged for him to go undercover overseas. She knew that the assignment would take him away for months and it did.'

It was Richard's turn to sigh. 'And, what?'

'And when he returned from, I think it was from Mali, he had a beautiful baby daughter.'

For a second Richard's face was still a picture of confusion, before the penny finally dropped. 'Ah, I get it!' he said in jubilation, which was followed by a much more sedate, 'Good lord.' Again, he thought how to word his next question. 'Did you want to give up your child?'

'Yes I did,' she answered immediately. 'Part of me wanted to keep her but I knew that I didn't *need* her. I think a child must be needed and her mother, her father's wife, needed her.'

'So you had an affair with a colleague who was married to your boss, you fell pregnant and they kept the child.' He was thinking aloud, and shaking his head at the same time. 'I think that's the Frenchest thing I've ever heard.' He smiled at her. 'It's also an incredible thing to live with; do you ever regret it?'

'I do not.' Again she replied immediately and was shutting out any semblance of doubt. 'Lionel Margaux is a beautiful and successful woman. I'm not sure I would have been able to offer that. Not then,' she added sadly, before shutting that down too. 'So, Richard, this has been a secret for many years and it still is.' Her face became very serious. 'How is it that you found out?'

Hard-pressed, Richard couldn't put a finger on it and said as much. 'It was just a feeling I had,' he said. 'I remember Alicia's first nativity play at school. Clare and I were there to see it, obviously. I, like all the other dads in the room, was just bursting with pride; she played an angel. I still remember her cardboard wings covered in cooking foil.' He smiled to himself at the memory.

Valérie was now as confused as he had been a few moments earlier.

'And?'

'Eh? Oh, well. Clare was just as proud, but there was something else about the mums in that room. It wasn't just pride, it was, I don't know, fear? Vulnerability? I don't know exactly. A sense that their daughters were going into a dangerous world? Dads always think they know how much danger their daughters are in, but only a mother

234

really knows. Anyway, maybe I read too much into it but I saw the same look on your face with Lionel…'

He couldn't be entirely certain, but he thought he saw moisture in Valérie's eyes which she wiped away immediately before shaking her head in wonder. 'You are a remarkable man, Richard,' she said, on the verge of expressing the emotion that he felt sure, or at least hoped, was there.

They stood awkwardly for a few moments before Valérie put her arms around his neck and kissed him warmly on the cheek.

'Ow!' Richard cried, ruining the moment with some violence.

'What? What is it?' Valérie asked, not unreasonably.

'Something digging into my neck!' He stepped back and pointed at her jumper. She unfolded the knitted wool at the top of her black roll-neck, revealing something that hit the light. 'It's that bloody brooch again! I thought you'd just put it in your pocket?'

Valérie pulled out a second, identical brooch from her trouser pocket. 'I did,' she smiled. 'Did you really think I could attack you, Richard?'

Chapter Twenty-Seven

The next morning Richard still didn't know where any of this left him. In darker moments he even considered the possibility that Valérie had kissed him tenderly on the cheek just so she could stab him with her brooch. The point being to show him, in a roundabout – possibly lethal – way, that it wasn't her that had attacked him in the music room. It had definitely been a woman though. It wasn't Lionel, she didn't look to have that much strength about her; nor Jennifer, though he couldn't say exactly why he doubted that option. Sacha was clearly unwell, which left Stella. Stella Gonzales had given Valérie her brooch in the first place, the same image that was hanging in the reception, he remembered again, and Stella had about the same build as Valérie.

All of which begged the question, what the bloody hell for? Why attack *him*? Why attack anyone for that matter? Then he remembered Amorette's query on his first day, 'Where are all the Spaniards?' she'd asked. Where indeed? Running around the chateau at night attacking innocent bystanders that's where.

It was very early in the morning as he now wandered around the chateau. There had been plans to start filming shortly after breakfast but Friedman had cancelled them. 'It wouldn't feel right,' he'd said and though everyone agreed, Sacha, despite her obvious physical weakness, had made it clear that they were now seriously behind schedule and over budget. 'I don't give a damn,' was the cigar-chomping response. 'We're not leaving this place until it's finished!' And while all the actors had rallied around with the traditional 'the show must go on' fervour, Sacha had just shaken her head sadly. This was her first film for Hollywood and she'd had a look on her face that had said it was very likely to be her last, and that she didn't mind if that wasn't her choice. She'd said goodnight to everyone, with a separate plaintive goodnight for the dead Amorette Arthur, and had gone back to her trailer.

Richard now made his way cautiously to the chateau reception. There was no reason to be so cautious, no one else was about, but if he'd learnt anything over the past few days it was that relaxing at any point could prove painful. What was it Valérie had said? O-O-D-A: Observe, Orient, Decide, Act. Richard was working on his own version and was happy to call it O-O-D-A-R. Observe, Orient, Decide, Act, Run. The picture was still up in reception and there had been no attempt to hide that it looked out of place. A pencil etching of an open book, held up with hands bound by chains. It looked like a declaration of some kind, though he couldn't make out the wording, only two Roman numerals VIII and IX.

'The Cortes de Cádiz, the start of the return of freedom for Spain.' Richard nearly jumped out of his skin and briefly had time to swear at the very idea of O-O-D-A and his inability to live by it. He ducked and raised his hands to his eyes in self-protection just in case Stella Gonzales decided to finish what she'd started the night before. 'I am sorry about last night, Mr Ainsworth, really. I thought you were someone else.' Her sultry Spanish accent was exactly the kind of thing that would immediately get through to Richard, but he determined for once not to be quite so shallow and say that everything was just fine, don't worry, you hit away.

'Someone you did not like, that is clear.' Valérie appeared from nowhere and Richard, although grateful for the potential back-up, was beginning to wonder if he'd lost the use of all five of his senses.

'Somebody wanders around this place at night and, I don't know, they might be violent,' Stella replied, a little sheepishly.

'I've noticed the same!' Richard said tartly.

'Not me, somebody else.'

'Well, you'll do!'

'I said I am sorry!'

Valérie stepped between them. 'Do you know who it is?' she asked Stella.

'No. I have not seen this person, only heard them.' Valérie nodded, and shot Richard a quick, disbelieving look.

'I believe you lost this,' she said and handed one of the two brooches to Stella. 'It is also the Cortes de Cádiz I see. What does it mean?'

Stella took the brooch in the palm of her hand and closed her fingers around it. 'The Cortes de Cádiz was a Spanish parliament that met to show the end of the French invasion and occupation in the Peninsula War,' she said. 'It was the start of democracy in Spain, the start of the real Spain. We have fought for that freedom ever since, all through Franco.' Her passion for the subject was almost religious in its zeal.

'We?' Richard asked sceptically.

'I am a member of the Caballeros de Cádiz. It is up to us to defend the history of democracy in our country.'

'By attacking me?'

'No, by maintaining its presence in this film.' Valérie and Richard looked at each other in disbelief as Stella raised her eyes to the etching on the wall. 'That is my job,' she added, as behind her back Richard twirled his finger at his right temple. Stella turned around suddenly and Richard covered his eyes. 'Amorette helped me to do this,' she said quietly.

'She helped you to do what, madame?' Commissaire Lapierre stood in the doorway of reception with his hands behind his back and Richard was relieved that he wasn't the only one who hadn't noticed him arrive.

'She encouraged me to help with the historical accuracy of this film, monsieur, that is all.' She nodded at Richard and Valérie, then at the Commissaire. 'I have to go,' she said, 'Mr Friedman wants us to watch some of the rushes this morning.'

She left swiftly, and a look of confusion came across Lapierre's face. 'What are these rushes?' he asked.

'Uncut footage from the film,' Richard explained. 'They'll watch over some of the stuff they've filmed.'

Turning to Lapierre, Valérie asked, 'What is the news, Henri? How was Amorette Arthur killed?' Valérie was impatient for information and the look on her ex-husband's face was a contrite one.

'Madame Arthur was probably murdered,' he avoided eye contact.

'I could have told you that information, that is not news! What we want to know is how was she murdered?'

'Why would be useful too,' Richard chipped in.

The Commissaire looked from one to the other again. 'Do you know what indoramin is, either of you?' he asked, probably already knowing that they didn't.

'Well it sounds like a drug…' Valérie said impatiently.

'It *is* a drug, madame. It is a drug used mainly for the treatment of *hypertension*, high blood pressure.'

'And Amorette Arthur was on this drug, or was this another concoction from Reed Turnbull's bag of tricks?'

'Both, monsieur. Indoramin is prescribed for people with high blood pressure and for men with prostate problems. Both Madame Arthur and Monsieur Turnbull have prescriptions for the drug.'

Valérie was thoughtful. 'That doesn't really help,' she said caustically. 'But together that would make quite a large amount would it not?'

'It would.' The Commissaire was starting to build in confidence. 'But a large amount is not needed; two and a half thousand milligrams could kill a human being. That, madame, is less than a teaspoon.'

'But you said probably murdered?' There didn't seem much doubt in Richard's mind.

'She may have taken an overdose! She may have made herself these profiteroles with her indoramin and then…'

'…And then taken herself away to convulse to death in the peacock's coop? Don't be so silly, Henri! It was murder and you know it.'

The Commissaire put his hands behind his back once more and walked towards the large windows overlooking the ornamental gardens. He sighed like a man who had a boulder on his chest. 'I am inclined to agree with you, madame. My instinct tells me that it is murder but I ask you, where is the proof? I do not like coincidence any more than you, but each death has occurred *naturally* with their own medication; Monsieur Corbeau was different. I need more proof than we have and...' he whirled around surprisingly nimbly, 'I want to know who you suspect!' He pointed a finger at the empty room: Valérie had already dragged Richard away and outside.

'It is no wonder so few crimes are solved these days!' Valérie was practically frog-marching Richard towards Ben-Hur Friedman's apartment. 'The police have the speed of snails. Of course it's murder, Henri knows that it's murder and that's why he needs us.'

'He needs us?' Richard was sceptical.

'Of course he needs us! You heard him...'

'Not all of him.'

'He was really begging for our help. He knows that we can work more quickly without all this paperwork and manners and diplomatic approach. Don't you see, Richard? He was *begging* for our help!'

Richard did not see it that way at all; in fact even though he hadn't been around for the end of whatever Commissaire Lapierre had been saying, he was pretty certain it would have been the opposite to Valérie's conclusion of it. This wasn't the place to thrash it out though as they were now at Friedman's apartment and Valérie was opening the French doors without bothering to knock.

'Hey! Come in!' Friedman was looking increasingly weary and his attempts at enthusiasm were beginning to show signs of being heavily forced. 'We're going through some of the rushes,' he said. 'I like to do this before the big final scenes, I find it helps.'

'We have only one more scene to film.' Sacha, who was looking brighter and on the road to recovery, nevertheless looked relieved at the prospect of the end finally nearing. 'Talleyrand's death scene,' she explained quietly.

'I make my deal with God!' Burdett exclaimed from the depths of a deep armchair. 'Or, is it the devil?' he added dramatically.

Richard took up a position next to Stella at the back and asked how things were looking.

'Great!' It was the boundless energy of Samuel Friedman who replied. 'It's looking really great. I think Reed may get a posthumous Oscar nomination!'

'Like James Dean.' Richard couldn't help himself.

They all watched in silence for a while. Brian Grace nodded to himself, assessing the quality of camera and lighting no doubt. Stella looked tense, presumably seeing if her rather absurd attempts to add a Spanish influence were obvious or not, though Richard noticed nothing out of place. Sacha was quiet and made some notes while Jennifer Davies and Gilbertine were only interested when they came on screen. Lionel looked vacantly out of the window and Valérie concentrated on watching the faces in the room. It felt less like the 'rushes screenings' of old that Richard had read so much about, and more like a party of mild acquaintances sat around watching a DVD.

Richard felt Stella tense beside him and he noticed that the tableau on screen showed a fiery Reed Turnbull berating Jennifer Davies in his all too familiar bullying fashion. It took Richard a few moments to realise it was part of the film and not their off-screen relationship captured for posterity.

'This is really great, Unc!' Samuel obviously liked what he saw. 'You're back in the game!'

'Do you think you'll carry on the family tradition, Samuel, and become a Hollywood producer like all the Friedmans before you?' Jennifer gave the young man a maternal smile.

'I hope so,' he replied. 'I'm not cut out to be a medical intern anyway.'

Friedman senior nodded slowly. 'It looks OK so far,' he said. 'But you can't always tell…'

'Here we go!' Brian Grace interrupted.

'I wasn't going to say anything, Brian,' Ben said apologetically.

'You didn't need to. You always bring up that turkey. The footage looked great, but there was no story. I had to try something!'

Valérie looked to Richard for an explanation.

'Are you talking about *The Sidewalk Romantics*?' Richard asked, a picture of naivety.

'You've heard of it?' Brian sounded shocked.

'Well of course,' he said, hoping that he wouldn't have to add any detail. 'It's become a cult classic.'

'Ha! I had no idea. That movie killed off my directing career. Still, I wasn't the only casualty of that.' He didn't seem to bear a grudge though, not as far as Richard could tell.

'Do you mean the director you replaced?' Valérie asked, looking even more innocent than Richard.

'Yeah. Poor guy. Friedman's grandad had him sacked, he was an alcoholic and going way over budget, but he didn't take it well. Not well at all. He kept turning up at the set after he was sacked, begging for any kind of role. He even tried to bribe us, said he knew where we could find riches beyond our dreams!' Grace laughed. 'The poor guy was nuts. I wonder what happened to him. I can't even remember his name now. Ben, what was the name of the director I replaced on *Sidewalk*?'

'Huh?' Friedman was still concentrating on the screen.

'You know, the fella who I took over from directing?'

'Oh, er, Masker was it? Alex Masker I think. This looks great, Sacha!'

It all felt very odd to Richard. They were in the midst of death, natural causes possibly, suicide more likely, murder almost certainly and yet they were all so wrapped up in their own world. It felt wilfully delusional and for someone who had lived and breathed the Hollywood Dream Factory for so long, he now wondered who was more captivated by it – the consumers or the creators.

'Ah.' Dominic Burdett noticed himself on screen, bowing to Reed Turnbull as Napoleon. 'There they are, the old war horses.' He had tears in his eyes as he spoke and the entire room turned towards him. 'There aren't many of us left.'

'He was truly a giant,' Friedman said quietly, 'and a friend.'

'Pah!' shouted Burdett suddenly. 'The instruments of darkness tell us truths, win us with honest trifles, to betray us in deepest consequence.' He stood up and made for the door. 'Macbeth,' he added theatrically and marched out, leaving nobody at all sure, as usual, if he was drunk Burdett or sober Talleyrand.

'Richard,' Valérie whispered in his ear. 'I think I have a plan.'

Chapter Twenty-Eight

'Yes. And supposing that I do not want to help you?' Stella Gonzales had her arms folded, suggesting a go-to truculence that had taken years to perfect.

'You of course do not have to, we are not the police…' Valérie let the final word hang, dripping as it was with threat, but it didn't seem to make much difference. 'You tell her, Richard!'

The last thing Richard wanted to do was to have to squeeze his way into this tectonic intransigence and so far he had wisely hung back. Valérie had now shoved him centre stage. 'Well, er, I do think Valérie has a point, you know?' Both women looked at him in disappointment and he rubbed the back of his head, showing where Stella had injured him the night before. 'I wouldn't want to press charges of assault,' he said, trying to sound innocent, 'but I'm sure that the Commissaire would be interested in talking to you about your role in all of this.'

'My role?'

'Yes,' Richard sensed an opportunity, 'your role as some kind of paramilitary wing of the Spanish Tourist Board for instance. Which I'm still not sure I quite believe.'

Again, both women looked at him, but this time there was a sense of bewilderment and eventually Stella shook her head, but responded positively nonetheless. 'What do you want me to do?' she asked, slightly deflated.

Valérie pounced before she changed her mind. 'I want to record Dominic Burdett as he talks in his sleep.'

Stella's eyes narrowed. 'Why?' she asked, not unreasonably and Richard was grateful for the fact that she had because he might have done the same.

'Because I think he has a lot to say, but doesn't know that he's saying it,' she said, as if that were explanation enough. Stella looked from Valérie to Richard, hoping that it would be Richard who could give some explanation to Valérie's enigmatic statement. It wasn't long before she realised that that would be a long wait and in the end she just shrugged her shoulders and relented.

'OK,' she said eventually. 'But I am not breaking into his trailer, someone else will have to do that.'

'Of course!' Valérie beamed. 'We have someone else for that.'

***

'You want me to do what now?' Clare no longer thought that any of this was a joke, and even had a look of bored resignation in her eyes which Richard hadn't seen since, well since their wedding day it now struck him.

'It's very simple, Clare,' Valérie explained. 'Dominic Burdett has taken a shine to you and we'd like you to use that trust and help us to set up a microphone in his trailer.' Again, Valérie's wide smile wasn't as disarming as she thought it was and without taking her eyes off her, Clare asked Richard a direct question.

'Why?' she asked him.

'I, er, well… honestly? I don't know,' he replied, and as honest as it was, it was woefully inadequate.

'Is it dangerous?' She looked him directly in the eye this time.

'Oh no,' Valérie answered for him, 'not at all.'

Clare nodded her head slowly and then matched Valérie's smile. 'Why not?' she said. 'I'm not doing anything else tonight.'

***

Richard, Valérie and Stella watched from Lionel's darkened trailer as Clare, with some difficulty, led Dominic Burdett back to his trailer. Lionel was back at the *chambre d'hôte* under the watchful guard of Madame Tablier and Passepartout, while the rest of Valérie's usual operatives were dotted about the chateau and the grounds, with orders to report even the slightest disturbance. The physical problems Clare was enduring seemed to come from Dominic either being very drunk or childishly pawing at her like a fumbling, desperate teenager. She had her instructions and those were to get the actor back to his trailer and hide the small microphone and booster set somewhere that was both open and discreet, and then get out. Then Stella, with surprisingly little equipment, and the others could listen in to and try to decipher the actor's overnight ramblings. Richard couldn't help thinking it was a long shot, but also had to admit that there was very little else that they could physically be doing other than wait around for the murderer to make a mistake, and that was far more dangerous. Besides which Clare was doing a very good job and finally managed to squeeze a swaying Burdett in through his trailer door.

Richard felt tense now as he saw the door shut behind the two of them, one of them still being, albeit in name only, his wife. Valérie, unusually for her, felt his tension and put a hand on his shoulder and squeezed. Stella, wearing headphones, interrupted them.

'OK, she has turned the battery pack on and I am picking up their voices,' she said, a hint of excitement in her voice.

'Can we hear too?' Valérie asked.

'Yes, hang on.' Stella changed a couple of cables while Richard was still looking at the door, willing Clare to get out. Then he heard her voice and it was so clear, she might have been in their trailer with them.

'...I've already told you, Mr Burdett, I'm a married woman.' She didn't sound in any danger, she sounded actually more like a disappointed teacher.

'And I told you, dear lady, that I am a married man. At least I think I am. Do you know, I can't for the life of me remember.'

'You could look yourself up on IMDB,' Clare said, and Richard knew this was a little dig at her listening husband. 'Now, I'll hang this jacket just here, it's filthy and smells, by the way.' There was a sound like Clare was trying to clean the jacket. 'I know you have the big final scene tomorrow, so why not get some rest?' There was some noise of movement, a glass or something being knocked over and Richard froze. Then came the unmistakable sound of a man in some physical difficulty, followed by someone falling onto a bed. A very calm Clare came over the speaker. 'There, can I get you anything else?'

'Some new testicles,' winced a contrite Dominic Burdett.

'Goodnight, Mr Burdett,' she said and Richard watched her exit the trailer. She shut the door behind her, took a deep breath and gave them a thumbs-up. She then made a signal that she needed a drink and went off to find René.

'Now we wait,' Valérie said edgily.

The wait wasn't a very long one. Burdett obviously got up off his bed and began crashing around his trailer, presumably looking for something and which, judging by the clink of bottle on glass, he quickly found. They then heard him turning pages, which they assumed was his script, a copy of which Richard had brought with them to see what was real and what wasn't. Though he still wasn't sure what difference that would make to their investigation. They heard him take a long drink.

'Ah,' the actor said eventually. 'So, old boy, the final big one tomorrow, eh? And then you're done.'

'It's going to be handy if he keeps up a running commentary all night,' Richard whispered, though obviously the microphone was only going one way.

'Let's make it a good 'un then.' He coughed to clear his throat. 'And so the great survivor, the thread that has bound together France this last turbulent fifty years, must go.' As he spoke the words would become fainter and then return to full volume.

'The microphone must be at one end of his trailer,' Stella explained.

'People say that I betrayed France, but I never,' he coughed again, 'I never betrayed a government that did not first betray itself! I never put myself in the balance ahead of my country. All I did, I did for France.' The voice grew weary and faltering, signalling that Talleyrand was dying. Then it came back stronger. 'Some guy,' he said loudly. 'He does what the hell he wants all his life, then signs a last-minute deal with God.' He put his glass down loudly. 'Could you do that, Dominic, you old fraud?'

Stella, Valérie and Richard all looked at each other. Was this just late night self-pity or was there a specific reason for guilt?

'Well, Charles-Maurice de Talleyrand-Périgord, you'd have done well in the movie business!' His voice changed back to character. 'A diplomat who says "yes" means "maybe", a diplomat who says "maybe" means "no", and a diplomat who says "no" is no diplomat.' It was one of Talleyrand's most famous quotes. 'For diplomat read movie producer. Dominic Burdett, movie producer. Pah!' There was a moment's silence, followed by a gulp of drink and the glass being refilled. 'Good friends will always stab you in the front!'

'Is that in the script?' Valérie asked, not without good reason as the man was all over the place.

'I hope not,' Richard said, 'it's Oscar Wilde.'

'Oh.'

Burdett's voice came through the speaker again. 'You were a good friend, Napoleon, but better that it end like this. Either that or die by ignorance, rotting in the sun, watching our own movies on late-night TV.'

'What is he talking about, the silly man?' Valérie went to look out of the window rather than needlessly huddle around the speaker.

'I'm not sure, but I think he's confusing Reed with Napoleon in the same way that he confuses himself with his role, Talleyrand.'

Valérie shook her head and repeated that she thought he was a silly man. 'If he is our murderer, he could plead insanity and get away with it,' she added. Richard half-wondered if that was the point.

'Hang on though, you may have something there,' he said. 'If he's blurring the roles, it may be because he's blurring the stories too. Just as Talleyrand was supposed to have betrayed Napoleon, Burdett may have betrayed Turnbull.'

'Or killed him?'

'Or killed him.'

'Do you think that he killed Reed Turnbull?' They had almost forgotten that Stella was there too. 'And Amorette?'

'I do not know,' Valérie said carefully. 'He has guilt about something, but I do not know if that is his character or the man.'

'Or both,' Richard added.

A phone rang and it was a few seconds before they realised that it was Burdett's phone. 'What do you want?' he asked gruffly. They could hear a muffled voice in the background. 'Now? Can't it wait? We've got to be up early… I don't care. I have one scene, then we're done, I'm out. Whatever it is can wait now. Besides,' he laughed, 'it's not safe around here, or haven't you noticed?'

There was a hard edge in his voice that hadn't been there before, it sounded almost threatening and thuggish like a stereotypical gangster, a 1940s gangster, the Hollywood version at least, and Richard wondered aloud if he was now playing another role. If he was, it was certainly possible that with all Dominic Burdett's roles, he had done extensive research on the subject. He said goodnight to whoever it was talking to him, turned off the light and fell onto his bed.

'What do we do now?' asked Stella.

'We wait,' Valérie said, shrugging her shoulders. 'We wait for him to start talking again.' Her walkie-talkie crackled. 'Yes?' she answered briskly and then quickly moved the instrument away from her ear as Martin's voice came across too loud and too clear.

'Er, Valérie old girl, sorry to bother you and all that…'

'What is it, Martin?' she snapped back.

'Well, yes, you see. I've been attacked. Have you got any bandages there please?'

Richard and Valérie took a quick glance at each other and then both shot out of the trailer door.

Chapter Twenty-Nine

The look on Martin's face was an uncomfortable combination of self-pity, and a very English 'Yes, I'm put out by this, but I'd rather not make a fuss.' He looked like a toy teddy bear whose face had been badly repaired. But if Martin was trying not to cause a bother, Gennie was prepared to make the fuss for him.

'We've always been very pleased to help out before,' she began, tending to Martin's superficial head wound.

'And it's always been rather fun,' Martin added apologetically.

'But this has all got a bit dangerous for us. Martin's in pain. What's going on?'

She looked pleadingly into Richard's eyes and he immediately felt as conflicted as Martin. On the one hand, he didn't really know what was going on as that was, at the moment, very much Valérie's department. But on the other, he had had the gross misfortune to see and spend time in the couple's 'pleasure' dungeon and pain seemed very much their thing.

Valérie, after a quick check on Martin, had left Gennie to the first aid of her husband, and was wandering around the large underground kitchen area. There were two rooms, both with high arched brick ceilings, enormous ovens built in the adjoining wall, copper sinks and large preparation tables. The walls that weren't covered in gleaming copper pans and utensils had framed sketches of some of Marie-Antonin Carême's most famous and most flamboyant creations and they looked more like prototypes for outrageous ladies' wigs rather than foodstuffs. The largest drawing was of the *croquembouche*, the profiterole pyramid which had been recreated for the meal at which Reed Turnbull had died. On one of the tables was a modern book of Carême recipes and some recently bought ingredients. It looked for all the world like someone had been disturbed mid-creation.

'Tell me again what happened, Martin,' Valérie said. Her tone suggested that she was on the verge of a great discovery and just needed one more piece of information.

'Well, er, I was just doing the rounds upstairs and I heard some clattering going on down here…'

'And you came rushing down?' Valérie asked. 'That's very brave!' She knew that by appealing to Martin's ego, she could mollify the couple.

'To be honest,' a sheepish Martin said, 'I thought Gennie was in trouble. We'd decided to split up…'

'Which we won't do again!' Gennie grabbed her husband's hand.

'Never fear, old girl.' Martin smiled warmly at her.

A touching scene it may have been, and it certainly moved Richard, but Valérie was impatient for any snippet of information. 'And then?'

'Well all the lights were on and I heard, you know, like I said, some clattering. Like someone was looking for the right pan or something, so I knew it wasn't Gennie.

Anyway, I thought I'd contact her, and get back-up. Is that what they call it, back-up?'

'I'd call it that,' Richard said encouragingly before Valérie could step in and tell Martin to get a move on.

'So I went down the corridor, was telling Gennie where I was and the next thing, bosh! I get a crack on the head for my troubles.' He gave a wan smile while Gennie rubbed his head lovingly.

'What is going on?' she repeated, this time to Valérie, who had her arms folded and a very serious look on her face.

'I think I know,' she said slowly. Which went some way to relieving the tension for Martin and Gennie but which was news to Richard.

They all knew Valérie well enough, however, to know that she was going to give nothing away until she was absolutely certain she knew. Even if they had felt inclined to ask what she was thinking, they were interrupted by her walkie-talkie. It was Stella.

'Madame,' she sounded urgent, 'come quickly, he is talking.'

Richard and Valérie left an apprehensive Martin and Gennie in the kitchens and made their way through the lower ground exit. As they passed Friedman's apartment he saw the producer slumped asleep on a divan, glass in hand resting on his stomach and his lap covered in paperwork. Valérie saw him too and whispered, 'Well, he seems safe enough.'

'Lucky that he is,' Richard said, following her over the bridge. 'If he goes, then the whole film really does collapse. He's holding this thing together like a proper old-school Hollywood producer.'

Clare appeared at the other end of the bridge. 'What's going on *now*?' she asked, not unreasonably. 'I saw you two running over here, is everything OK?'

'Martin's been coshed,' Richard explained dramatically. 'He'll be fine though.'

'Of course he'll be fine,' Clare said, caustically. 'He likes pain.'

'Oh, Clare…' Richard admonished her, to which she just replied with a shrug.

Valérie was a few yards ahead by now, signalling for them to keep up.

'What's got into Modesty Blaise now?' Clare asked, using a film reference that was so arcane it was like a secret language between them. They both hurried to catch up with Valérie.

'Apparently Burdett has started talking.' Richard would like to have added more, but that was all he had.

'Your microphone is working very well,' Valérie added as they reached the trailer door.

'*My* microphone?' Richard got the distinct impression that Clare wasn't dealing with this situation very well at all. It was everything she hated: not being in charge, not having any control and not having much of a clue as to what was going on. As such she was fighting the only way she knew how, territorially, and she put her arm through Richard's as he stood hands on hips trying to get his breath back. 'My microphone,' she repeated.

Inside Stella was crouched over her equipment, but there wasn't much noise coming through it, other than that of a gentle snore. She looked up at them apologetically, as if she could have done more to keep the ageing actor awake.

'He has stopped?' Valérie asked, her disappointment obvious.

'Yes,' was the equally frustrated reply. 'It wasn't much, but I recorded what there was.'

Richard gave a sigh of relief not just that Stella had had the foresight to record Burdett, but because Valérie had looked on the verge of blowing a gasket and the news calmed her down a little. Stella rewound the recording as Clare sat on Lionel's bed.

'Why is what Dominic Burdett says so important?' she asked wearily.

It was Valérie who responded immediately. 'I think he holds the key to all of this, and is more than likely involved but…'

Richard interrupted, '…he has such a weak grasp on reality, or at least difficulty in distinguishing it from fiction, that he could give the game away. Whatever that game is.'

Clare nodded.

'OK,' Stella said. 'Are you ready?'

'By involved,' Clare's speech was deliberately slow and immediately the warning alarms went off in Richard's head; he was a frigate and an enemy submarine was now directly underneath him. 'Do you mean he could even be the murderer?'

Just that one sentence seemed to last about half an hour.

'Oh yes!' Valérie was getting impatient with what to her was frivolous conversation.

Clare stared hard at her now very estranged husband. 'So you put me in danger, Richard?' Her voice was ice cold.

'Richard!' It seemed that Valérie hadn't heard Clare's question. 'We must concentrate.'

Stella pressed some buttons and there was a hissing noise from Burdett's recorded microphone.

'The quality is not very good,' Stella again apologised. 'I had to turn the gain up. I think he was facing away from the mic.'

Valérie shook her head dismissively, concentrating on the fuzzy noise. Then he started to speak.

'Ah, Talleyrand,' he began, evidently not wholly conscious. 'Talleyrand, Talleyrand, Talleyrand.' There was a pause while they all hoped for a bit more. 'What have you done?'

'Does he mean Talleyrand or himself?' Richard whispered and Valérie shrugged, shaking her head.

'TREASON!' was the sudden distorted shout through the equipment. 'Is a matter of dates.'

'That's definitely a line from Talleyrand,' Richard confirmed. 'It's in the script.'

'That poor girl… what did you do to her?' Burdett groggily droned and Richard mouthed the word 'Amorette' to Valérie, who just shrugged in response. 'What did we all do to her?'

'I am very pleased you recorded this, madame,' Valérie thanked Stella, but was interrupted as Dominic Burdett continued with his somnolent monologue.

'I have betrayed you, my friend.' It sounded like Burdett was slipping into a deeper sleep. 'I have betrayed you both.' They heard the sound of gentle weeping. 'But we were digging in the wrong place!' Valérie looked to Richard for an explanation but he couldn't work it out and shook his head to say so. 'We have lost everything for nothing! And worse… we have lost each other!'

'If that's a script, it's not from this film,' Stella said, her own excitement growing.

Valérie began hurriedly typing the words into her phone. 'I want to see if this is a script or his own conscience talking,' she said hurriedly.

'Stella is right, it's definitely not the script for this film.' Richard was certain of that. He was also vaguely aware of a slight draught behind him and he went to close the trailer door which had swung open. 'I tell you what it could be though!' He clapped his hands in delight, then quickly apologised for making too much noise. 'It could be from the script of *The Sidewalk Romantics*! Burdett and Turnbull fall out over a robbery that in the end they didn't commit.'

Valérie stood up quickly and held her bright phone in Richard's face. 'Brilliant, Richard!' she cried. 'And you are quicker than IMDB!'

For a brief second Richard felt something of Burdett's sense of betrayal: that Valérie would lean on his internet-based arch enemy stung, frankly. But pride quickly won over when he realised he'd actually beaten his nemesis anyway. He gave her a look as if to say 'was it ever in doubt?' but she was already crouching down and listening for any further damning evidence from Burdett. Instead he turned triumphantly towards Clare; this was a victory long in the making and the moment needed registering between them. But Clare wasn't there, she had gone.

'There is just one thing though,' Valérie said pensively and not giving any indication if she'd been aware of Clare's leaving. 'If Burdett is our killer, who attacked Martin?'

But Richard's mind was temporarily elsewhere.

Chapter Thirty

'From what he says in his sleep, maybe he was working with Reed Turnbull.' Richard stirred his coffee as René placed a basket of aged croissants between him and Valérie. Richard tried bouncing one off the table to test its edibility.

'And then he killed Amorette because Reed had confided in her?' Valérie also picked up a croissant and put it back immediately, a look of personal insult on her face.

'But then who is his accomplice now? We know he couldn't have attacked Martin last night, and Stella, who also has previous, couldn't have attacked him either.'

Valérie stirred her coffee. 'We are still looking for someone else.'

The sun was approaching mid-morning heat, and the quiet bustle of the set was in full swing. Alain Petit and Madame Tablier, who had delivered both Lionel and Passepartout earlier, were doing things that Richard couldn't fathom with screwdrivers and gaffer tape and as content as any couple he currently knew, though he doubted that they were actually a couple. It was no more possible to see Madame Tablier plucking at the lute of romance than it was to see Valérie eat one of René's cannonball croissants. If it was romance you wanted, then Gennie still fussing over Martin on a shaded patch of lawn was the solution there. The actors were in make-up with Jennifer in her dual role as make-up artiste and being assisted by Clare, who still hadn't spoken to Richard since she'd been convinced that he had dangled her as bait. Sacha and Friedman were poring over the script on a table further away and Grace, Stella and Samuel were moving equipment about. There was a nervy excitement in the air, a last day of school feel that, despite three deaths, Richard felt was probably not that different to the usual last day on the set ambience.

Richard and Valérie watched them all and were thinking the same thoughts. Which of them was Burdett's accomplice? And that was assuming, as Richard had pointed out on a couple of occasions, that they had drawn the right conclusions from the scant, bordering on lunacy, information that Dominic Burdett had unknowingly provided. And, as relevant as anything else, why? Richard felt that the answer, as things generally do, lay in the past, the film that they had all made together. But there was something else, a raging against the dying of the light. Burdett's reference to rotting in front of a late-night TV watching his younger self was a telling one.

Valérie interrupted his thoughts. 'Who pays for all of this?' she asked, and swept her arm wide. 'Is it the producer, Friedman?'

Richard mulled this over. 'I doubt it. This kind of thing, especially with costumes, runs into millions and millions of dollars. And I don't think Friedman has that kind of finance personally.'

'So where then?' It was clear from the tone of her voice that where was inextricably linked up with why.

'Well, lots of different sources,' Richard began. 'There'll be a range of film finance companies, all investing for a stake of the profits. There will be smaller investors, trying to get into the business. In this instance the French government will have invested as it would be good for jobs and tourism, product-placing, official product-placing that is, not Stella's guerrilla version. Then there's advertisers, costumiers… the list is endless really.'

'But not Monsieur Friedman, nor Monsieur Turnbull, nor Monsieur Burdett?'

'I can't see it.' He shook his head. 'They're unlikely to have that kind of money anyway, none of them have had a hit in years.'

She thought some more about this. 'So how do they make their money?'

'They will be paid a salary, or given a percentage of profits. It's more about getting back to where they feel they belong I think, at the top of the greasy Hollywood pole.'

'And do you think this film will do that?'

'No.' His answer was immediate. 'Not at all. It just doesn't fit and,' he looked about making sure he wasn't overheard, 'it's not good enough. Overblown, over-acted, historically inaccurate…'

'So you no longer think this is all an act of sabotage?'

'I don't know who would gain from that at all. The old hands need a hit and the younger ones, Gilbertine, Sacha…' He shot a quick glance at her.

'…Lionel,' she finished the sentence for him.

'Lionel. How would they benefit from crashing the thing? No, there is nothing to be gained, nothing at all.'

'So why then? Why all of this? It cannot be just vanity, Richard, there must be something else? Something going on behind the film itself.'

'You mean like the story of *The Sidewalk Romantics*? Down-at-heel thieves with a cover?' He thought about this. '*After the Fox*,' he said, as if she wasn't there.

'What is that?' she asked impatiently.

'*After the Fox*. It was a Peter Sellers film, where he pretended to be a great film director, but it was just a front to carry out a daring robbery under everyone's noses.'

'And?' She leant forward in anticipation of their breakthrough.

'Well, it has some good moments,' he said in a dismissive manner, before realising that she wasn't asking for a critique. 'Oh, I see. What was it Brian Grace said about riches?' he scoffed and she shrugged.

'There must be something, why is someone roaming the place at night, in the cellar, the kitchens… what are they looking for?'

It was Richard's turn to shrug his shoulders. 'Talleyrand made a fortune by investing in wine, maybe there are still some bottles left?'

'But what would that be, a hundred thousand euros? Even if they have themselves not invested, the return is too small for too great a risk.'

He nodded. 'Maybe we're thinking about the wrong era? Valençay is more than Napoleon and Talleyrand. The original script was about the Second World War and what was it Amorette said about Turnbull…?'

'The Louvre Museum!' Valérie grabbed his wrist. 'The Louvre Museum hid priceless artefacts here in the war!'

Richard suddenly put his coffee down. 'We need Burdett's phone!' he cried, and then admonished himself. 'We need Burdett's phone!' he repeated in a whisper. Valérie gave him a blank look and then she connected with what he was saying.

'Of course!'

'Whoever called Burdett late last night *could*, and I mean *could*, be his accomplice.'

'But it would be almost certain?' Valérie clearly wasn't in the mood for this 'could' nonsense.

'No, it wouldn't be conclusive at all. But it would be interesting.' He overrode her attempt to interrupt. 'And that number is more than likely stored on his phone as a recent call.'

Their deliberations were interrupted by Samuel Friedman who called everybody on set. 'You go,' Valérie said, a glint in her eye. 'I am going for a walk.'

He knew exactly where she would be walking to and for once didn't see the harm in letting her go as everyone else would be on set, so she had a free passage.

The set was best described as 'moodily lit'. This was Talleyrand's death scene, his reconciliation with God, his final peace treaty as it were and one which added to his reputation for political expediency. Samuel Friedman temporarily lay on the bed in place of the awaited Burdett, while Brian and Stella were adjusting the lights to create more shadows on the wall behind. They weren't happy with the effect so far.

'Can we lose these books?' Brian asked, his impatience showing. 'I can get a much better contrast if we have a lighter background.'

'I think it works as it is,' Sacha said, still not fully recovered and clearly a ball of stress.

'Friedman!' Brian shouted, going over the young director's head.

The producer had been watching from the side, the inevitable cigar in his mouth, which he now removed. 'I think we should take our time and get this right,' he said. 'There's no need to rush, Sacha, forget the budget, forget time. I know you, you'll make this perfect.'

'OK,' she said. And Brian Grace immediately started moving some books.

'Can somebody give me a hand here?' he shouted over his shoulder.

Richard went to help him and lifted a few himself. 'They're not exactly contemporary, are they?' he joked as he did so. They'd obviously all been chosen for their colour scheme, which matched the chateau bedroom, and placed beyond the visitor ropes so away from scrutiny. 'This one,' Richard pointed it out to the disinterested cameraman, '*Pêche à la mouche*, *Fly Fishing*, ha! And this, *Peugeot 403 1959: entretien and réparation*.'

Grace ignored him. 'Can we get some ornaments on these shelves instead, something that'll give me some shadows?'

'Oh, I might keep this one!' Richard was suddenly off on a reverie. '*Le Dictionnaire du cinéma*, Jean-Luc Peppin,' he said to himself and sat down in a quiet corner, hooked.

'Ornaments!' Brian Grace demanded again and Stella Gonzales appeared with some ornate photo frames and a metal-forged statuette of the Cortes de Cádiz. Richard made a mental note to tell Valérie that, but for the moment was happily flicking through his find.

Nearly half an hour later and Brian, Stella and Sacha were still rehearsing camera movements and it was clear that they weren't happy.

'The shadows are everything in this scene,' Grace was saying.

'They're not as important as the actors and the words,' argued Sacha, who had recovered her appetite and wasn't backing down whether her opponent was a Hollywood legend or not.

'Maybe if I sat up higher in the bed it would help?' said a bored Dominic Burdett as he finally approached, walking through the other actors who were sitting around on the fringes waiting to begin their work.

'You're supposed to be dying,' Sacha said, hoping to end the discussion.

'Madame,' Turnbull immediately replied in character. 'I am Charles-Maurice de Talleyrand-Périgord, I will choose how I die!' He threw off his long, flowing golden and hooded bed cloak and approached the bed wearing just a simple white robe. Then he lay on the bed, his face a pale mask and his eyes ringed with darker make-up.

Sacha looked at him, closed her eyes, shook her head and nodded her assent. Talleyrand was plumped up and Brian Grace got the look he wanted. A dying Talleyrand, silhouetted against the shelves behind him. All of which Richard would have approved of had he not been deeply into his book.

'OK, let's have some quiet on set!' shouted Samuel Friedman, before Richard loudly slammed shut the cinema book. 'Masquer!' he said, under his breath. '*Les romantiques de chaussée*. Masquer! So that's who you are!'

There was a commotion at the side of the set. 'I wish to come in now!' It was Commissaire Lapierre. 'I have urgent business.' He was waving a mobile phone in the air and Richard saw that Valérie was at his side.

'Can it not wait, please?' Friedman's frustration had been building all morning. 'Just five minutes, please, maybe ten?'

But the Commissaire was not to be put off and he strode to the bed. 'I need to unlock your phone, monsieur,' he said to a deathly Burdett.

'NOW?' Burdett sat suddenly bolt upright and pointed at the Commissaire. 'I am to make peace with my Lord and you interrupt my celestial negotiations with this?' He fell back on his pillows, suddenly stricken with pain and fatigue. 'Can France not exist without my intervention?'

'Please, just a few minutes, Commissaire, I promise.' It was the younger Friedman who led a frustrated Lapierre to the shadows. 'OK, kill the lights,' Samuel shouted.

'We kill all the lights, then the spot slowly comes on for Dominic,' confirmed Sacha.

'Talleyrand!' came the frustrated cry from the now dark bed.

'Silence on set!' The lights went down to almost total darkness.

'Rolling,' Sacha said with authority, 'and…'

'ARGH!' A scream went up from the bed.

'The lights!' someone shouted. 'Put on the lights!'

The spotlight on the bed came on to reveal Dominic Burdett slumped in bed, blood pouring from a knife wound in his shoulder, just as Richard felt somebody rush past him and duck behind the curtain at his side. Then the wall behind him gave way entirely and Richard fell backwards down a winding wooden staircase.

Chapter Thirty-One

Richard would never know what made him give chase. It certainly wasn't instinct, not one that he'd had before at least, but once he'd started he had no choice but to continue. The second he'd painfully reached the bottom of the staircase it seemed somewhat churlish to just rest there, besides which he didn't fancy sitting still as a potential target for whoever had just circus-knifed Dominic Burdett.

Voices from the floor above echoed down the staircase with Commissaire Lapierre's the loudest. 'Nobody move!' he bellowed. 'Not one centimetre. We have the exits to this room blocked, you will remain exactly where you are!' Nobody, it seemed, had noticed either the attacker or Richard disappear behind the large tapestry curtain. It did occur to him that maybe he should let them know, but that would inevitably waste valuable time in his pursuit. The problem with his pursuit, however, was that he didn't know which way to go. Whoever it was had a decent lead on him and, being back in the music room, he had at least two directions to cover.

Then the decision was made for him. Just as he was about to get onto his haunches, he felt a blow to the back of the head, a regular occurrence that he was becoming increasingly resentful of. The attacker had attempted to leap over him, presumably having hidden in an alcove on the stairs, but hit Richard as they jumped, rather like an Olympic hurdler crashing a barrier in the home straight. At least it gave him the opportunity to know which way to go, but as to who he was chasing he was none the wiser as the fleeing culprit was wearing Dominic Burdett's hooded dress robe. The rope belt and the cloak flowed gothically behind as they ran down the corridor towards the courtyard and an easier escape.

'Oi!' shouted Richard, as if that would make a difference, but he got up quickly and followed. Instead of turning immediately left towards the exit though, the sinister figure stopped, as if making their mind up. It was a few milliseconds but, with the decision made, they did turn left and Richard, just a moment later did exactly the same, only to be confronted by the hooded figure rushing straight at him, then leaping at his midriff like a rugby player and crashing him through centuries-old wooden-framed windows and outside, before rolling down a short embankment.

For a second after they had landed, Richard lay winded, trying to get his breath back. He'd broken the fall of his assailant and felt like he'd been hit by a car. Groggily he watched as the figure ran through the side-door entrance into the kitchens and cellars and knew he had to follow, just hoping that the lights were on or he was quite likely going to end up being brained by a copper pan. The lights weren't on, and Richard made a mental note that the next time Valérie d'Orçay involved him in one of her cases he was going to buy a crash helmet. Cautiously he descended the steps and into the darkness.

Without the electric light, the kitchens were even colder than usual, and they felt more like a cave than the famous *cuisines* of Marie-Antonin Carême, once the pride of France and the centre of its diplomacy.

'You can't escape, you know?' he shouted into the darkness, knowing it was futile to do so but hoping that his quarry would give their position away. 'I have you surrounded. No, we, we have you surrounded. Shut up you idiot,' he added under his breath. He brushed against something on the wall which rocked from side to side like the pendulum on a grandfather clock, metal scraping the brick as it did so, which made for a fearful echo down the arched corridor. From memory he remembered it was a long-handled antique bed-warmer, shaped like a modern pizza paddle but with a heavy copper pan on the end.

Barely had a day gone by in Richard's adult life that he hadn't daydreamed he was some kind of cinema hero, out to save the leading lady from dastardly villains. He thought he had covered all scenarios, all periods and all costumes, from a goatee-bearded medieval knight, through to a laconic Midwest sheriff, a heroic wounded captain in the war, a beaten-up shamus in a rough area of downtown LA, and an aluminium-wrapped spaceman saving the earth from alien invasion. What he had thus far failed to envisage was himself sweating profusely in an underground kitchen, winded, breathless and carrying an eighteenth-century bed-warming pan as a weapon. Not for the first time the difference between real life and the Hollywood version of it had let him down considerably.

'I think you should know I'm armed!' he shouted again, his voice echoing and travelling down the corridor. At first there was no reply and then, just too late, he saw a copper mug come hurtling out of the shadows and hit him squarely on the forehead. 'Ow!' he cried. 'Right!' and he attempted to lift the copper pan above his head like it was a medieval flail and attack. 'Bloody hell that's heavy!' he winced, as he immediately dropped the idea and the pan to the ground.

The hooded figure took this opportunity to run down the corridor towards the wine cellars. Richard heard the footsteps and saw the shadow as they passed under a skylight. Cautiously he followed. At least down this end of the underground kitchen area, thanks to the skylight, he would have a chance of dodging any further projectiles aimed at his head. He was careful to avoid the shaft of light and found himself at the bottom of the stone steps that led up to the banqueting hall. The only noise now was his heartbeat, a thunderous noise that sounded more like a ship's turbine engine.

He decided to try again. 'Look,' he said, crouching down, just in case. 'You can't hope to get away from this now. You're trapped here. Why not give yourself up?'

'To you?' Despite the voice being muffled and therefore impossible to tell who it belonged to, Richard knew a mocking tone when he heard one and felt the necessary effrontery.

'Well, I'm the one that's got you trapped here!' he replied, unable to hide the pique in his voice.

This time there was no reply, but he could now see the figure, also crouching behind a display of empty bottles. Whoever it was looked like the splintered image in a kaleidoscope, but still he couldn't see for sure who it was. He knew who it was though and decided to take a gamble.

'I know who you are, you know? I've worked it out. I even feel some sympathy for you.'

It was a few seconds before there was any response and for a horrible moment Richard thought that he'd allowed his quarry to escape. He heard a bottle smash to show that whoever it was was still there.

'You know nothing!' the voice mocked, it was a theatrically deep voice like a woman pretending to be a man, or a man pretending to be a woman pretending to be a man. He sighed; he was over-complicating things.

'Was he your grandfather?' There was no answer. 'He went to Hollywood and the system chewed him up and spat him out like thousands of others. But they used him, didn't they?' He heard footsteps shuffling on the stone floor. 'They took his ideas, then wrote him out of the film. Then they left him with nothing, just a broken man.' He paused, and took another deep breath. 'I'd be upset too, Sacha Vizard-Guy!' He gave the name a heavy theatrical boom, which reverberated off the stone walls as though there were a dozen people making the same accusation.

For a moment there was silence, leaving Richard to wonder if he had either got it completely wrong or the figure behind the bottles was stunned by his detective work.

'How did you know?' came the whispered question eventually.

'*The Sidewalk Romantics*,' he said. 'It was a remake of a French film, *Les rêveurs dans le caniveau*. Ben's grandad bought the rights, even hired your own father to recreate his own film for the American market, but it didn't work out, did it?'

'They lied!' was the throaty scream in response and Richard saw a bottle hurtling towards him just in time and rolled out of the way. He felt the hem of the robe brush his face as once again he was bundled out of the way.

'Sacha!' he shouted up the stone staircase. Grudgingly he got to his feet and gave chase once more, but kept his arm across his face as protection. He made it to the top and into the banqueting hall, which had been the set on the first day. There were so many places to hide – under the table, behind a desk, more ceiling-to-floor tapestry rugs – that he doubled back into the vestibule for safety and then heard more stairs being leapt above him, two at a time and knew that his suspect was now heading upstairs and he ran after her.

'Give it up, Sacha!' he said cautiously as he reached the top, hoping to get an indication of which direction to take. It wasn't difficult to make the decision when he heard the smashing of glass to his left, in Talleyrand's treasure room. He flattened himself against the wall by the doorway and was about to step inside when he felt a hand on his shoulder.

It was only later that he would regret screaming quite the way he did, but at the time it seemed like a perfectly reasonable reaction. His senses were at optimum level and he was in very real danger. He had a right to scream. That it was Valérie's hand on his shoulder was really neither here nor there in his opinion.

'What are you doing, Richard?' she asked, the excitement in her voice was at glass-breaking level, as was her concern at the cuts on his forehead.

'I have our murderer,' he said triumphantly. 'I have her cornered in there, and I'm going in!' The heroism in his voice was perfectly weighted, his lifetime of daydreaming gallantry and bravado had led to this moment and he was ready. 'Sacha Vizard-Guy,' he said nobly.

Valérie looked at him. She wasn't really the melting let-the-man-get-on-with-it leading lady material if he were honest, but he knew when someone was impressed, and she was impressed. Two swords slid on the marble floor and stopped at Richard's feet. Slowly he bent down and picked one up, holding the jewelled handle.

'Choose your weapon,' Sacha's voice came from the shadows within and Valérie picked up a sword for herself.

'Is this a good idea?' she asked, not unreasonably.

Richard held the sword in front of his face and decided it was time to channel some of the greats. There was Errol Flynn as Robin Hood, Oliver Reed in *The Three Musketeers*, Tyrone Power as Zorro…

Suddenly the hooded figure leapt at them from the darkness of the treasure room, knocking them both over on the way to the top of the stairs. Richard was up immediately and decided, in an instant and on seeing the thick tapestry that adorned the side wall, that this was his moment.

In 1926 Douglas Fairbanks had made cinema history as he abseiled down a ship's sail by plunging his sword into it and letting gravity take its course. An audacious Richard, hyped up on movie knowledge, adrenalin and a sense of injustice, leapt over the head of the fleeing murderer and at the tapestry itself, plunging his sword into the centuries-old fabric.

It was a valiant effort. The sword though, merely a ceremonial effort and not much more than a letter opener, bent on hitting the wall which Richard did too very shortly after, again knocking the wind out of him. He fell backwards off the wall and onto the robed figure knocking them both flying. Valérie was there immediately with her sword, just as her weaponed opponent stood up. From where he lay, he watched as Valérie expertly toyed with her combatant, pushing them back and drawing them forward with supreme swordsmanship, a grin on her face that Errol Flynn himself would have been proud of. He was also vaguely conscious of a crowd gathering in the reception area watching the duel.

Valérie lunged forward and cut the rope that held the heavy cloak together, it fell open. Then she lunged again and with a wristy flick twisted her foe's sword and snapped it out of their hand. Then she pulled her sword back, leapt forward and pinned the hood of her opponent to a wooden panel behind. The cloak fell away from her opponent, revealing who it was.

'You?' Richard cried, losing consciousness as he did so, and just as Ben-Hur Friedman sank to his knees in defeat.

Chapter Thirty-Two

Valérie led a groggy Richard back into the banqueting hall and sat him down at the head of the table. At the other end sat a downcast Ben-Hur Friedman, flanked by two gendarmes, one of whose uniform was covered in braids and was of noticeably higher rank than the other. The scene looked like a summit to end a war between two bruised nations, though the irony of that being ostensibly what Friedman's film *The Servant Master* was about was beyond Richard for the moment.

There was an air of disbelief in the rest of the room; most of its occupants were seated, except for Valérie, the Commissaire and Madame Tablier, who obviously didn't think highly of the forces of law and order and was keeping guard by the main entrance. Sacha looked on the verge of tears and Richard, sitting to her right, wanted to apologise for getting it so wrong but was interrupted before he could do so.

'I can't believe it, Ben!' Jennifer Davies couldn't keep it in any longer. She was visibly upset, wrenching at a handkerchief in her lap and, like the other actors, still in costume. 'I always thought you had a good soul.' It was like her belief system had come crashing down.

Slowly Friedman turned to her and forced a smile. 'Maybe I have, maybe that's why I failed in Hollywood.' Jennifer began to cry and it was Lionel, sitting next to her, who put her arms around her and hugged her close. Lionel Margaux looked stronger now than at any time in the previous few days, as though a weight had been lifted from her. Richard, beginning to recover some of his senses, suspected that a decision had been made and that soon French cinema would lose one of its major stars.

Commissaire Lapierre gave a small, attention-grabbing cough. 'Ladies and gentlemen. We have formally arrested Monsieur Ben-Hur Friedman for the murders of Monsieur Reed Turnbull and Madame Amorette Arthur. Before I take Monsieur Friedman into custody, I want to establish exactly what happened here today.'

Everyone started talking at once, but it was Clare's voice whose was the loudest. 'You might start, monsieur,' she said clearly, and in English, 'by also charging him with attempted murder!'

Lapierre raised his eyebrows and balanced on the toes of his feet with his arms behind his back. 'Of whom, madame?'

'Of Charles-Maurice de Talleyrand-Périgord!' Dominic Burdett stood, albeit unsteadily, as he made this proclamation. There was a bloodstain on his shoulder but clearly the thrown knife hadn't made much of an impact other than superficially. 'I was his loyal servant,' he added, breaking with emotion before slumping back down again.

The Commissaire's eyes narrowed. 'Yes, make a note of that, Capitaine,' he instructed.

'Actually, no,' Clare said, again with a determination that couldn't be ignored. 'I was referring to my husband!'

There was a murmur around the table and it became clear that the majority of those present didn't know that Clare had a husband. 'Him!' She pointed at Richard who at that moment was mopping his bleeding brow with a table napkin.

'Eh?' he said, suddenly aware of the attention. 'Oh, well. Yes, I suppose so.' He paused. 'But what about Monsieur Corbeau?' he asked the Commissaire, much to the obvious disappointment of Clare who had perhaps expected more in the way of acknowledgement from her heroic, even if estranged, husband.

The Commissaire sighed but it was Valérie who intervened. 'That was natural causes, Richard,' she said, gently putting a hand on his shoulder. Without thinking, he put his own hand on hers, and nodded sadly.

'He was a hundred and two,' he said quietly, before becoming suddenly aware of a cold front coming from the chair next to him, as Clare's icy stare almost turned him to stone. He removed his hand from Valérie's.

Gennie, who up until now had been sitting quietly and demurely with Martin on a chaise longue in the corner, couldn't contain herself any longer. 'Someone also hit my husband!' she said, almost in tears.

'There, there old girl.' Martin managed to be both stoic and warm at the same time, and put his arm around Gennie, pulling her in more closely and kissing the top of her head. Richard was now beginning to see things far more clearly as the fog dissipated from his brain and it occurred to him, not for the first time, that for all their peccadilloes, perversions and polyamorous activity, Martin and Gennie were about the most functional couple he knew. 'But really, Val, Richard?' Martin was on the verge of pleading. 'What's been going on?'

This set off a wave of heated discussion around the table, except for Gilbertine, who seemed so bored by the whole thing, probably a little lost with the language, and was plaintively eyeing up a plastic ornamental *croquembouche* in the centre of the table. Alain Petit, sitting next to him, was inevitably playing with a set of screwdrivers.

Everyone quietened down and all eyes turned to the Commissaire, who again balanced on his toes as if he were about to run away. 'Yes,' he began slowly and, blushing ever so slightly, started to pace the room. He approached Valérie and an idea came into his head, his eyes brightening at the thought of it. 'There are still one or two details that I would like, er, confirmed,' he emphasised the last word. 'Perhaps madame, would like to tell the full story?' He spread his arm wide to give her the floor and all eyes were on her.

'Thank you, Commissaire,' Valérie said graciously, stepping forward slightly. 'I am sure you will learn a great deal.' The Capitaine sniggered, then tried to turn it into a concealing cough.

Lapierre flushed with anger and pursed his lips. '*Allez-y,* madame,' he hissed and moved into the shadows.

Valérie walked a few more paces, partially circling the table as she gathered her thoughts. 'In truth,' she began, 'I cannot piece it all together by myself. But Richard, my partner,' Richard kept his eyes to the front, not daring to look to his right, 'has been working on another aspect of the investigation and can add any extra information.'

Richard gulped and sincerely hoped that that was going to be the case.

Valérie put her hands together as though in prayer and bounced her index fingers off her lips. 'The death of Monsieur Corbeau was important and only Richard saw that,' she began slowly, again ordering her thoughts. 'I admit that I felt Richard was over-reacting at first and as the Commissaire has said, it was natural causes. The war hero finally loses a battle to time itself.'

Richard was impressed; this was a theatrical side to Valérie he hadn't seen before and even Ben-Hur Friedman, ground down in his own self-pity, followed her around the room and hung on her every word.

'It was very sad,' Jennifer Davies said, not missing the opportunity to act up to the required emotion.

'It was, madame,' Valérie pounced, 'and yet, with all your chakras and holistic whatnot, you did not really feel it, did you?' Her pronunciation of the informal English noun was pure Peter Ustinov as Hercule Poirot and Richard wondered if she'd been secretly raiding his DVD collection when he wasn't looking.

'How do you mean?' Davies was immediately affronted.

'It was a death, madame, yet you, so sensitive to atmosphere and *vibe*… it made no big difference at all.' Jennifer reddened in anger but before she could interrupt, Valérie started again. 'I am not accusing you of anything, madame, really. But it just – and please take no offence – is yet another layer of artificiality in all of this pretence. Nothing, absolutely nothing, is what it seems.'

'Welcome to the movie business,' Brian Grace said sarcastically. 'Of course it's artificial, it's what we do!'

'Speak for yourself!' Burdett languished in his chair trying to give off an air of practised authenticity.

'You're the biggest fraud of all!' Grace shot back.

'Gentlemen, please!' The Commissaire stepped forward. 'Please continue, madame.'

'One person did feel it, and only one person. Someone who knows more about the artificiality of film than any of you, but he felt it. Richard saw that first. Do you remember? You said that it was all like a profiterole. You can see what is on the outside, but have no idea what is inside.' Richard nodded, eyes front, while everyone looked at him. He hoped that this wouldn't be the moment he would have to explain everything to the rest of the group. He also noticed a slight smile on Clare's face, and the vaguest of nods.

'Well done, old man,' said a supportive Martin from the corner.

'Yes, well done, Richard,' Gennie added.

Richard, inevitably flustered, said a few vague, 'Oh, you knows', though in truth he hadn't much of an idea where this was leading.

'Richard sensed,' Valérie continued to circle the table, 'that things weren't right. And he told me about a film called *Following the Fox...*'

'*After the Fox.*' Richard couldn't help himself. '1966.'

'It's like a form of Tourette's,' Clare said, but she smiled warmly as she did so.

'*After the Fox.* That's right.' There was a brief flash of impatience in Valérie's eyes, but it soon passed. 'It is a film about a fake film that is hiding a crime.' There was a murmur as people started to cotton on to what she was saying.

'But this is a real film.' Brian Grace was slightly insulted by her suggestion.

'And that is precisely why it is so clever, monsieur.' Valérie very clearly put out any fires of insubordination and carried on. 'This is a real film, but it is also hiding something. And it did not become a crime until greed took over. Which I think was also the intention all along. But we will come to that later.'

'But what is it that Monsieur Ainsworth saw that nobody else did?' The Commissaire was clearly under the impression that Valérie was bumping up Richard's role in all of this.

'He saw, Commissaire, that the film wasn't very good and that nobody seemed to care.' This time there was no argument or discussion, just an embarrassed silence. 'Why would that be? Because the film was an excuse to be here.' She spread her arms wide. 'In the Chateau de Valençay.'

'I thought we only came down here from Paris because Lionel was being threatened?' Grace was trying hard to control his temper.

'That was the convenient excuse that suited a number of people, Stella Gonzales for instance, and her, I'm sorry, but… frankly absurd role in trying to ensure that Spain is represented in the film.'

'It is not absurd!' Stella said angrily.

'Oh it is,' Valérie said dismissively. 'Who would invent something so silly and easily checked? No, the Caballeros de Cádiz really do exist.' Stella looked defiantly around the table, but nobody challenged her.

'I don't get any of this,' Jennifer threw her arms up. 'What has this got to do with Ben and Reed and Amorette?'

'Riches,' Valérie said simply. 'Now, Richard, tell them about *The Sidewalk Romantics*.'

He took a deep breath, relieved that he was on home ground. 'Well, it wasn't very good. In fact it was worse than that, it ruined a lot of careers. Brian Grace was never trusted to direct again, Reed Turnbull and Dominic Burdett were forever tainted by it, and have never really recovered.' In the corner Burdett wailed. 'Jennifer Davies, the same. Sorry,' he added.

'I was told I was too old to play a woman in her mid-twenties.' She shook her head sadly. 'I was thirty-one at the time.'

'It killed my grandaddy,' Friedman said sadly.

'And it killed your chances of being a big-shot producer too, Ben,' Grace added cruelly. 'You were in charge of that picture, everyone knew it, you made all the decisions.'

'And it destroyed Alan Masquer,' Richard said quickly, 'who we now know…'

Valérie quickly interrupted him. 'You came to Valençay in search of something, Monsieur Friedman, something you believe had been hidden.'

'Hidden for centuries, no doubt,' the Commissaire scoffed.

'No, Henri,' Valérie corrected him. 'For decades. Since the Second World War when the Louvre Museum hid some of its treasures here in the chateau itself.' She turned to Friedman. 'I am right, monsieur?'

'*The Lacemaker*,' Friedman said quietly. 'Johannes Vermeer.'

'But that is in the Louvre Museum,' Lapierre said dismissively.

'No!' Friedman retorted angrily. 'It is here. What hangs in the Louvre is a copy, a good copy, but a copy. The original is here somewhere, copied during the war and then hidden. Fifty million dollars!'

'How do you know it's here?' It was Richard who asked the question for everyone else.

'Because Alan Masquer's father worked here in the war. He was part of the team that curated the Louvre pieces here.'

It all seemed a bit far-fetched to Richard. 'And you waited twenty-five years to come here and look for it?'

'Of course not! Samuel was going through some of my grandaddy's things, old boxes, memories…' Samuel hadn't said a word so far, he had sat there stunned and disbelieving as his world, built around the hero-worship of his uncle, came crashing down. He nodded at the memory, but remained silent. 'There was a letter, unopened, from Alan Masquer.'

'He had made the original French version of *The Sidewalk Romantics*,' Richard said, helpfully. 'And…'

'That's right.' Friedman snorted. 'But he wasn't doing a good job. I sacked him, put Brian in charge. This letter was from him to my grandaddy begging for his job back and saying that if he rehired him, he could lead him to the Vermeer. It would be the prize of his collection.'

'The letter was a fake.' There was almost a mocking tone in Valérie's voice. 'Cleverly placed to tempt you and it worked. But you could not do it alone, so you went to old friends, equally unsuccessful by now. Reed Turnbull and Dominic Burdett. You would produce a film, a real film, the three of you, but you would search for the painting.'

'And presumably they had a falling out?' the Commissaire asked.

'Yes,' Valérie said. 'Reed Turnbull began an affair with Amorette Arthur, but did not tell Monsieur Friedman, who suspected that Turnbull and poor Amorette were trying to double-cross him. That is why he killed them. He also knew that Dominic Burdett was now a liability and would have killed him too. He tried earlier today and also tried to tempt Monsieur Burdett out late last night.'

'Is that who hit Martin then?' Gennie asked angrily.

'Yes, it is,' Valérie confirmed and Gennie began to rise off the couch, but Martin pulled her back.

'Steady on, old girl,' he said calmly.

'Poor Amorette,' Valérie continued, 'that was a cruel, unnecessary thing to do.' Friedman shrugged, but showed no remorse. 'It was Amorette you saw walking with Monsieur Friedman, Madame Davies. You said that you saw him with his arm around Monsieur Burdett and that Monsieur Burdett had stumbled. It was a dying Amorette Arthur you saw being walked, carried, to the peacock coop. She was wearing the tunic of Talleyrand, the tunic that Clare had noticed was so filthy in Monsieur Burdett's trailer. Amorette Arthur was poisoned with her own blood pressure medication, just as he had done with Reed Turnbull, mixing his medication with Viagra. Then you smeared her face with chocolate, a ridiculous thing to do. Obscene. Unnecessary.'

A heavy, awkward silence descended on the group and nobody wanted to catch anybody else's eye.

'I am not guilty!' Dominic Burdett shouted. 'I knew nothing about these murders.'

'That is yet to be established, monsieur,' the Commissaire said menacingly. 'Come,' he walked over to the actor, 'you will come with us for now.'

'There's just one thing.' It was Clare who spoke. 'You said the letter to Mr Friedman's grandfather was a fake. Who faked it, and when?'

'Ah.' Valérie seemed grateful for the question. 'Richard?'

He had known this was coming for some time, but it still made him jump and he just hoped that his own conclusions were the correct ones. 'Sacha Vizard-Guy,' he said quietly, just in case he was wrong.

Again a murmur went up around the table; even Gilbertine said something in astonishment.

'It is true,' the young director said quietly, but also with a touch of defiance.

'You are the daughter of Alan Masquer,' Richard added. 'I should have seen the connection earlier, even the name Vizard. It's another word for mask, Masquer.'

Sacha sat still but her eyes bored into the bowed head of Ben-Hur Friedman. 'He destroyed my father, broke him. And I have watched ever since how pathetic his life has been. A talentless failure, living on a famous name. My father would be proud of me, your *grandaddy*,' she spat the word, 'would despise you!'

Friedman jumped out of his seat, his eyes fiery in anger and before anyone could react he was almost at Sacha's throat. The others were briefly distracted by Samuel Friedman leaping from his seat and shouting at Sacha, 'You used me!'

It was Richard who swiftly intervened; quickly manoeuvring himself between producer and director, he splayed Friedman's arms out wide and poked the startled murderer in the eyes. Friedman fell to his knees and a startled Sacha slumped back in her chair. As did an exhausted Richard.

Chapter Thirty-Three

'So Sacha Vizard-Guy was behind it all then?' Clare asked as they drove back in the limousine.

'Yes,' Valérie and Richard said simultaneously.

'No, you say.' Richard gallantly stood down.

'Sacha was pulling the strings, but she did not know how far it would go.' Valérie looked oddly distant as she explained. 'She must have been planning this for years, but I think even she underestimated the level of greed and desperation with Monsieur Friedman.'

'And she must have befriended Samuel Friedman in Hollywood and somehow placed the fake letter where it would be found?' Clare shook her head in wonder.

'Yes.'

'And at the same time made it known that she had a script for sale to the right producer, probably via Samuel, that was based somehow in Valençay. It's very clever,' Richard added.

'It would make a good film.' Clare snorted. 'You could write the script, Richard!'

'I never liked any of them.' Madame Tablier sat like an angry child in the corner of the limousine. Her entire face was drenched in disdain, not just for movie people in general, but the limousine as well.

'Oh come now, Madame Tablier,' mocked Clare. 'I think you had a soft spot for Alain Petit.'

'Pah!' was the dismissive response. 'Another man and his broken promises!'

'What did he promise you?' Martin's voice came loud and clear through the intercom.

Briefly confused as to where the question had come from, the old woman looked to the ceiling, then her eyes became wistful with a look of longing. 'He said he'd show me how to rewire a standalone electric generator,' she said quietly, then quickly added, 'bloody liars the lot of 'em.'

After a brief uncomfortable pause it was Gennie's voice that broke the silence from the front of the car. 'But Martin said that Sacha was definitely sick, that she had food poisoning. Was she pretending?'

'No, Gennie,' Valérie answered. 'She took something to make her unwell, I think. When Monsieur Friedman killed Reed Turnbull she knew that her game was getting out of hand and she made the decision to remove any suspicion from herself.'

'Her grandfather, the one who worked here in the war, he must have known Monsieur Corbeau.' Richard was still piecing things together.

'I think so,' Valérie said. 'Which is why she showed such concern when he died. The only one who did, as you said.'

'You say that it was all a game.' Clare was hanging on Valérie's every word.

'I think that is how it started, yes. A serious game though.' Valérie nodded sadly. 'She had planned everything in such fine detail. The friendship with Samuel, the fake letter, the script for sale, encouraging Lionel to "stalk" herself for – I don't know what – motivation?'

'But,' Richard sighed, 'she couldn't control the actions of those she'd set up. She suspected that they would destroy each other somehow, and I think she was willing to sacrifice her own career for that. But when it was Amorette that was killed, she knew she had gone too far but didn't know how to stop it.'

'In a way that is similar to Monsieur Friedman, Ben-Hur Friedman. He was driven insane thinking he could find the Vermeer painting, restore his fortunes and the name of his grandaddy. I ask you!' she blurted suddenly. 'A grown man calling somebody *grandaddy*!' She cuddled Passepartout to recover her composure.

Clare reached into the small limousine fridge and pulled out two half-bottles of champagne, which she gave to Richard to open while passing around some flutes. Madame Tablier inspected her glass to make sure it met with her hygiene standards, which it did, and Richard poured everyone a small drop.

'Well,' Clare said, raising her glass. 'I have to concede, you two make a formidable team. Well done!'

Richard smiled at her, as did Valérie while Madame Tablier pulled her face at the taste. 'Thank you,' Richard said, warmly.

'Yes, thank you, Clare.' Valérie raised her glass in return and it was clear that a mutual respect had built between the two and Richard didn't know if this was a good thing or even more terrifying than mutual antipathy.

'So what's next for you two?' Clare beamed. 'I really didn't know there was such excitement to be had in the Follet Valley.'

'Well,' Richard took a sip of his champagne, 'I'd like to go back to making breakfasts for a bit, I think. There tends to be less violence in that.'

Valérie was silent for a moment. 'I may need to go back to Paris for a while,' she said, looking at the floor. 'I have some things I must sort out.'

Clare noticed the look of near panic on Richard's face.

'Can I clean your room out then?' Madame Tablier asked eagerly.

The limousine pulled up at Les Vignes *chambre d'hôte* and they all got out. Richard hung back, offering to help Madame Tablier out of the car, but was angrily rebuffed. Clare hung back too as the others went into the salon.

'Richard,' Clare said in a businesslike manner, wiping dust of his jacket lapel. 'Now listen to me, and listen carefully. If you don't make a move on Madame Valérie d'Orçay soon, I may just do so myself!' She patted his cheek mockingly and he didn't know whether to be grateful or petrified, but she turned away not waiting for a response.

Feeling a little stunned and not much fancying company either, he tip-toed around to the hen coop and stood, feeding his ladies, lost in thought. Suddenly a blast of gas flame made him look up and there, some fifty metres above, were Patrice and Lionel waving to him as they floated away.

'I think she will be very happy, you know?'

Valérie, as usual, had appeared silently from nowhere, startling him into scattering more hen seed than he wished.

'I hope so,' he said, a trifle stiffly. 'Are you really going back to Paris?' he asked, trying not to sound desperate.

'Yes,' she replied bluntly. 'I am going to put my apartment up for sale, and move down here permanently.' She smiled up at him.

'That's, well, how…' he stammered, nodding like he had the tremors. 'Good news,' he managed finally. Valérie giggled at his side and put her arm through his. 'I know what you're going to say,' he smiled. 'That I am *very Eengleeshe.*'

She laughed. 'Yes, Richard, you are. But well, nobody is perfect.'

Preview
Death in le Jardin

Chapter One

'Ah, spring!' Richard Ainsworth said out loud. He was trying to inject the right note of optimism and hope that the word spring was supposed to provoke. Then he took a deep breath, said '*bloody* spring' under his breath and ventured outside into the fresh morning. Richard had views on spring and they weren't entirely positive. In fact, he was downright suspicious of the whole thing.

Spring was a mantrap which rolled around once a year looking to catch the optimist off guard with its promise of regeneration and new life. As a rule, Richard was quite some way down the street from optimism but was wary nonetheless. It was a glorious, warm day but as if guarding against an enemy, Richard kept his jumper on over a buttoned-up polo shirt, muttering to himself under his breath as he pulled on his stiff wellington boots. It wasn't that he was against regeneration and new life *per se*, just that those things brought with them the burden of responsibility and inevitably, backbreaking hard work.

Every year. *Every year.*

Like clockwork, the bleak Follet Valley winter would just suddenly end and, within the space of what seemed like hours, new shoots, rampant and vigorous, would sprout everywhere, going off like floral fireworks. Weeds would grow through his gravelled driveway literally before his eyes, his leylandii hedges would break free of their finely edged shackles and look like an untrimmed beard. And the grass, oh the grass, he moaned, that would need cutting on an almost daily basis. He had of course tried to embrace the recent fad of leaving your garden to grow wild, thereby encouraging nature to look after itself and promote the insect population, but it wasn't his style and wasn't necessarily his choice to make anyway. He ran a high-end B&B, a posh *chambre d'hôte*, and generally his clientele liked their nature to look shipshape, its borders smart and its insects preferably at somebody else's arm's length.

None of this would really matter if the garden was small and manageable of course, but it wasn't. It was just under a couple of acres and Mother Nature regarded it as a large blank canvas just to be Jackson Pollocked with flora whenever his back was turned. He sighed and took in the view. *What were they thinking?* he thought to himself, not for the first time, *what were they on?*

'They' were he and Clare, but it was mainly him. Wounded by redundancy, booted out of a film historian job he loved by the rampaging desire for digitalisation and the internet, specifically the world-ruining IMDb. com, he had salved his ego in the purchase of the biggest bloody property they could afford. Which in rural France meant very big indeed and, in comparison to southern England, at dirt cheap prices. Clare had warned him that the maintenance would be too much, that he'd regret it in the long run, almost as if she knew then that she herself wasn't going to be in it for the long haul. And she'd been right on all counts. Not that he would ever admit that to her, even now, now that they were separated and she was living back in the UK.

'Me?' he'd said, a brash confidence papering over fragile wounds. 'I am a man of the soil.' And off he had gone to buy a ride-on lawnmower, one more fillip for the male ego. His heart sank at the memory. The ride-on mower. His enthusiasm for the machine had lasted perhaps two of the early spring cuts. It was the most uncomfortable contraption he'd ever ridden and after a couple of hours of admittedly rapid grass-cutting he'd stagger off the thing and feel like he'd spent the afternoon trapped in a tumble dryer. Clare had been right about that too.

'You're just not a gardener, dear,' she said, every time she heard him swearing somewhere on the property. 'You don't have green fingers.' She would then back this theory up by claiming that because there were so few films about gardening, he had nothing to draw any heroics from, no grounding in the subject. She would then turn the page of whatever glossy magazine she was perusing and take a triumphant sip of an early evening cocktail.

'Not true,' he'd argue. '*The Spanish Gardener*, Dirk Bogarde, 1956. *I Confess*, Hitchcock, 1953. Peter Sellers, 1979, *Being There*…'

'For which he should have won the Academy Award, yes, yes, dear, so you say. Top me up will you?'

Clare. The letter was still sitting in the kitchen, unopened after ten days. It was an official-looking brown envelope with Richard's name and address typed on the front. Anyway, he assumed it was from Clare because the sender's address was stamped on the back. 'Forshaw-Banks' it read in pale blue print, 'Solicitors'. Followed by an address somewhere in Woking. Only bad news travelled by old-fashioned mail these days so he was guessing that Clare, not for the first time, had taken charge of the situation and the inevitable grinding wheels of divorce were turning. Well it could wait, was his barely considered opinion. If it was a divorce petition then he knew it would all be fairly amicable, they were still good friends after all, communicating often; and if she wanted half of everything she was welcome to it, in fact she could have the whole lot of it in his opinion, just as long as he didn't get custody of the ride-on mower.

'She has a new boyfriend,' their daughter Alicia had warned him, the tone in her voice more than hinting at disapproval. 'He has a sports car like the one your girlfriend has.'

It had taken Richard some time to work out who she meant by 'your girlfriend'. He was pretty sure that if he had a girlfriend he would have known about it, but it was now the assumption of pretty much everyone they knew that he and Valérie d'Orçay were what used to be called 'an item'. They weren't, but like owning a ride-on mower, the prestige of the assumption was good for Richard's delicate male psyche so he affected a sort of 'gentlemen never tells' type air and hoped no one would actually ask him a direct question.

From a distance it was, he had to admit, an easy assumption to make. Valérie and Richard behaved, on the face of things, like a couple. Or at least what had become Richard's notion of a couple. She bossed him about and he more often than not did as he was told, secretly happy to be bossed about. What social life there was to be had in rural France was passed together; Richard's friends had become her friends. They even, in theory and certainly to the outside world, lived together since Valérie and her pampered Chihuahua Passepartout had taken up permanent residence, though in the largest of the B&B bedrooms, not the main house. For free too, but as they were now business partners as well, he was putting that down as a tax break.

Business wasn't booming though, he ruminated as he dithered his way to the dreaded ride-on lawnmower shed. In fact they hadn't had a job in months. Granted, private investigations and personal security work was always going to be a tough sell in a quiet agricultural French backwater like the Follet Valley, but Richard – and he would never admit this to anyone, probably not even himself – missed the excitement of their adventures. It was fair to say that his initial foray into the world of personal security had got off to a rocky start; three deaths on his watch wasn't the launch anyone was looking for, but it all seemed a long time ago now. Two whole seasons in fact, and while he had kept the reduced capacity B&B going, it had all become a bit dull, a bit safe. No doubt, Clare would say, a bit Richard.

Valérie on the other hand kept a professional hand in on her own full-time job as a bounty hunter and likely assassin; the facts of the latter had never been properly established and Richard had never felt like addressing it full on. Every so often she would disappear for a few days, sometimes to visit her apartment in Paris which was still for sale, sometimes for work and always leaving strict instructions for Passepartout's personal menu. Richard could piece together her work movements by checking on the internet whether a fugitive on the run had been captured or a rogue tin pot dictator had disappeared. She offered him no further information than that and he was far too English to ask for any. He was just relieved when she returned.

He stopped by the chicken coop to check on his hens. 'Morning, ladies,' he said with genuine warmth and was greeted with a comforting chorus of contented clucking in reply. 'Sleep well?' He opened the gate and went in to check on their water as they fussed happily around his feet. Clare's letter, Valérie's dangerous profession, money worries and the dull descent into a sedentary middle age, from an admittedly not very great height, could all be forgotten when he was with his hens. They were his happy place, his balm. Joan Crawford and Lana Turner pecked at his feet while Olivia de Havilland lagged behind, eventually joining the others though clearly limping as she made her way over to Richard. He bent down to pick her up, putting the calm bird on his lap as he sat down on the hen coop bench.

'What's up, old girl?' he asked gently and she cocked her head in response. 'Why are you limping then?' She flattened her back as he stroked her and he saw the culprit immediately as a small section of bramble hung aggressively off her right foot. He pulled it off gently, making his own clucking noises as he did so, trying to comfort the animal. The bramble was a rogue element of a larger bush that had sprung up right next to the coop ladder. 'Bloody spring!' he said loudly, and after placing

302

Olivia back on the ground, he stood up ready to attack what he now saw as the epitome of his seasonal nemesis, Mother Nature herself.

'Bloody spring!' he repeated, almost as a battle cry, as he cupped his hands like a murderous strangler ready to choke the life out of the floral invader and injurer of his beloved Olivia.

'Richard, what are you doing?'

Valérie's mixture of concern and bemusement, a look echoed with frightening accuracy by the nestled Passepartout, momentarily put Richard off his stride. Though not enough to actually stop his act of revenge on the bramble which went ahead anyway and with predictably painful results.

'Ow! Bloody hell!' he cried, and staggered backwards, a look of horror on his face as blood began to drip from a cut on his right index finger. 'I'm bleeding!' he said redundantly.

'Yes,' was the equally useless reply. Even Passepartout seemed to nod in confirmation.

There was an awkward silence as Richard sucked childishly on his torn finger and Valérie, who had no mothering instinct whatsoever beyond that for tiny dogs, tried to look away as Richard crumbled into a man child.

'Bloody hell!' he repeated, though now it was more a whine than a rage.

'Richard, I am worried,' Valérie said eventually.

'Pah.' He shrugged. 'I'll get over it. It's just a bit of blood.'

Again a look of confusion crossed her face. 'No,' she said quietly, 'not about that.' She pointed at his stricken hand so he folded his arms in a gesture of embarrassment, hiding his finger. Richard didn't consider himself a scruffy individual but Valérie always made him feel like one. She wore beige jodhpurs, a cream turtle neck jumper and a tweed jacket; her brown suede Chelsea boots looked brand new. She looked like she was off to a society gymkhana.

'Have you lost your horse?' he asked attempting a casual air to distract from his bramble tantrum. She narrowed her eyes in response, looking at him now not only with no sympathy whatsoever but with an expression that indicated her confusion had now replaced by the obvious conclusion that Richard was an idiot. 'Never mind,' he added quickly, as usual internally admonishing himself for trying humour on her. She took life too seriously for such frivolities as jokes and sarcasm.

'I am worried about Madame Tablier,' she said eventually. 'I have not seen her this morning.'

In his anti-spring fever Richard hadn't realised that his *femme de ménage*, and permanent fixture since he'd moved to France, wasn't there. There had been no guests staying the previous evening so he hadn't had to prepare breakfast, but Madame Tablier was always, always there and now he felt guilty for not noticing. Even if there was nothing to do, no reason for her to be at the B&B at all, she would have been there anyway having taken on the role of Richard's protector. Richard didn't need protecting in his opinion, but Madame Tablier thought otherwise having concluded almost on first sight that Richard was a danger to himself.

'I'm sure she's OK,' he said unconvincingly.

'Well, we are worried aren't we, *mon petit*?' Passepartout didn't look overly concerned to be fair.

They were interrupted by the throaty roar of a large-engine motorbike as the aforementioned Madame Tablier, in full cycling leathers, pulled up beside the couple, scattering the hens.

'I'm late,' she said in what Richard knew passed for an apology from the doughty old woman. 'I've been to a funeral,' she added quickly. 'My brother-in-law.'

Richard and Valérie looked at each other wondering how to respond. Madame Tablier didn't do schmaltz or platitudes.

'I didn't know you had a brother-in-law.' Valérie was testing the water.

'I don't anymore.'

'Well, you don't have to stay today, Madame Tablier, if you want to be with your... er, family.' Richard thought he may as well play at being in charge, ridiculous notion though it was.

'No. No need. There's nothing can be done now he's in the ground, is there?' She wandered into the chicken coop.

'How did he die?' Valérie asked, presumably showing a professional curiosity.

'Ha!' snorted the old woman. 'He went and got his head chopped off, didn't he?' She bent down and ripped up the bramble bush that had caused Richard so many problems, then realised that jaws had dropped and eyes were staring so she looked up. 'What?' she asked innocently.

Preview

Death in le Jardin
(A Follet Valley Mystery 4)

On the surface, Richard Ainsworth has life where he wants it. Middle-aged navel gazing and Olympic levels of procrastination are exactly what rural life in France should be about.

Then crisis hits his posh B&B when redoubtable housekeeper, Madame Tablier, is accused of murder. Even more surprisingly, it's the murder of a former fiancé, turned brother-in-law. None of which the stubborn old woman denies.

Valérie d'Orçay is having none of it and their investigation leads them to a strange tourist garden village, where backbiting, recriminations and even former colleagues provide a deadly scenario more tangled than knotweed.

COMING SOON

Also available

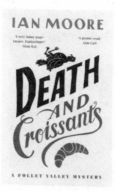

Death and Croissants
(A Follet Valley Mystery 1)

Richard is a middle-aged Englishman who runs a B&B in the fictional Val de Follet in the Loire Valley. Nothing ever happens to Richard, and really that's the way he likes it.

One day, however, one of his older guests disappears, leaving behind a bloody handprint on the wallpaper. Another guest, the exotic Valérie, persuades a reluctant Richard to join her in investigating the disappearance.

Richard remains a dazed passenger in the case until things become really serious and someone murders Ava Gardner, one of his beloved hens... and you don't mess with a fellow's hens!

OUT NOW

Also available

**Death and Fromage
(A Follet Valley Mystery 2)**

Richard is a middle-aged Englishman who runs a B&B in the Val de Follet. Nothing ever happens to Richard, and really that's the way he likes it.

Until scandal erupts in the nearby town of Saint-Sauver when its famous restaurant is downgraded from three 'Michelin' stars to two. The restaurant is shamed, the town is in shock and the leading goat's cheese supplier drowns himself in one of his own pasteurisation tanks. Or does he?

Valérie d'Orçay, who is staying at the B&B while house-hunting in the area, isn't convinced that it's a suicide. Despite his misgivings, Richard is drawn into Valérie's investigation, and finds himself becoming a major player.

OUT NOW

About the Author

Credit: Richard Wood

Ian Moore is a leading stand-up comedian, known for his sharp, entertaining punditry. He has performed all over the world, on every continent except South America. A BBC TV and radio regular, he was a Champion on Richard Osman's *House of Games* and stars in Radio 4's *The Now Show*.

Ian lives in rural France and commutes back to the UK when occasion demands. In his spare time, he makes mean chutneys and jams.

He is also the author of the Juge Lombard series of mysteries, and two memoirs on life in France contrasting with life on the road in the UK. *À la Mod* and *C'est Modnifique*.

Acknowledgements

Everybody thanks their family, right? Sometimes you suspect that they do it because they're afraid of the repercussions if they don't. I get that. But without the love, support and 'keep your feet on the ground, Charlie Big Potatoes' that I get from Natalie, Samuel, Maurice and Thérence, none of this would be remotely possible. Writing can be a lonely experience but once you emerge from under your creative rock, you demand company. It takes a special group to always be there when that happens.

To the team of professionals who make this all possible, I am eternally grateful. My agent Bill Goodall and all at Farrago Books: Pete Duncan, Rob Wilding and Matt Casbourne and to Abbie Headon, for always being there. Danny Lyle and Becca Allen for the proof edits and the sales team who have been magnificent.

None of this would have been thinkable without any of those mentioned above, but it would be churlish also not to tip my hat in the direction of Napoleon Bonaparte himself. Given the chance he may admit to a few errors on his part, but he had the foresight and good taste to install the political genius Charles Maurice de Talleyrand-Périgord at the Chateau de Valençay and feed my imagination. A special thanks to the chateau itself then, just fifteen minutes from home and which emerged from the pandemic lockdown without fanfare and where I was able to wander around on my own planning this book.

Note from the Publisher

To receive background material and updates on further humorous titles by Ian Moore, sign up at farragobooks.com/ian-moore-signup